BREATHE

BY DOUGLAS A. VAN BELLE

SPECIAL EDITION COVER
BY JEFF FENNEL

Other Novels by Douglas A. Van Belle

Barking Death Squirrels
Random Static, Wellington New Zealand

The Care and Feeding of Your Lunatic Mage
Andromeda Spaceways, Melbourne Australia

And From Intergalactic Media Group in 2017
The List

First Published in New Zealand and New York by

Intergalactic Media Group
http://inglmedia.com

National Library of New Zealand Cataloguing-in-
Publication Data
Van Belle, Douglas A. 1965-
Breathe-World Science Fiction Collector's Edition/
Douglas A. Van Belle
ISBN 978-0-473-36063-4
1. Title

Acknowledgements

The first acknowledgement should probably go to my publisher, Andrew Pillay. When he told me he loved Breathe and he wanted to use it to kick off his new Science Fiction imprint, that gave me the extra encouragement it sometimes takes to get a novel like this finished. He also knew I was lying every time I said I was only a few weeks from finishing it, and he planned appropriately. And my editor, Juliet Buchanan, deserves the second shout out. I don't actually drift randomly between American, Canadian, British and Kiwi English, it just looks that way. My name is Doug and I am the undisputed king of typos.

Speaking of typos, I can't overstate the value of the feedback from the people who braved those grammatical atrocities and read through the unedited final draft. Liz McLay, Jean-Sébastien Riox, Gerard Van Belle, and Samantha Van Belle; your comments on the science, the characters, and countless other details added up to a huge difference.

Prologue

The future is defined by neither hope nor despair. The future is carved from the past by Occam's razor.

It was hardly a sunrise at all. The feeble ruddy glow that trickled down from Jupiter during the night just became the harsh, colourless twilight that passed for day on Ganymede. For some reason Luke had expected something similar to a Lunar sunrise. He had expected that first ray of the sun to be brilliant. He had expected that instant of transition between night and day to be dramatic to the point of unbearable. He should have known better. Ganymede rotated a fair bit faster than the moon and from Jupiter's orbit the solar disk was just one twenty-fifth the size it was back home. It should have been obvious that the pathetic little bastard would just pop up over the edge of the world.

Feeling oddly annoyed, Luke packed the last of the airtight plastic shipping containers on the cart, and started pushing his last delivery towards the base.

There wasn't all that much to Aquarius. After eighteen months of construction, a glasshouse and two wings of living and working quarters were all that had been added to the original hub module. But the grand future of the first human outpost beyond the Belt had already been carved into the rock-hard ice. The low angle of the sunlight highlighted all the foundation pads, sub-level vaults, and utility runs that had been excavated, and as he descended from the small rise at the edge of the landing pad, he could see the truly impressive scale of what was only the first phase of construction. A second hub module was being built on the north side of the existing hub, and it looked like they had flattened enough ice to extend that into a line of ten or so hubs and associated wings before they reached the huge circular cut that could only be meant for a dome. A dome in the first phase construction – someone clearly expected this far-flung little outpost to become the first city in the outer system.

As he approached the big airlock at the end of the engineering wing, Luke realised that he was rushing and forced himself to slow down. Getting out from under a roof and walking under a big sky was the one thing he missed the most since he'd traded construction for cargo, so he turned the cart away from the airlock and slowly pushed it past the idle construction minions. The months on Ganymede had been unkind to the big, insectile robots. They had all the typical wear and tear that you would expect to see on heavy equipment, but they looked like they were ten years old, not two. Every leg, arm, and panel was beaten, battered, and at least a little bit bent, and there was a hell of a lot of improvised refunctioning and other kludges that he recognised as the work of an engineer trying to wring every last bit of use out of dying machines.

Luke rounded the end of the personnel wing and followed the gravel pathway that led to the airlock at the end of the glasshouse. He kicked at the gravel as he walked and watched it scatter. The difference between lunar basalt gravel and water ice gravel was remarkable. They may have looked the same, but the ice was bouncier and it scattered farther. He gazed at the distant curving ridge and the mirrors that reflected extra sunlight into the glasshouse. He tried to admire the majesty of Jupiter looming overhead. It was all a wasted effort. There was no salvaging his last few hours on Ganymede. No matter how hard he tried, he just couldn't shake the disappointing sunrise out of his head.

Actually, it wasn't the sunrise itself that bothered Luke. He was upset that he just couldn't seem to stop expecting a frozen pissball orbiting Jupiter to be like Luna. He knew why it kept happening. With a barren, grey-on-grey landscape and an almost identical surface gravity, Ganymede looked and felt like the moon. Combine that with the decades he'd spent working on Luna, and most would think that it was perfectly natural for his every instinct and expectation to be tied to Earth's moon. However, any spacer would tell you that there was nothing natural about working in a vacuum, and all of his experience should have taken him in the exact opposite direction. His instinct should have been to think through every detail, then question every assumption, and then think it all through again.

Over the years Luke had said 'little surprises are lethal surprises' more often than 'hello' and 'goodbye' and 'please pass the salt' combined. It was his mantra. He muttered it to himself every time he closed his helmet. He said it to every man he ever sent into an airlock. He used it as his signoff to signal the end of every call, memo, briefing, or meeting. That was the man who was annoyed for not anticipating the lame sunrise. That was the man who had been caught off guard at least a dozen times over the last few days because he let himself get distracted and didn't think through the differences between Ganymede and Luna. That was also the man who then walked right into what was probably the biggest surprise of his life.

He was still stewing as he went through the big airlock at the end of the glasshouse, and when the inner airlock door opened, he was hit by Mozart, cranked up well beyond loud. That was a bit unexpected, but the thundering music was just the setup.

The glasshouse, like the rest of Aquarius, was stuck in the seemingly eternal state of half-completion that was typical for a construction site. Still, despite the fact that the sections closest to the airlock were still barren, it was obvious that it was meant to be far more than the typical feel-good patch of garden. Firstly, it was huge, at least a hundred metres from the airlock to the hub, maybe closer to a hundred and twenty. Secondly, it was clearly being set up to maximise the density of production. The sections down by the door to the hub were already a riot of green. They were a textbook example of intensive agriculture, and with a huge aquaculture pond in the middle of each section, the glasshouse was eventually going to produce one hell of a lot of food.

All of those thoughts, along with the irritation Luke always felt when surrounded by unfinished work, flitted through his head as he stepped into the glasshouse. He didn't see anyone working down amongst the green so he blithely assumed that Zoey, or more likely, Olivia, had forgotten to turn off the music when they left for the night. That sent his head tumbling into the puzzle of how someone could have just forgotten to turn off music that was playing so loudly, and as a result, he didn't spot the naked woman until he almost tripped over her.

It should have been physically impossible for such a scrawny little woman to produce such a tremendous noise, but there it was, yet another surprise for Luke. Zoey's startled, shrieking scream was truly deafening, and it just kept going. Simple physics said that there just couldn't have been that much air in her little lungs, but somehow she sustained that scream long enough for him to realise that he was staring at the naked woman, decide that staring at her was probably impolite, and turn away.

"Jesus Christ, Luke, you scared the shit out of me," Zoey huffed as she fumbled with her clothes.

"Yeah, I kind of guessed that," Luke said. "You know, from your screaming and shrieking and all that. I'm kind of clever that way."

The fumbling stopped, and after giving it a couple seconds to be sure it wasn't just a pause, Luke turned back around and stepped right into the longest and most uncomfortable moment in the history of the universe. Zoey, for perhaps the first time in her life, seemed to be at a loss for words, and neither of them could even manage a snarky joke or crass comment.

"Well," Luke eventually said. "I gotta say, Zoey, I didn't peg you as the type of girl who would like this sort of shit."

"And I didn't peg you for the kind of guy who would think that only pretty girls like to lie out in the sun," she snarled.

"First, don't pull that not-very-passive, passive-aggressive 'tell me I'm pretty' bullshit on me," he snapped right back at her. He was annoyed by what was her typical reaction to just about everything, but also relieved to escape the universe's most uncomfortable moment. "I've been married longer than you've been alive."

"Wait." Zoey frowned, puzzled. "I thought you just married Tara a couple of years ago?"

"Yeah, we had our first anniversary while we were bringing you out, but if you figure in all the, uh... practice wives it took for me to finally get it right, it adds up to one hell of a lot of years of dealing with bitchy bullshit."

"That is some charmingly misogynistic maths you've got going there."

"And second," Luke continued, pointedly. "I was talking about the music. I had you pegged for liking that thumpa-thumpa, 'I'm so sad I want to die' crap, not strings and brass classical."

"Oh." Zoey frowned again.

"Yeah, apology accepted."

"I didn't apologise."

"It was as close as you were going to get, so I decided to just help you out a bit."

Zoey was about to come back at him with something caustic, but he cut her off with a dramatic gesture at his cart and a few magic words, "Now do you want your personal freight allotment or what?"

And with that, the moody, mercurial little woman was transformed into a kid on Christmas morning. She grinned and gave Luke a quick peck on the cheek before scrambling eagerly over to his cart.

Luke couldn't help but chuckle and smile. One thing that had been obvious to Tara, and something that he had eventually figured out over the course of their long drift out here with Zoey, was that there was a bright and genuinely nice young woman hidden behind the scowl, snarl, and black hair dye. Luke thought that Zoey was a bit too comfortable with the wild-child end of the spectrum of irrational chick bullshit, sprawling naked on the floor of her glasshouse being a case in point, but she was still a nice young woman.

Luke gave the blanket and pillow on the floor a belated double take, and then looked around at the glasshouse. The lights were all off, but the glasshouse was lit up as bright as a spring day on Earth, and it was warm. He turned towards the source of the light and closed his eyes, half amazed and half annoyed with himself for stumbling into yet another surprise.

"Wow," he said. "I guess you sprawling naked on the floor wasn't quite as crazy as I thought. That actually feels like the sun." Luke looked around for the IR emitters but couldn't spot them.

"I was not sprawling. I was sunbathing," Zoey said. "It's probably all in my head, but lying out for a couple of hours in real sunlight actually helps with the whole grump and funk thing."

"You can call it what you want, but shifting the vocabulary won't change the fact that you were sprawled across the floor like a cat that fell asleep during a yoga class," he said, teasing.

Zoey stopped shuffling the cases long enough to give Luke a single finger salute. "And for your information, that is the sun."

"That can't be just the sun." He squinted at the mirrors on the ridge. The futility of building a glasshouse under such a feeble sun was another thing that he should have realised. "Even with mirrors to augment the direct sunlight… Jesus, how big are those mirrors?"

"It takes about twenty thousand square metres of mirror to reflect enough light and heat into a glasshouse this size to get something close to a mid-latitude, Earth-like intensity." Zoey set a small case on the floor and went back to moving cases and checking their manifest tags. "But there's room for something like five hundred square kilometres of mirror on that ridgeline, so a couple of hectare's worth looks pretty small."

"Five hundred square kilometres of mirrors?" Luke muttered.

She had to have that wrong. The ridge was a fairly long arc left by a big and very old impact, but it couldn't have been more than twelve hundred metres tall; none of the surface features on Ganymede were more than about twelve hundred metres tall. The water ice might look and feel like stone, but it wasn't stone. It couldn't support the extremes of relief that you found on rocky worlds, so the mountains, scarps, and deep craters that were common elsewhere just sagged into hills and swales on Ganymede.

"Yeah, they're going to build a bunch of huge as shit mirror towers all along the ridge," she said. "It's the whole reason they decided to build Aquarius here."

Perhaps she had the number right after all. They'd have to be damn tall towers, but it would be easy to build mirror towers that were several thousands of metres tall on Ganymede. The thin film mirrors that they'd developed for solar sails weighed almost nothing, the gravity was low, and with no atmosphere there was almost no need to brace for horizontal stresses other than the pressure from the light itself. A simple, old-fashioned carbon-fibre scaffolding design could easily do the job.

It was plausible, but Luke's mind reeled as he worked through the maths. There were a hundred hectares in a square kilometre, so five hundred square kilometres of mirrors meant they were planning for, or at least imagining a hell of a lot of acreage under glass. "Twenty five thousand glasshouses like this one? That can't be right."

"Most of the glasshouses will be bigger than this, and set up for industrial-scale growing," she said. "But yeah, that's the rough number."

"And it's a number that's way too big for just producing a few lemons, blueberries, and other luxury perishables that you can't grow without a little gravity, soil, and real sunlight."

"And that's only part of the story." There was a bit of wicked in her smile. "If you add the aquaculture ponds and what you can produce with factory-scale hydroponics under artificial light, and yeast, and algae, then it's pretty damn obvious that Aquarius is meant to produce one hell of a lot more food than it needs to be self sufficient."

"Don't pan for gold, sell the miners eggs." Luke chuckled. "Looks like someone back at Corporate actually learned something in their history classes."

"Prostitution was actually the biggest money maker during most of Earth's gold rushes, but if Aquarius was meant to be a deep space whorehouse, they would have never contracted the glasshouse to a woman who so clearly lacks the appropriate assets." Zoey grabbed her chest, looked down, and made a comically disappointed face and shrugged at Luke. "So the safe bet is that the real plan for Aquarius is to supply overpriced food to everyone who scurries out to claim a chunk of the Jovian moons."

"And you're the first Aggie in." He was impressed. "You clever, clever girl."

Zoey checked the shipping tag on the last case on Luke's cart, checked it again, and frowned. "Luke, where's the rest of my stuff?"

"That's all of it." He nodded at the small case she'd set aside. "Corporate cut the personal allotments in half for this trip."

"Those bastards!" Her curse was heartfelt.

"Hey, cutting your allocation lets them add six more kilos worth of very important stuff to the four hundred tonnes of construction supplies that I brought out."

"But I need my stuff!" She looked truly desperate.

"Oh, I know you do sweetie…" Luke loaded the last word with all the paternal affection he could muster. She hated the entire category of pleasantly nondescript adjectives that people used as name substitutes, but she loathed 'sweetie' with all the fire her heart and soul could muster, which was a lot. After a long moment passed without a foul but poetic reference to his mother's intimate inclinations, he realised that he had again missed something. That was getting tedious.

"You didn't find Tara's package, did you?"

Zoey's bewildered expression confirmed that she hadn't.

"Seriously, Zoey? You didn't notice that Tara added six kilos of 'This is farm shit, honest' to the shipping manifest?"

"Olivia checked the shipment in." Zoey smiled and rolled her eyes, shaking her head. "But that does explain a couple of rather odd questions she asked me yesterday."

"Well those must have been some profoundly odd questions if they somehow stood out from the rest of the lunacy that tumbles out of that girl's mouth."

"Yeah, Olivia can be…" Zoey gasped. "Oh my God, I told her that farmers fertilise things with shit. Please tell me she didn't put it in the fertiliser hopper."

Zoey ran over to a pallet and immediately spotted the small cardboard box sitting on the plastic bags of ammonium nitrate. She ripped the box open and sighed like a woman in love. "Oh Luke, you and Tara are life-savers."

"Honestly, Zoey, how do you manage to eat chocolate by the kilo and stay all scrawny and waify?"

Zoey laughed heartily even though she knew that Luke was only half-joking. He really did like that girl.

Delivering most of the rest of the personal allotments was uneventful. With only a dozen or so people on the base, Aquarius was still small enough that Luke didn't really have to worry about security. So even though it was 3 A.M. on the base clock, and all the reasonable people were asleep, he could just leave the cases where the right person would find the right one first thing and be done with it. Unfortunately, the one person he might have actually wanted to avoid was the one person other than Zoey who wasn't asleep.

Luke was painfully aware that engineers tended to be a socially awkward and generally odd bunch of human-shaped animals, and adding spacer to that mix pushed it up a notch, but Karl Hansen was in a league of his own. He doubled down on the odd, added a touch of manic, and drove it all home with a complete and utter inability to understand the concept of inappropriate. He could be a hell of an engineer when the whim struck, but he was still a long ways out there. When Luke entered the repair shop there was some kind of collage of artsy-but-creepy, oddly angled pictures of nude women cycling across all the computer monitors in the shop, and Karl was using a laser cutter to carve a slogan into the wall.

In addition to the simple fact that vandalising the base was almost as inappropriate as the erotica on the computers, carving something into the wall was also a criminally inappropriate way to use an extremely expensive tool. Still, whatever hack Karl had done to control the depth of cut was damn impressive. Laser cutters usually had just two settings, 'blaze away you glorious bastard' and 'rip right through that shit'. Delicate simply wasn't in their DNA, and Luke had no idea how Karl could possibly have tweaked the thing so it only burned a few microns off the surface of the foamsteel wall. It was impressive as all hell, but still a gross violation of at least a half dozen regulations.

Luke recognised the half-finished quote immediately. Most engineers knew it. "The future is defined by neither hope nor despair. The future is carved from the past by Occam's razor."

"It means that the simple solution is usually the best solution," Karl shouted over the shrieking hiss of vaporising steel.

"Yes, Karl, I know. I've read Kerstoff's textbook on practical and applied engineering," Luke shouted back.

"Really?"

"Karl, I used to be the Chief Engineer for Hadley Rille."

"The city?"

"No, I was the Chief Engineer of a lunar canyon."

Luke's sarcasm was wasted on Karl. Karl just nodded, as if he'd been politely corrected, and turned his attention back to his amazing act of vandalism.

"And that isn't really what that quote means," Luke shouted.

That got Karl's attention. He shut off the cutter. "But that's what the book says it means."

"Yeah, Kerstoff uses it to introduce the idea of parsimony as an engineering ideal, but he's quoting someone else, and the original author never intended it to mean anything like that."

"But that's what the book says it means," Karl insisted.

"Karl, didn't the words 'hope' and 'despair' ever strike you as odd for a quote about engineering and design?"

"No."

"Well they should have, because that is actually a quote about literature, not engineering."

"Literature? What could Occam's razor possibly have to do with literature?"

"The book where Kerstoff got that quote is called Where the Hell is My Flying Car? and it's all about why writers and filmmakers have always been so shitty at predicting the future," Luke explained. "Authors always write about what they hope the future will look like, or what they fear it might be. They never seem to understand that in the real world, we only use new technologies in ways that do something we couldn't do more cheaply or more conveniently without them. We can make flying cars, but the skies back on Earth aren't full of them because it's far cheaper and easier to make something that rolls along a road on wheels and axles. That's what's meant by Occam's razor in that quote, and that's the reason we still use screens and keyboards for most of our computer work, and hydraulics to move heavy things, and screws to fasten things."

"That does make a lot of sense," Karl said. "I don't know if it helps any, but I've read a lot of those old stories and it makes sense."

"Why the hell are you carving that old quote into the wall anyway?"

"Reading it over and over again helps me figure things out. You know, like the really hard, complicated things that I've been trying to figure out for weeks. So I decided to put it on the wall."

"What's to figure out?" Luke gestured at what were literally piles of damaged tools and equipment lying around the shop. "Just dig in and fix shit."

"It's not that kind of problem." Karl glanced nervously around the room before admitting, "It's a people problem."

"Ah, the people problem. The cruel joke that God plays on engineers." Luke felt sorry for Karl. He hadn't wanted to run into Karl, and if that was how a fellow engineer felt, he couldn't imagine how the people stationed on Aquarius felt about the odd, awkward, and annoying man. "Well, the first rule is that you never try to find an engineering solution to a people problem. But in this particular case, the engineering advice about digging in and fixing stuff still kind of holds. People notice when things come off the repair log, and that alone solves a lot of the people problems that engineers have to deal with."

"I've tried repairing extra stuff and doing favours and nice stuff for her, but when I drop things off she just says, 'Thank you' and that's it. If I try to stay and talk or something, she just looks at me like 'why are you still here?'. Sometimes she even says, 'Why are you still here?'" Karl looked at Luke, all but pleading. "How can I ever get someone to like me if I can't ever even talk to them?"

Karl's problem wasn't a people problem, it was a woman problem, and Luke felt truly sorry for him. He thought he could guess which 'her' he was talking about. Doc was married, Zoey would probably scare him, and Kai would definitely terrify him. That left Olivia, and it didn't take much imagination to see just how hopeless his situation was. An engineer who was captivated by Olivia's cherubic charm would have no hope of escaping as she pleasantly, and probably unintentionally, crushed his awkward, hapless, and socially inept soul.

"Yeah, I know all about that kind of people problem," Luke said. "Back when I was Chief of Engineering, I figured out a kind of strategy for when I talked to people, and it helped a lot. If I didn't want to talk to someone, I would make sure I picked a time when they were busy to drop by to fix something or deliver a repair or whatever."

"But I want to stay a little so we can talk and stuff," Karl objected.

"And when I wanted to talk, I picked a time when I was pretty sure they weren't going to be busy, so they had nothing better to do than chat for a bit."

Karl's jaw dropped and he gestured at the half finished quote on his wall. "That makes so much sense, and it's so simple."

"Yeah, it's so obvious that once you see it you can't believe you didn't already know it, but it also only solves half the problem."

"What's the other half?"

"Well, I'll bet that part of the reason she doesn't seem like she wants to talk to you is because you don't know much about things she likes to talk about. So you also need to make sure that you're all set to talk about something that she likes."

Karl nodded, then frowned. "Like what things?"

"Depends." Luke shrugged. "I used to keep a little database on all the people I worked with, and whenever I found out that they liked something, I kept track of it. Then when I had to call them or go to a meeting with them or something, I could check what they liked and look something up so I could mention it and get things started if I wanted to talk to them."

For several seconds, Karl just stood there, absolutely still. He didn't even blink, or move his eyes, or breathe, and then, without warning, he leapt into frenetic action, rushing over to his computer console and working like a man possessed. Everything else was forgotten, including the half-finished laser-etched graffiti.

"Karl."

Karl looked up at Luke, and his eyes darted to the one small plastic case that was still on the cart. "Is that my personal allotment?"

"Yes, Karl, but…"

Karl darted over and opened the case. He made a small gesture of triumph at whatever it was he saw inside and darted back over to the console.

"Karl!"

Karl stopped, confused.

"You need to finish that!" Luke pointed at the quote on the wall. "I can't stand knowing that something is half finished, and knowing that it's not finished because I interrupted you would bug the living shit out of me. So would you mind finishing it, now?"

"Oh yeah, sure." Karl restarted the laser cutter, and Luke waited for him to finish carving the quote before he left. It wasn't until a full day later, just after Tara had finished making the slingshot burn around Europa and they'd settled in for the long drift home that he realised Karl had spelt 'despair' wrong.

That was going to irritate Luke forever.

Chapter 1

Why the hell do a couple of little cleaning robots think they need twenty kilos of minced onions?

John thought he ran the base. He thought that the little chart he'd made that put him at the top of the chain of command gave him a fistful of trumps in his morale-be-damned crusade to get the surface crew to finish out every minute of every shift. He was wrong. Simon's roughnecks loved their rugby more than they loved their mothers, and nothing short of an act of God was going to stop them from watching it. In fact, when it came to their precious international test matches Mitch only gave God himself a fifty-fifty shot at keeping Kai and the boys from finding a way to plant their arses in front of the broadcast. That was why, even though there was a full two hours left in the afternoon shift, Mitch was already pulling the first batch of game day finger foods out of the oven and wondering where the hell they were. The pre-game blather was already in full song and there was still no sign of the surface crew.

They were late enough to cause Mitch a bit of worry. He had planned all his Saturday cooking around the presumption that Kai and the boys would again thwart John and find an excuse to end the day early. For the rugby mad Kiwis, he had put together a collection of mini egg rolls, mini pizzas, samosas, and other things that seemed like junk but would, in aggregate, pass as a decent meal. Mitch had also already made emergency dinner salads for Zoey and Olivia, just in case it was one of the weeks when Zoey decided that rugby was a barbaric spectacle that she had to boycott by convincing Olivia to start their usual Saturday night movie early. All of that early cooking had freed a good hour for him to prepare the something special he'd promised for Doc. She wanted to surprise John with dinner in their quarters followed by whatever prim rituals the oddly prudish woman thought constituted a romantic evening.

However, if some dark miracle had allowed John to upend the natural order of things, it was going to throw Mitch's whole evening into the shredder. He could keep the buffet of game day snacks warm for a little while, but certainly not for two hours. They would be inedible after that long, and then he'd have to cobble together something close to a normal after-shift meal, but that would use up all the time he had set aside to cook for Doc. He could maybe just give Doc the salads he'd made for Zoey and Olivia, but that certainly wasn't what Doc expected him to make from the prosciutto, capers, unusual cheeses, and other fancy ingredients she'd brought out with her personal freight allotment.

Fortunately, before Mitch could despair any further, he heard Edgar's bellowing laugh from down by the hub, and he literally sighed in relief. Dumping the batch of mini egg rolls into a big bowl, he took them out to the table nearest where the hall passed through the lounge. He knew he took the extra favours and feel-goods he added to his job a little too seriously, but he also knew that little things really made a difference for a small crew that had been stuck on a distant moon for well over a year.

The lounge itself was an odd space. Much to the consternation of base and ship designers, the human animal reacted poorly to living in overly regular spaces. People liked nooks and crannies and open places that served no real purpose. Removing a wall here and there had become the standard way of creating that kind of variety in living spaces outside of the Old Well, and that was how the base lounge had been created. The crew had simply decided not to install several walls near the middle of what was now the personnel wing, turning the kitchen, mess hall, and break room into one large and oddly-shaped open area. A dedicated kitchen would have reduced interruptions and made it easier for Mitch to manage the housekeeping systems that he also had to run, but he still liked the makeshift common room. It was really just a wide space in the hallway, so at some time every day, often several times a day, almost everyone passed through, creating a nice, social focus for the base. Mitch thought that sort of thing was far more valuable than a workspace free of distractions.

"Ah, good-on-ya bro," Paul said as he grabbed a handful of mini egg rolls and started shoving them in his mouth. "Love these buggers."

The others in the crew followed Paul's lead, not that any of them were the kind who needed any encouragement to consume food on offer. The bowl was empty in the blink of an eye, just as Mitch had expected.

Simon's lone surface crew was the typical collection of mismatched this-and-that kind of people. Paul was small and wiry, but he ate like a horse and his booming voice filled every room he entered. Edgar was a giant of a man, but he ate like a mouse, and except for his laugh, he was as quiet as a mouse as well. Cuzzie looked like a brute but acted like a giddy puppy, and he claimed to have enough cousins to populate a small country. If something had been done by a human being, one of Cuzzie's cousins had been there or done it. Tui acted like an idiot half the time, but Mitch knew that he had an Art History degree. Useless as all hell, but clearly not the sort of thing an idiot picked up. And Kai was probably the oddest of the group because she actually was the stereotypical foul-mouthed bitch of a crew foreman that she seemed to be.

"Why don't you guys go ahead and take a quick run through the showers before kick off?" Simon suggested. "I'll help Mitch get things moved around for the game."

"Yeah, boss's right, bro, you stink like yesterday's shit," Paul said, smacking Edgar upside the head.

The crew continued down the hall towards the bunks and locker rooms, roughhousing and insulting each other all the way.

"You guys are cutting it a bit close this afternoon," Mitch said to Simon as he nodded a request for the wild-haired old construction manager to help him shift a table. "You had me a little worried that John had won this round."

"Just the opposite, actually," Simon said. "It seems that John finally figured out that Kai and her boys have an infinite number of technically legitimate safety issues, obscure Polynesian religious holidays, and other things that they could use to shut down pretty much any shift they fancy."

"So he gave in and just let them end the shift early?" Mitch frowned. "That doesn't sound like the John I know."

"Oh, John didn't give in," Simon said, jovially. "Honestly, why would he want to win some good will and boost morale when he can generously agree to let the crew make up the missed hours by giving him some comp time?"

"He doesn't really think he's going to get any comp time out of them, does he?" Mitch asked, rolling his eyes.

"He might think it, but the dumb bastard's actually going to lose hours." Simon chuckled sadly. "The whole crew has started keeping track of every single second they spend doing anything that might possibly be considered work so they can claim comp time for it. I drew the line at Paul trying to say that taking a shit was prepping for surface work, but it's still adding up pretty damn fast. So I'm probably going to lose an entire afternoon shift, maybe even a whole day every week."

"Shit." Mitch gestured Simon towards a second table. "John could solve the whole problem and make everyone happy and keep every minute of ice time if he just shifted the base clock by a couple of hours so the games started at 6:30 instead of 4:30. And I've gotta say that matching dinner time with the games would make my life a hell of a lot easier."

"Yeah, shifting the clock would be the smart thing to do," Simon agreed as they moved the second table and created the optimum rugby-watching lounge configuration. "But you suggested it, so it will never happen."

"What a pitiful excuse for a base commander," Mitch grumbled. "Even if he is married to the CEO's daughter, I still can't believe that anyone back at Corporate would be stupid enough to put him in charge of Aquarius. It's almost criminal."

"He has been a nightmare, but pretty soon he'll be exactly the right kind of base commander for Aquarius," Simon replied.

"You planning to give him an involuntary brain transplant or something?" Mitch pretended to take the idea seriously. "Because I've been thinking along the same lines, but I'm pretty sure it's a little bit illegal."

"The union bosses back in the Old Well just signed off on John designating the glasshouse as an isolatable, fully functional wing," Simon said, smiling. "So our self-contained living spaces are now, officially, triple redundant."

"Which means we can finally start expanding the crew," Mitch finished the thought.

"Six new surface crews, a thousand tons of new equipment, and a half-dozen experienced support staff have already started the drift out." Simon's smile grew into a grin. "So in ten weeks or so, John will be delegating pretty much everything important to someone else, and the only thing he'll be handling directly is the corporate bureaucratic bullshit."

"Well, I guess I gotta admit that John is pretty damn good with the corporate bullshit end of things." Mitch tried to sound sceptical, but he was smiling right along with Simon. If there was any arena in which you could say that John was actually blessed with talent, it was playing the corporate bureaucracy game. "So we just have to hold out for a few more weeks and hope his new flock of flunkies will be competent."

"And not like our new intern," Simon said.

"Oh yeah, definitely not like our new intern," Mitch agreed. "Five days of him and I'm already counting down his six months."

A timer chimed, but when Mitch turned towards the oven and saw what his minis were doing, his jaw dropped. "Have you little buggers lost your bloody minds?"

Minis were the miniature versions of the big construction minions that the crews used outside. Colourful beetle-like plastic shells, power induction antennas that looked like ears, and big optical sensors designed to mimic eyes made them look cute, but they were actually some of the most versatile little robots around. They had surprisingly sophisticated AIs for such small machines, and there was an almost infinite variety of tools and implements that could be installed on their three tool mounts. The motorised rear mount was particularly useful. It was sometimes called a stinger on both the minis and the minions because it looked like a scorpion tail when it was unfolded out of the top of their shell. It could arch all the way forward to the front of the mini, and that allowed the little machines to bring a small power tool to bear on things held in the claws that were usually installed on the two front mounts. Add to that the fact that minis were capable of extreme precision in three dimensions, and a mini became a machine that could do anything from embroidery to cleaning toilets.

For the most part, Mitch only used his minis to clean things, but for some reason the two he used in the kitchen had taken it upon themselves to climb up on the stainless steel prep-counter and chop the living shit out of the big box of onions that Zoey had brought over from the glasshouse. The minis were actually doing a pretty good job of it. They both had a third claw mounted on their stinger, and one was using that extra claw to help peel the onions while the other had used it to grab a knife and was merrily chopping away.

"Command stop!" Mitch shouted, and the minis froze.

"Did they decide to do that all on their own?" Simon asked.

"Yeah," Mitch replied as they walked over to the minis and their monumental pile of onions. "All my minis have an annoying tendency to do a lot more stupid little things than you'd expect, but an onion mountain is a bit odder than usual. Their random bouts of stupidity have always kind of fit the jobs they're supposed to be doing, like when the minis that clean the bathrooms sprayed Zoey's perfume all over the toilets, but this is odd. Honestly, why the hell do a couple of little cleaning robots think they need twenty kilos of minced onions?"

Simon picked one of the minis up, pushed a few of the little buttons hidden on its belly, and squinted at a little readout. "Well, it looks like they're murdering your onions because someone added some kind of culinary training to their basic task matrix."

"And by someone, you mean Karl, right?"

"Assuming that you didn't do it in your sleep or something, yeah," Simon admitted. "He's probably the only person on the base who could find a way around the security that's supposed keep anyone from messing with the training mode of someone else's AI."

"I'm going to kill him," Mitch grumbled. "Of all the people on this base, he should damn well know how hard it is to get these things trained up just like you want them."

"It was probably just his way of saying thank you for making sure he gets fed even though he never shows up for meals," Simon said. "And if you're going to blame anyone, blame John. He was the moron who decided to buy the household models instead of the industrial ones."

"Is that why they break down so much?"

"Yeah, the domestic versions are nowhere near as sturdy. That's part of the reason we're behind on all the interior detail work; we just can't keep enough of the little buggers on the job long enough to get anything done. But the real problem is that the learning and reward parameters burnt into their AIs are tweaked to try to make them playful and curious," Simon explained. "Which is fine if all you want is a glorified toy that helps with little fiddly things around the house, but when you try to get them to focus on consistent work, it's a big problem. An industrial AI's base reward matrix is biased towards repeating and perfecting tasks, but these have an emphasis on finding new things to do, and they give themselves positive feedback for doing them. And when you try to force them to stick to a limited range of tasks, they get frustrated because they're not getting the reward for doing new things, so they sometimes fall off the drift and do things like build an onion mountain."

"Those minis are not approved for food handling," declared Abhrakasin, their uptight and infuriatingly proper new intern, as he walked imperiously into the lounge. Somehow, the young man managed to turn that simple and uninflected statement of fact into an accusation of incompetence. "That is a violation of the housekeeping regulations in the Aquarius charter."

He pulled out a data pad and began filling out an incident report.

"You have got to be shitting me," Mitch growled.

"I do not shit people," Abhrakasin said. "My primary responsibility is to observe and advise on the implementation of policy and procedure. I have observed a violation. Now I must advise the management."

"And if I poisoned your food that would probably also be a violation of housekeeping regulations, right?" Mitch asked, sarcastically.

"Yes it would," Abhrakasin said, humourlessly. "I advise against it. Multiple violations may be considered in aggregate if disciplinary sanctions are deemed appropriate."

"Simon, would you mind trying to wipe that extra programming out of these minis for me?" Mitch asked. "I need to run grab some poison before the game starts."

"Sure," Simon said, agreeably. "Just unlock their command default for me, so I can access the programming and teaching mode."

Located at the very end of the engineering wing, Karl's repair shop was as far away from the lounge as a person could get without leaving Aquarius. Supposedly it was out there on the end of the wing because that was the best place to build the high-ceilinged oversized module and airlock that he needed in order to bring the minions inside for repairs. Karl had always assumed that made sense, but after spending three straight days and nights using his diagram of the base to turn his new plan into reality, he wondered if that explanation was true. It might just have been the lack of sleep, but he couldn't stop thinking that his shop was way out on the end of the wing simply because nobody liked him.

Aquarius was a modular base, but not in the common sense of the word. The big octagonal hub was the only section that had been constructed elsewhere and dropped into place; everything else had been built in situ. 'Modular' referred to the style of base or free-floating station where a dozen or so standardised subsection designs were used over and over like building blocks. Aquarius's glasshouse wasn't just a wing that extended 120 metres out from the west side of the hub; it was a run of ten identical Type 3 glasshouse modules built one after the other in a line. The personnel wing on the southwest side of the hub was made from six Type 1 room modules and twenty Type 2 room modules built around eight hall modules. The engineering wing that extended to the south of the hub was similar to the personnel wing but with the addition of Karl's shop tacked on to the end.

Karl had never really thought that much about the location of his shop until he updated his diagram of the base to include the new hub that they were building on the north side of the existing one. The minute he did that, he realised that his shop and the second hub were variants of the same Type 2 hub modules. So, if they could build a whole line of hub modules off the north side of the original hub, then obviously they could have built a second hub first thing. If they had done that, then Simon and the surface crew could have used that second hub as a staging area and Karl could have used it as a temporary shop. That would have made all the difference in the world.

It was incredibly difficult to work on machinery out in a vacuum, so by the time Simon and the crew got around to building the repair shop, Karl was already months behind. Ten out of their fourteen construction minions were damaged in ways that limited their use, and several of them were so badly beat up that they needed a significant rebuild to restore anything close to full functionality. From there it had been a constant, round-the-clock scramble to keep enough machinery on the ice to let the crew work at full speed, and once he was stuck spending every possible hour scrambling to keep those machines going, the broken minis had quite literally started to pile up. At least half the minis on the base, maybe as many as two-thirds, were sitting in his shop, waiting for repairs.

It was an impossible backlog and everyone hated him for it, but if they had built that second hub first, there would never have been much of a backlog at all. Repairs were so much easier and so much faster in a pressurised shop that just having that space for a few hours a shift during the early months would have made it easy for him to keep up. And like Luke said, everyone likes an engineer who clears the backlog.

Building the second hub first made so much sense to Karl that he couldn't help but obsess over his suspicion that all his problems were due to them not liking him and wanting his shop as far away from the rest of the base as they could put it. He realised that he had wandered away from the computer console, and cursed himself. "Focus, Karl. You need to focus."

Minion Seven made an annoyed noise, and Karl didn't have to look at the message it sent to his computer console to know what it was saying.

"I know you want to go out and get back to work," Karl said. "But I've got to get this done first."

Minion Seven responded with a demanding buzz.

"I'll get you fixed tonight."

A sceptical braap.

"I will, I promise. I just have something really important that I need to do before the afternoon shift ends."

Minion Seven made more angry noises and sent a long message scrolling rapidly over the top of the collage of voyeuristic pictures cycling across one of the big secondary monitors mounted over Karl's computer console. The minion shifted and pointed its stinger-mounted welder out the large window to where six other minions were powered down just outside the airlock, waiting for major repairs.

"I said I'll get you fixed!" Karl entered a command into his console and Minion Seven powered down. "I'll get you all fixed."

Karl tried to take a deep breath and focus on what he was working on, but couldn't. He hadn't slept in three days, and when he let himself get too tired, any lapse in concentration was like letting a dog slip the leash to chase squirrels and pigeons. His mind darted like mad, bounding after thought after thought until he was lost in a forest of ideas and imaginings, and it kept going and going. He had no idea how long it took to calm himself down, but eventually he found himself standing in the middle of the mess that was his shop, repeatedly reading the quote he'd carved into the wall.

He had to backtrack to figure out what he'd been working on. Minion Seven? No. The huge backlog of minis waiting for repair? No. He looked at the console and the diagram of the base on the central monitor. The modules. His shop and the new hub were the same module. He could have had a temporary shop a year ago, but that wasn't why he was thinking about the modules. That wasn't what was important about the modular design of the base. Redundancy of the modular systems and the intentional isolation of the safety systems: that was what was important about the modular design of the base.

Modular bases were ideal for situations where there wasn't regolith you could grind up to make one of the concrete equivalents that were needed to pour an organic-style structure. The consistency of the modules made it possible to standardise all their parts, including the components that went inside the modules. So it was easy to get a factory to crank out a set variety of wall panels and door mechanisms and airscrubbers and all the other things you needed. A modular design was also ideal for situations where fires or pressure loss were an ongoing concern. Emergency pressure doors were usually built into the connections between the modules, making it easy to confine any problem that might arise to a very small portion of the base.

That was it. That was the thought he needed to get back to. The focus on isolating the modules extended into the design of all their safety and control subsystems, and that was what had been such a nightmare for Karl and his little plan. He had finally managed to get past all of it, but it had been a hell of a lot of work.

Karl was about to initiate the huge program he had created, but he stopped, took a deep breath, and took one more run through his checklist. The distraction of the argument with Minion Seven had him a little rattled. He was breaking at least a thousand rules and regulations, so he had to make sure he had everything perfect, and he had to have a backup for everything that could possibly not go quite right, just in case. He also had to do it before the end of the shift. That way he could be sure she would be in the glasshouse, and more importantly, if he did it during the shift, Kai and the boys would be on the surface, in their suits. Having them out there was his double backup just in case all his other just-in-cases didn't cover everything. Triple redundancy wasn't just the number one safety regulation, it was a good idea.

He went through his checklist a third time. 'Shower' was written near the bottom, and it wasn't checked off. He glanced at the clean set of coveralls sitting on the edge of his computer console, then sniffed at his armpit and was desperately thankful for his third run through the checklist. He stank. Women hated body odour.

He checked the time. It was too close to the end of shift for him to run all the way to the men's locker room at the end of the personnel wing, but he had a shower in his shop for chemical emergencies. That shower wasn't really meant for washing up, but he must have planned to use it all along. That would explain why he had put a big note on it that said 'shower'.

Olivia was cute, flirtatious, and buxom. She was almost always overflowing with good cheer, and when that was added to the fact that she said some of the most inane and offbeat things, most people immediately dismissed her as some kind of bubble-headed bimbo. That was a mistake. Not only was there a surprisingly intelligent young woman hidden under the blonde hair and tragically misinformed prattling, but to describe her as a simple bimbo would miss the fact that she was actually a slightly too adult version of the fairy-tale princess from a children's cartoon.

When the door between the hub and the glasshouse opened, Mitch could hear her singing to the glasshouse minis.

"That's right, that's right, that is so, so right," she sang. "In soil we sow or roots don't grow."

Yes, Olivia was a fairy-tale princess and the minis were her friendly forest creatures. A few of the minis had little circular saws mounted on their stingers and were giving the citrus trees their first pruning, but most of the fifty or sixty little robots that were assigned to the glasshouse were gathered around Olivia, who was sitting daintily on the floor. The minis were chittering excitedly and playfully scattering dirt everywhere as they helped her transplant seedlings from hydroponics trays into small soil-filled pots.

"Hi, Mitch!" Olivia exclaimed with a childish wave of her soil-covered hand. "Look bugglyboos, it's Mitch."

The minis scattered even more dirt and spilled some of the pots as they scurried around, waved, and made happy noises.

"So why ya in here, Mitch?" she asked. "We don't have much ready to pick right now, but Zoey says we can dig up some potatoes next week."

The minis made enthusiastic noises.

"Oh yes, digging potatoes will be a fun new thing." Olivia smiled at one of the minis, getting an excited reaction from it. "Won't it?"

"I just need some of Auntie Zoey's world famous swill." Mitch walked over to the still that he had helped Zoey build, and grabbed one of the empty wine bottles that Doc had been so tickled to donate to their not-all-that-clandestine defiance of Corporate's prohibition against alcohol.

"Oh wow! It's world famous now!" Olivia was genuinely excited. "Really?"

"Ganymede is still a very small and very empty little world, Olivia." He started to fill the bottles from the hidden little tap, and wondered if they should make an effort to camouflage the still a bit better. He and Zoey had installed it behind the master irrigation manifold, and it was reasonably well hidden in amongst a labyrinthine tangle of irrigation hoses and pipes; but it wouldn't be that hard to find if you were looking for it, and Abhrakasin seemed like the kind of person who would decide he needed to find it.

"Actually, Mitch." Olivia switched to a sweet, primary-school-teacher voice. "Ganymede is still just a moon. It'll be a long while before it grows into a real world."

"So I hear, Olivia. So I hear." Mitch popped a plastic cork in the first bottle and started filling the second. "The rugby starts in a little bit. Are you going to watch it with us this week, or are you and Zoey going to have an early movie night?"

"No movies tonight," Olivia said. "Zoey had a thing she had to get done or something, but watching the boys watch rugby is almost as much fun as a movie."

"Yeah, sometimes they are as entertaining as the game." Mitch took a small sip before he put the cork in the second bottle. It made his eyes water like only high-proof alcohol could, but it was smooth and a bit tangy, a hell of an improvement since their first batch way back when. "Is that lemon?"

"And some limes from our first crop. Zoey says they go together." Olivia finished planting the last seedling and set the little pot down with a flourish. "Okay my little buggly boos, that's all for today. Shut yourselves down."

The minis all made disappointed noises.

"Oh, go on. You know that Zoey doesn't want you working when no one's in here. Last time you were very naughty and ruined all her tomato plants."

The minis shut themselves down as Olivia leapt dramatically to her feet, dancing and prancing as she hurried to catch up with Mitch before he left the glasshouse.

Half the people on the base had no idea that Doc's given name was Beatrix, and for her, that was a point of pride. In most workplace cultures a nickname was a signifier of inclusion, and being accepted as a contributing partner in the establishment of Aquarius meant everything to her. That was part of the reason she loved John so deeply. He had never really understood why she wanted to prove that she could be part of something like this, but he had agreed to take an assignment out here with her anyway. She could not express how grateful she was for that, which was a big element of why she was so excited about the little extra surprise she had for him. John always enjoyed the wine her father shipped out to her, as well as the caviar and other things he missed from home, but he was going to adore the lacy intimates and the cute little matching chemise that her mother had finally sent out in her personal freight allotment.

She lowered the lights in the quarters she shared with John, and watched her reflection in the mirror as she untied the bow at her neck and experimented with different poses as she took the chemise off. She had already decided that she would remove her dressing gown before dinner and torment him by dining in nothing but her new lingerie, but she was also toying with the idea of pushing it further. She had never really tried to undress seductively, but the new chemise was perfect for it. It was an old-fashioned, apron style silk gown. It was open all the way down to the middle of her back, and she could slip it off her shoulders simply by untying one single bow at her neck. All she had to do was find the pose that would give him the perfect taunting glimpse of the lacy intimates underneath. She wanted that proper balance between naughty and nice as she made him wait for her to let the chemise drift slowly to the floor.

Karl's hair was still damp as he stepped through the door separating the engineering wing from the hub. The hub was a mess of tools and supplies, but it was an altogether different kind of mess than his shop. The mess in the shop lingered and gathered dust, but the hub had become the staging area for the interior work on Aquarius, so the mess was always transient. Nothing was ever in there for more than a week or so.

His unruly mind grabbed hold of that thought and ran wild with it, darting frantically through countless random details and tangential bits and pieces, spinning out logical deductions, offering up realisations, and creating a relentless torrent of ideas so far outside of the box that the entire concept of boxes may as well not even exist. That was just the way it always was for Karl. He could take an imaginary step back and drift along with it, waiting for something interesting and useful. Or, with a little effort, he could rein it in. Or, if he really tried, he could even bend it to his will, and get it to grind away on a problem or puzzle he needed to solve. But the one absolute was that the chaos was always there. Even when he slept, his mind churned.

The door to the glasshouse seemed to grow bigger and loom ominously over him as he approached it. It was exactly the same as the doors to the other two wings, but for some reason it suddenly felt like the fortified entrance to an old-time castle. He fought the instinct to wallow in his imaginings about maidens in castles, and took a deep breath. That didn't help. He took another breath and tried to look confident. All the books said that women like quiet, calm, pleasant, and confident men. He needed to be those things. The problem was that he was none of them, and he knew it. Everyone knew it.

He pulled the packets of seeds out of his pocket, shuffled them a little, and focused on his plan. It was a good plan. He'd got the idea for the seeds straight out of a novel where a guy gave a girl a small present and admitted straight away that the gift was just an excuse to visit. That had seemed really romantic and confident, and worked so well that Karl just had to give it a try. And then what Luke had said about finding a time when she wouldn't really have anything else to do but talk, that was genius. That was why he had worked so hard to set this up. It would work. It was a perfect plan.

It took several more moments before he managed to hit the button to open the door to the glasshouse, and several more seconds passed before he stepped through.

The glasshouse was brilliantly lit and it was a mess. There was dirt all over the floor, leaves and twigs were scattered all around Zoey's citrus trees, and there were pipes and fittings and scaffolding and other construction stuff everywhere. Simon must have decided that it was time to finish installing the catwalk and all the fixtures that would follow the peak of the glasshouse roof.

Karl's untamed mind was so intent on darting from detail to detail that he was ten steps into the second section before he realised that the glasshouse was empty.

"Oh shit."

He checked the time, then turned and ran.

The first of the engineering challenges confronting Karl's plan was the safety system that prevented more than one of the hub's pressure doors from being open at any one time. That, however, had also been one of the simplest of the puzzles for him to solve.

When the countdown on his console reached zero, his computer connected to the hub module's local network and simulated the yet-to-be-installed control system for the locked-down pressure door that would someday open to the wing being built off the southeast wall. Once that imaginary door controller was established in the local system, it told the other pressure doors around the hub that it was sensing full pressure on both sides of the door, so it was bringing itself online. The other doors around the hub then initiated the subroutine for integrating the new door into their local control network. Syncing all their pressure sensors was part of that process, and that took all the sensors offline all at once. That sensorless moment only lasted a few milliseconds, but that was more than enough time for Karl's computer console to reset the calibration baseline for all the sensors in all the doors. When the controllers tried to bring those sensors back on line, the readings were all well outside the range of expected variation across the hub. That caused the door controllers to default to test-and-reset mode. From there it was an easy hack for his console to keep them stuck in that mode, take direct control, and open all three of the pressure doors between the hub, the glasshouse, and the two wings.

Taking control of the hub doors was relatively simple because the hub's control systems were designed to integrate with multiple hub modules so they could be linked together. As a result, there were several communication channels dedicated to, or open to, accepting commands and information from outside the module.

It was even easier to take control of the doors to the individual rooms around the base. All of those doors could be locked from the inside, so there was an override function that allowed base security and medical staff to open a locked door during emergencies. Technically, Karl wasn't allowed to access that mode, but that was an easy nut to crack.

The other door and safety systems, however, were completely different beasts, and they turned out to be a monster of a problem. To prevent exactly the kind of remote manipulation that he was attempting, the emergency pressure doors that were meant to isolate the individual modules of the halls and glasshouse during emergencies were intentionally cut off from external inputs. The doors fed status data into the base network, but they would only accept data input through the hardwire links that connected them to the doors and sensors in their own module and the sensors in the immediately adjacent modules. That had seemed like the insurmountable barrier that it was supposed to be until Luke had told Karl what his favourite quote actually meant.

Wires were an old fashioned technology, but they were still used all the time because they were often the best way link systems together. The patch cable that Karl had strung between his computer console and the hazard sensor in the shop ceiling was crude and obviously makeshift, but it linked his console directly into that physically isolated emergency system. There were still some challenges, but he eventually figured out what kinds of contradictory data queries he had to send from the pressure sensor to get the emergency isolation system in the first hall section to shift into a standby mode. From there, it was a simple matter of mimicking that to the next hall module and repeating the process. It took nearly a minute to daisy chain that process all the way down to the ends of the personnel wing and the glasshouse, but it worked. By physically connecting his computer console into that isolated system he was able to take all the pressure sensors in all the halls offline, and that would keep the hall and glasshouse section isolation doors from shutting, leaving one last challenge.

Karl's collection of sub-routines and commands set off a general quarters alarm and then started a countdown to the final element in his plan.

It was ten minutes into the first half of the game when Karl ran through the lounge on his way down to the bunk rooms and locker rooms. It was odd to see him outside of his shop, kind of like seeing a mouse scurry about the kitchen in the broad daylight, but everyone was too busy enjoying the game to think much of it. The first rush to gobble down the snacks was slowing, the first and second rounds of drinks were segueing into the third, and the crew's vile defamations of the referee's parentage were just reaching the level of complexity and subtlety where Mitch had to start calling them poetic. Olivia, with an assist from Zoey's swill, was giggling uncontrollably about something, and Edgar was laughing at her. It was exactly the afternoon that the crew needed after a long week of dangerous work.

Pleased with himself, Mitch put a batch of lemon tarts in the oven and took a long slow sip of his drink, savouring the flavour and the scene.

When the general quarters alarm sounded, the first reaction in the lounge was annoyed frowns and shared glances. No one moved or looked like they were inclined to move, as the commentary on the video feed blared on.

"What the hell is that all about?" Paul eventually asked, annoyed.

"It is the general quarters alarm," Abhrakasin said as he hurried in from the direction of his bunk, data pad in hand. "Safety watch must suit up. All remaining base personnel must immediately proceed to a refuge."

"We know the fucking procedure for a GQ drill, you little prick!" Kai shouted at him. "What we don't know is why the hell we're having one right now."

"You think maybe John's shitting on us?" Cuzzie asked, not really directing the question at anyone in particular.

"Call a GQ drill just to ruin our game?" Kai nodded. "Yeah, that seems like exactly the kind of petty arsehole thing that prick would do."

"Regardless," Simon said, finally rising from his seat. "A drill is a drill and we'll get beaten over the head with the regs if we don't dance the dance. Paul, Cuzzie, Tui, with me. Let's get over to the engineering wing before the pressure doors start closing."

Once Simon, Paul, Cuzzie, and Tui were out of their seats, they walked briskly towards the hub and the engineering wing beyond, but Kai, Edgar, and Olivia had still made no effort to get out of their seats when Doc strode into the lounge.

She was still buttoning her lab coat as she rushed to the sickbay. Unlike the others, whose only responsibility if they weren't on safety watch was to make sure there were at least four people taking refuge in each wing, Doc and Mitch were assigned to the sickbay. They always took refuge there and they had the additional responsibility of making sure it was ready for a medical emergency. Mitch gestured to Doc to make sure she knew he'd join her as soon as he finished pulling the half-baked lemon tarts out of the oven. She nodded, but the look on her face couldn't have been interpreted as anything other than embarrassed. It took a second glance for Mitch to realise that Doc's legs were bare and there was a fringe of grey silk and lace spilling out from under the bottom edge of her lab coat. He gave her a reassuring wink and nod. It was meant to make her feel a little bit more comfortable, but it just made her blush and fluster, and that caught the attention of Edgar.

"You'd freak the shit out if I told you that you look hot in that get up, wouldn't you Doc?" Edgar asked, conversationally.

Doc went from flustered to mortified and picked up her pace, desperate to get to her sickbay.

Mitch tossed the pan of tarts on the counter and hurried after Doc, giving Edgar a good smack upside the head as he passed him. "Dumbass."

"What?" Edgar complained. "Chicks are supposed to like it when you tell them they look nice."

Kai gave Edgar a second smack upside the head. "Not like that, dumbass."

Mitch caught up with Doc just as she opened the door to her sickbay, and he couldn't help but groan when he saw what was inside.

"John, sweetie, what are you and Zoey doing in my sickbay?" Doc asked, confused to the point of befuddled.

Chapter 2

No shit that's not supposed to happen.

Karl's final hack had been the most difficult to figure out, but in the end it was the simplest and crudest of them all. The airlocks were even more isolated from the other emergency and control systems than the section pressure doors. The inner and outer doors of each airlock were interlinked, but that was it. The only connection the airlock door controllers had with rest of the universe was the status update they sent out to the base network. They had no mechanism whatsoever for accepting any input from anything other than their own sensors and door controls.

From the moment the first outlines of his plan had taken shape, the airlocks had been its nemesis. Even as he solved the other problems and put the elements in place, it had seemed like it would be impossible to get the airlock doors to do what he needed them to do; but once he figured out how to shunt the emergency section isolation system into standby mode, the solution for the airlocks had become obvious.

Karl solved the problem of accessing the airlock controllers by running a couple of wires from his console out through the patch block to the surface, and then down to the surface crew's airlock near the middle of the engineering wing. Once he had established a hardwire connection between his console and one of the airlock door controls, he had direct physical access to the controller itself, and with that he could activate a plethora of repair, testing, and emergency modes, and use them to do pretty much anything he wanted.

The only real challenge was finding a way to get the outer door to stay just a little bit open. Airlock doors were made to be either open or closed. Anything in-between was so contrary to the whole purpose of an airlock that the motors themselves were hardcoded to only stop when fully open or closed.

Karl's solution to that was to make one of the doors think it was closed when it wasn't. His console opened the outer door, took the whole system offline, and reset one of the motor's parameters so it thought it had been installed in a slightly narrower doorway. Bringing that motor back online, he ordered the door to close, and when it reached the position where the motor expected it to hit the doorframe, the console spoofed the signal from the door seal sensor and it stopped. Once that was done, the computer shut down the door by putting the controller back into repair mode.

Opening the inner door was then relatively simple. His console just initiated the emergency cycle. The whole point of the emergency cycle was to make it possible to get someone out of the vacuum as fast as possible, no matter what. The last thing anyone wanted was for someone to die because of one of the plethora of conditions that might cause a safety system to prevent an airlock door from opening and letting someone in. So, the emergency cycle ignored the status of the other door and the status of the pressure in the airlock as well as all the other safety protocols, and when it was triggered it just slammed the door open or closed as fast as the motor could manage.

The emergency cycle command wasn't quite the complete solution. Like everything else, there were multiple redundant safety measures built into it, and one of those redundancies was that it only gave you five seconds before it reset the controller to its normal function. However, those five seconds only ticked off when the controller was online, so the last command in that phase of the program put the inner door's controller in repair mode. That stopped the countdown before it really even started, and left the inner door open with the outer door just slightly ajar.

Air rushed out, but with the rate of air loss limited by barely opening the outer door, Karl hoped to spread the pressure drop out over three or four minutes. That was about as fast as he thought he could get to the ten percent drop he needed for triggering a full lockdown without causing ear pops or a noticeable breeze or anything else that might alert the others on the base to what was happening.

From an engineering perspective, his work was brilliant. It was a masterful symphony of kludges, hacks, and workarounds. From any perspective that a normal human being might choose, it was a profoundly stupid way to get a couple of hours to chat up a girl. In fact, by any reasonable standard, Karl's plan was absolutely insane.

The general quarters alarm shut off, its last echo leaving a silence so tense it was tangible. With every breath, Mitch expected all hell to break loose, but it didn't. Doc just didn't seem to recognise what was right in front of her. The ruffled hair, the bare feet, the guilty look on John's face as he swallowed nervously, Zoey's fearful expression as she finished pulling her coveralls onto her shoulders and slowly pulled the zipper from her navel to her neck; Doc seemed unable to recognise what any of it meant. It wasn't until Zoey glanced guiltily at the bra she'd accidentally left on the floor that Doc finally understood, and even that took a long moment to sink in. Doc stared at that forlorn little tangle of utilitarian underwear for several seconds before her jaw dropped and her eyes went wide.

"You mousy little whore," Doc whispered, incredulous. "In my sickbay?"

Zoey backed away, terrified, but when Doc's fury boiled over it was aimed at John.

"You filthy son of a bitch!" Doc pushed off from the door jam. Even if she hadn't caught everyone by surprise, there would have been no way for John to move out of her way. Momentum took on a life of its own in low-G. There just wasn't enough down to get any kind of traction, and your feet tended to shoot out from under you if you leaned over to try to make a quick change of direction. Shoving off from something solid was about the only way to make a sudden move, and there was nothing within John's reach.

The shoulder Doc threw into John's chest would probably have been illegal on the rugby pitch, but Kai and the boys would still have applauded the way she managed to transfer so much of her momentum into and through the collision.

John flew backwards, crashing through a cart full of medical supplies and scattering the little plastic drawers, sending their contents flying from one corner of the sickbay to the other. The collision with the cart was spectacular, but it hardly slowed John down; it just twisted him around and sent him head first into the big yellow emergency supply cabinet. His head left a dent in the metal door as he bounced off and staggered back into the middle of the room.

Dazed and disorientated, John grabbed Zoey and accidentally threw her to the floor in his desperate effort to regain his balance. He finally caught hold of the surgical table and managed to get his feet back under him just in time to flinch away from Doc's roundhouse punch. She caught him with a glancing blow across the cheek. The impact was enough to snap his head to the side, but he avoided the worst of it. That was a bit of luck for Doc; if she had connected, she would probably have broken her hand.

John lifted an arm up to deflect Doc's second punch, and then he covered his head and cowered.

"This kind of behaviour is inappropriate for a married man!" Doc howled her oddly maternal curse as she pummelled John with a wild flurry of vicious, closed-fist punches.

"What the hell?" Kai muttered from the hall.

"John was throwing a leg over Zoey," Mitch explained. "In Doc's sickbay."

"Jesus, he really is dumber than shit, isn't he?" Kai chuckled, and after a moment, she and Edgar both wandered in to watch.

"Honey," John said, trying to sound authoritative as he scuttled a couple of steps away from Doc and held up a hand as if he expected that gesture to stop her. "I don't want to hit a woman, but I swear, if you don't stop this..."

Doc lunged forward and landed a solid punch square on John's nose, sending him stumbling head first into the emergency cabinet for a second time. John bounced off again and went back to cowering.

"You go, Doc!" Kai cheered her on. "Give the cheating bastard what he deserves."

"Kai, please don't," Mitch pleaded. "This is going to be bad enough as it is."

"Her punchin' the shit out of him is good, Mitch." Kai nodded at the teary-eyed doctor who had gone to flailing away open-handed on John's back. "Uptight bitch like Doc holdin' onta that kind of rage, that's how you get axe murderers and shit."

"I know, but that doesn't mean you should spin this up and risk encouraging Doc to push it too far," Mitch said. "It's not like she's going to be able to avoid John or Zoey tomorrow."

"Or the next seventy tomorrows," Kai said.

"Actually, it's probably more like a hundred and forty tomorrows," Mitch said. "Next ship's already on drift, and I can't imagine they put someone on it who could replace Doc."

"Two to a refuge!" Abhrakasin shouted at them from out in the hall.

"And it just keeps getting better," Mitch muttered.

"This is a violation of drill protocol." Abhrakasin entered the sickbay and waved his data pad in the air. "You must respect the drill."

"Respect this, you little shitstain." Kai gave Abhrakasin a single finger salute, then pulled the finger back into a fist.

"Olivia!" Karl's desperate shout echoed in from the hall, carrying over the sound of Doc's sobs and her slaps at John's back. "Have you seen Zoey? I can't find Zoey."

"She's in the sickbay," Olivia said, cheerfully.

"Oh my God," Karl gasped, sounding panicked as he grabbed Olivia's shoulders. "Is she okay?"

"Oh yeah." Olivia pointed at Zoey, who was cowering in the corner of the sickbay. "She's just watching the fight."

"The fight?" Karl stepped into the sickbay, bewildered.

"No, get out!" Abhrakasin stepped in front of Karl and tried to push him back into the hall. "Two to a refuge."

"Yes! Zoey, two to a refuge." Karl beckoned to Zoey, trying to get her to head for the exit. "We should go to the refuge across the hall, together."

Doc finally ran out of steam. Gasping for breath, she took a step back from John and wiped her face, leaving a long streak of tears and snot on the sleeve of her lab coat.

"Okay, sweetie." John hesitantly held his hands out in a placating gesture. "Let's just take a breath and deal with this like civilised people."

"Fine."

The seething menace that Doc put into that single syllable sent chills through Mitch. John didn't seem to notice. He relaxed and stood up straight.

He even took a moment to straighten the collar of his coveralls and try to regain the dignity he imagined he had.

"Like the gentleman you are," Doc sneered, giving John just an instant to realise his mistake before her foot slammed into his testicles.

It had always been obvious that Doc was plenty athletic. She spent far more than the minimum required hours in the gym, and she had that ingrained grace and poise that comes from spending thousands of adolescent afternoons running around a field or court. Mitch would bet that a fair few of those afternoons must have involved football, because she clearly knew how to kick. She stepped into it and caught John with just about all the power a person could have put into it.

John doubled over, and that dropped his face right into Doc's follow-on punch. Again it was clear that, despite the earlier flailing, the woman knew something of what she was doing. She used the recoil from the kick to load the tension in her plant foot and sprang forward, using all the strength in her legs to help her drive the palm of her hand into the point of John's chin. His head snapped back and his body went limp as the blow lifted his feet off the floor and sent him flipping over backwards. Perhaps Doc's adolescent hours had included some form of martial arts rather than kicking a ball around a field. It certainly looked practised.

John's lower back hit the edge of the counter that ran the length of the outer wall, and his limp body offered no resistance to his momentum. He flipped up onto the counter and his head hit the big window with a sickening, hollow thud, leaving a smear of blood on the glass as he crumpled awkwardly and rolled slowly off the counter, slumping to the floor in a tangle of limbs.

"John!" Zoey shouted.

Mitch's worries about John's injuries vanished as Doc turned towards Zoey. She snarled like a monster that had just spotted its next victim, and Mitch reacted instinctively, tackling Doc just before she could launch herself at Zoey.

There had definitely been some martial arts thrown into Doc's adolescence. Her first reaction was to roll and use Mitch's momentum to throw him off.

Fortunately, wrestling had been part of Mitch's adolescent athletics. He also had at least twenty kilos over Doc, and he had the advantage of the first move. Doc made a swift swimming-stroke movement to free her arm from his attempt to trap it in his bear hug. That kept her arm free, but it also left it out away from her body, and Mitch took advantage. Releasing the grip on her waist, he thrust his hand up under her armpit and grabbed her hair. It wasn't quite a half-nelson, but it was close enough. He pulled that fistful of hair, and as it twisted her head, she exposed the elbow of her other arm. He grabbed it, established a chicken-wing hold, and effectively immobilised the woman. He held that for a moment, letting her struggle and squirm until she gave him the chance to shift his first hold, moving his hand to the back of her neck to put her in a proper half-nelson.

Doc fought like an enraged animal, but it wasn't going to do her any good; she couldn't break free.

"Stop it, Doc," Mitch growled. "You'd kill Zoey if you hit her like you hit John."

That just added fuel to Doc's fury. She shrieked, flailing even more vigorously. Mitch tightened his hold and settled in, waiting for Doc to burn through her rage.

———————

Paul and Cuzzie had been standing in the refuge long enough for Paul to become restless. That wasn't all that surprising; Paul had the attention span of a goldfish and the patience of an espresso-swilling puppy. He could get bored in the middle of a car chase, even if he was driving. However, in that moment, he had good reason to be unsettled. Compared to Paul, Cuzzie had the patience of a saint, and even he was starting to wonder what the hell was going on. The all clear usually sounded almost as soon as they had reported that they were at station in the engineering wing refuges, but this time there'd been nothing. Neither John nor the safety watch had even acknowledged their status update.

"Paul, get back in the refuge and wait for the all clear!" Simon yelled from the refuge across the hall and a section back towards the hub.

Paul took a step back and stood just inside the open door, fidgeting and grumbling quietly.

"General quarters, eh bro," Cuzzie shouted politely back to Simon. "Shouldn't all the section doors be closin'?"

"It's well past ninety seconds," Simon agreed. "They should already be closed."

Simon glanced around then leaned out the door of the other refuge and frowned at the flashing yellow light on the pressure and fire sensor mounted on the hall ceiling. The sensors were flashing yellow all the way down the hall. Cuzzie wasn't exactly sure what that meant, but he knew it wasn't right. And the door to the hub was still open. Come to think of it, the door out of the personnel wing had been open too. That also wasn't right. While this part of Aquarius was under construction, the hub was supposed to be programmed so only one door could be open at any one time, which was a pain in the arse when you were moving shit around, but also an important safety provision.

"Bro, check out the idiot tape!" Paul pointed at the yellow and black danger tape covering an exposed power induction relay.

The crew were supposed to drape yellow and black warning tape over every unfinished job that might be a hazard. However, with only the absolute minimum of interior finish work completed so far, there wasn't enough yellow plastic in the universe to cover everything they were technically supposed to mark. Still, they had gone through the motions and scattered a fair bit of it around, and the tape hanging over a missing wall panel was fluttering ever so slightly.

"Bro! The airlock." Paul leapt out of the refuge and ran for the airlock prep area. "Look, both the doors are open!"

"No, Paul!" Simon shouted. "Get back in the refuge!"

Cuzzie knew that Simon was right. Every third item in the emergency procedures manual said that once they were in the refuges, they were supposed to stay in the refuges; but those procedures also said all kinds of shit that assumed that the emergency pressure doors between the sections would work like they were supposed to, and right then, nothing was happening like it should. He was two steps down the hall before he realised he was rushing to help Paul.

"God damn it, Cuzzie! Don't be stupid!" Simon shouted at his back, furious.

Paul hit the emergency cycle button on the inner airlock door controller, but door didn't budge, so he leapt inside and tried the same thing with the outer door. That was a stupid thing to do; if it had worked, it was a fifty-fifty chance whether it closed the door or yanked it all the way open. As it was, nothing happened, so Paul tried the manual wheel.

Cuzzie went for his vac suit. The suit-first instinct had been drilled into him since forever, and Simon would totally finesse the GQ drill report a little if he could pretend that Cuzzie had been in a suit all along. Also, it just made sense to grab the suit. If Paul couldn't shut the door straight away, the only way he would go back to the refuge was if Cuzzie was in his suit and it was obvious that he was ready to take over and get the door fixed no matter how long it took.

"Leverage, Cuzzzie!" Paul shouted. "The wheel is jammed or something. Get me something to use for leverage."

Cuzzie's suit was hanging right next to the rack for the shovels, hammers, and other hand tools they used on the surface. They were a typical surface crew, so none of the tools were actually in the rack, but there were plenty in the general vicinity. Cuzzie was almost standing on a metre-long pry bar.

"Cuzzie, seriously bro, I've almost got it!" Paul shouted. "Hurry, man."

Cuzzie pushed off the wall and grabbed the pry bar off the floor in the same motion. He told himself that the five or six seconds that it would take to get the pry bar over to the airlock wouldn't make any real difference, but he knew better. Leaving the refuge was foolish enough, but running towards a breach without his suit was just plain stupid. Unfortunately, even as he was realising how idiotic it had been to follow the lead of a squirrel-brained dick like Paul, he also knew that it was too late to do anything about it.

From the moment he pushed off from the wall, he was committed. Even if he tried to turn around, he'd be at the airlock anyway by the time he managed to stop. So he kept his speed up with the shuffling low-G skip they called running, and stopped himself by grabbing the edge of the open airlock door. It wrenched his arm and shoulder, and almost sent him stumbling head first across to the far side of the airlock, but it did the trick.

A bright red, cast-iron wheel was connected to the same rack and pinion mechanism that the electric motors used to operate the doors. The manual override wheels were a bullet-proof and dirt-simple backup that would work even if something took out all the electronics in the entire galaxy.

Unfortunately, that manual wheel was never meant to be used to pit muscle and leverage against an active motor, but that was exactly what Paul did. He took the pry bar from Cuzzie, shoved it through the spokes of the manual wheel, and pulled with all of his strength. He was trying to force the outer door closed, but with the system in lockdown mode and thinking it was already closed, the motor was hell bent on holding that door it exactly where it was. Cuzzie could actually hear the strain of the motor over the howling of the air rushing to escape into the void.

Every sensor and door control unit had an icon on Karl's diagram of Aquarius, and all but one was flashing yellow. The icon for the last fire and pressure sensor in the last hall module of the personnel wing was a steady green, then it turned yellow and Karl's program sprang back into action. The response to that flash of yellow was simple; his computer reset the system. It would take 32,327 separate commands, carefully timed and sequenced, to accomplish that task, but that was nothing for a computer.

It was simply bad luck that Cuzzie was still in the airlock doorway when Karl's computer console began unwinding what it had done. Cuzzie had no intention of staying to help Paul, or even lingering to see if he could manage to shut the door. It just took him a moment to regain his balance after handing over the pry bar, and it was in that moment that the status light on the inner door's control panel changed from flashing yellow to steady green. It took a fraction of a second for the controller to come back online, and when it did, it executed its long-delayed response to Paul's earlier attempt to initiate the emergency cycle. The emergency cycle was meant to be a last resort, only to be used in a life-and-death situation. As such, it was stripped of all safety features, and the only design consideration was to move the door from whichever position it was in to the other as fast as the motor could manage; and that was very fast. The inner airlock door slammed shut, and Cuzzie didn't even have the chance to flinch before it smashed into him. The impact knocked him out and pinned him in the doorway.

Before Paul could turn his head to see what had happened to Cuzzie, Karl's computer console reset the controller for the outer door, catching Paul completely by surprise. He was pulling with all his strength when the motor suddenly quit fighting him, and he smacked himself in the face with the pry bar. As he was reeling from the impact, the controller came back online, and immediately executed its own delayed emergency cycle.

The result was gruesome. As the door shot open, the pry bar that was stuck through the spokes of the manual wheel was ripped out of Paul's hands. It spun all the way around, and the two-pronged claw on the hook-shaped end slammed into the soft underside of his chin. It ripped through his tongue, palate, and sinuses before emerging through the bridge of his nose. The impact lifted his feet off the floor, but the motor wasn't quite powerful enough to pull him all the way up and over, so the opening of the door stalled. The motor strained with all its power as he dangled several centimetres off the floor. Thrashing in blind panic and buffeted by the torrent of air rushing out through the airlock, he danced like a macabre marionette as the door motor burned itself out and exploded in a shower of sparks and smoke.

The timer in the emergency cycle routine for the inner airlock hit five, and door controller switched to normal mode. It opened a bit, allowing Cuzzie to fall to the floor, and then tried again to close, this time less forcefully than before. It repeated the action over, and over, and over, intent on closing.

In the decades since humanity began colonising space in earnest, a variety of nuances had been added to the concept of redundancy. Most importantly, 'different' and 'separate' had become essential elements of the word's technical meaning. When spacers, designers, and engineers talked about redundancy, they didn't mean just multiple copies of the same thing. They were instead discussing a collection of different and independent systems, mechanisms, or processes for performing a vital function. Inherent in that understanding of redundancy was the desire to ensure that no single failure could disrupt a vital function. Thus, the airlock could be operated with the integrated controller, the emergency cycle, and the manual wheels. Subsystems, such as the battery backup to provide power to the airlock, provided another layer of redundancy, and the airlock itself was nested inside a much bigger system for sustaining base pressure. Software firewalls protected each control system, limiting the chance that anyone could gain enough remote access to cause problems. Firebreaks, such as the physical isolation of the airlock, section door, and hub systems, provided yet another level of security. They kept any problem that might occur from spreading across multiple elements of the redundant system. The result was a structure intentionally set up so that it would take so many simultaneous failures to compromise its function that it was essentially impossible for anything short of a cataclysm to bring it down.

However, Karl's insane effort to create a situation where he and Zoey would be trapped in the glasshouse for a couple of hours had fundamentally transformed the very nature of the base's safety systems. The hardwire connections that he has used to centralise and integrate control of all the pressure containment systems served to link all of the doors, sensors, and controllers. It bridged all the firebreaks, and in doing so it transformed a robust redundant system into a fragile complex system. Complex systems were characterised by tightly integrated chains of interactive elements, and they were in many ways the exact opposite of redundant systems. Because complex systems were tightly integrated, it was difficult to compensate for failures, difficult to isolate problems, and almost impossible to predict how they might fare when damaged. The breakdown of almost any element could cause the whole thing to collapse.

All the power that was being pushed into the motor trying to close the outer airlock door had to go somewhere when the motor exploded. Some of it escaped as sparks, but most of it surged through the wire connecting the airlock to the computer console in Karl's repair shop. The result was a cascade failure.

A power surge was always a possibility when connecting a computer console to damaged machines to perform diagnostics, so the hardwire interface for the repair shop console was designed to act as a fusible link. It functioned perfectly, protecting the console, but that did nothing to stop the power from surging through the other makeshift wire that connected the console to the hazard sensor in the shop ceiling. The electronics in the fire and pressure sensors and the controllers for the section isolation doors were no match for that kind of power. Some of them simply burned out, but most exploded quite spectacularly. In seconds, the entire system was destroyed, and that left Karl's console with no way to reinitialise the systems that were supposed to isolate the hall and glasshouse sections.

The adaptive elements in the console's core programming were smart enough to recognise that they would never be able to finish that set of routines, so they jumped to the command sequence that would bring the hub door system back online. Again, the program stalled. It should have been simple. All Karl's program really had to do was to quit sending the false sensor data that kept diverting the hub doors back into test-and-reset mode. Once those doors started receiving the real data again, they would simply bring themselves back online, but the destruction of the ceiling pressure sensors gave them nothing to use to confirm that the sensors in the doors were functioning within operational tolerances. If Karl had used anything other than the test-and-reset mode to take those doors offline, it wouldn't have been a problem, but syncing the readings of all the various sensors in the hub was the whole point of that routine, so when the destroyed sensors offered nothing but an error message the synchronisation routine just kept trying again.

With that, the base's pressure retention system lost its last line of defence. The console was again smart enough to skip on to the next set of routines and bring the door controllers for the individual rooms back online. Once they reset, their sensors noted the low pressure and the room doors slammed shut, trapping Simon and Tui in their refuge, and the others in the sickbay. But that did not alter the fact that Karl's little plan had accomplished the impossible. The base was depressurising.

Everyone in the sickbay was staring at Doc, horrified.

"Settle down, Doc," Mitch whispered, soothingly. "You got your licks in fair and square, but now you need to just settle down."

Doc took a deep, gasping, shuddering breath, and it looked like she was about to escalate her futile struggle to escape. Instead, the fury suddenly abandoned her, and she sagged, limp and weeping. Tentatively, Mitch released her, and the only motion she made was to cover her face.

A collective sigh went around the room, and it seemed to grow almost supernaturally until there was a noticeable breeze. Confused, no one noticed the status light on the door control change from flashing yellow to green, but when it did, the door slammed shut.

"Oh my," Olivia said, melodramatically clutching at her chest. "That scared the living bejeezus out of me."

Olivia hit the big button on the door controller, and when the door didn't open, she frowned at it as if it were misbehaving and reached for the manual override wheel.

"No, Olivia!" Kai grabbed her arm and pulled it away from the wheel. "Look at the pressure in the hall. It's down, way down, and dropping like mad."

"That's not what's supposed to happen," Karl muttered, confused.

"No shit that's not supposed to happen," Kai snapped at him.

"Don't panic, Kai." Olivia attacked her with a fierce hug. "The guys in the other wing will fix everything and rescue us, just like we practice in the drills."

After a long confused moment, Kai stiffly patted Olivia on the back, looked over at Mitch, and said, "This isn't a drill."

The halls, hub, and glasshouse lost pressure quickly, but it was far from instantaneous. For the first five minutes or so, it was as a near-perfect example of a simple deflation model. The rate of loss slowed steadily as the pressure pushing the air out the door decreased, so the initial rush of air became a breeze, and then a sigh. At roughly the three hundred seconds mark, however, something changed, and the rate of pressure loss momentarily flattened out. The obvious explanation for that kind of sudden deviation from the mathematical model was that a door had failed and dumped a large room full of air into the halls, but the internal pressure data being recorded by the door controllers didn't fit that explanation, and for good reason.

As the pressure dropped in the glasshouse, so did the boiling point of the water in the aquaculture ponds. When the boiling point dropped below the pond temperature, the water began to churn and cold steam erupted into the void left by the escaping air. That surge of water vapour added just a bit to the pressure across the base, just enough to be measurable. It was nowhere near enough to compensate for the air that was escaping through the open airlock, so the pressure kept dropping, and that caused the water to boil even faster.

The phase change from liquid to gas sucked heat away from the water, and within seconds, the ponds were trying to boil and freeze at the same time. Roiling convection currents kept their surfaces from freezing solid, and that kept the ice from sealing off the flow of vapour into the near-vacuum. The ponds' automated systems were no match for such a dramatic loss of water and heat, but they tried. Pumping warm water into the ponds, they kept driving the convection currents, and that further delayed the inevitable freezing over of the ponds, dumping more and more water vapour into Aquarius.

That water vapour flowed out of the open glasshouse door, through the hub, down the engineering wing, and out the open airlock doors, and as the pressure in the base approached zero, the temperature of the ponds dropped until the vapour became a fog of frost. The frost melted when it touched warm surfaces such as walls and doors, then immediately evaporated back into the vacuum, stealing massive quantities of heat from every surface it touched. Soon all the surfaces exposed to the vapour were below freezing themselves, and the process started forming tangled icicle threads, thinner than a human hair. In a matter of minutes, everything was coated with icy fur and the hub was knee-deep in candyfloss snow. Once the very last dregs of air were lost out the airlock and the pressure in the base was down to the slightest whisper above zero, the ice fog started eddying down the personnel wing. It was a slower process, and there was far less frost deposited along that hallway, but it still created a fantastical winter scene as it stole heat and carried it outside.

The evaporative cooling of the ponds would eventually overwhelm the heating elements trying to keep the ponds warm, but the surface of the ponds would persist in a state of 'almost frozen over' for quite some time. Jets of ice vapour erupting out of cracks in the surface acted like tiny ice volcanoes, forming a miniature mountain range down the centre of the glasshouse. Most of that ice fog fell back to the ground nearby, but it was the nature of the vapour to drift, slowly but persistently, towards the fractionally lower pressure outside of the base.

Chapter 3

Numbers do not wiggle.

'Ominous' was the only way Abhrakasin could imagine describing the tricks of light, colour, and shadow that played across Kai's face as she watched the sunset. However, even as he selected the word, he knew it was inadequate. The last of the day's cold, harsh sunlight had been just bright enough to wash all hints of colour out of her face, and the sharp-edged shadows it cast across her features had turned her eternal scowl into a macabre grimace. It was a ghastly sight, but it was the transition brought on by nightfall that was truly disturbing. The sudden disappearance of the sun unleashed the Jupiterglow. Warm reddish beige replaced cold white, shadows vanished in the diffuse light, and her features suddenly softened, making her look youthful, almost cherubic. For the briefest of moments she looked disturbingly seductive, but before Abhrakasin's vision could fully adjust to the change in the colour of the light, she glanced at him. Her eyes actually seemed to glow. He knew it was just a trick of perception and reflection, but that flicker of burning red inside her eyes was still a demonic image straight out of a horror film. It deserved a descriptor that was far more emphatic than 'ominous'.

Kai scowled at him and he looked away.

There was a less extreme but still ominous feel to the rest of the scene in the sickbay. John was not dead. The crumpled heap of manflesh that had been their base commander moaned and moved a little, so he was clearly alive, but Abhrakasin suspected that he was seriously injured; at the very least he was severely concussed. That might be a problem. Doc wasn't about to tend to him, and no one else seemed interested in risking setting her off by showing any kind of concern. Doc's animal fury had burnt out, but the charred woman it had left behind was just as frightening. Seething silently, she rocked herself ever so slightly and stared unblinking at nothing. Her self-control felt so precarious that even Abhrakasin was not willing to offer aid to John, despite all of the procedures and norms of behaviour that clearly indicated that he should act. So if John needed some care, he might just be out of luck.

Across the room, Karl stood at the door, muttering to himself as he stared at the pressure gauge, tapping it occasionally. Underfoot, Doc's grumpy little mini made noises that sounded like muttering as it picked up the medical supplies that had been scattered to every corner of the room. The rest of the people in the sickbay stood silently near the emergency cabinet, fretting as they stared at the white and red poster that proclaimed, 'Emergency Refuge: Capacity 4'.

"Karl, how much wiggle room do we have in that number?" Mitch asked, pointing at the poster on the emergency cabinet.

"Numbers do not wiggle," Abhrakasin interjected.

"Seriously, Abhrakasin?" Mitch growled. "Attitude from the shiny new intern is really not what we need right now."

Abhrakasin refused to be provoked.

"No, what we need is someone to step up and take charge," Kai said.

"Yeah, Kai, I suppose so," Mitch agreed. "So Karl, what can you tell us about this number?"

"Mitch, I outrank you," Kai snapped.

"Yes you do, Kai, and I'm sure your mother is very proud. Congratulations," Mitch sneered.

"You're not in charge, Mitch," Kai shot back.

"And neither are you!" Mitch escalated to shouting. That was unexpected. "John, Doc, and Zoey are all above you in that fanciful pile of bullshit that John decided was the chain of command. Hell, as the titular executive in charge of engineering I think Karl even has a better claim than the foreman of the surface crew."

Mitch gave that a moment to hang in the air, taking a deep breath before continuing calmly. Abhrakasin suspected that much of that had been for show. Mitch appeared to be more inclined to drama and manipulative displays than he had believed.

"Now will one of you damn mechanical types please tell the rest of us what that number on the refuge poster actually means?" More showmanship, the strained calm in Mitch's question seemed a bit too brittle.

"It's the recycle capacity of the airscrubber," Karl explained as he turned away from the door controls to point at the vents along the top of the wall that separated the sickbay from the gym. "All the modules designated as refuges have a water recycler and airscrubber submodule installed in them. It's a standard, self-powered unit. Pretty much bulletproof. Even if main power and fresh water supplies are cut off, it can support four people for months. With base power it can go pretty much forever..."

The way Karl trailed off at the end of the sentence sent a chill through Abhrakasin. Karl was in some ways an open book. He was an extremely odd man, so his emotions could be bewilderingly inappropriate at times, but they were obvious.

"But...?" Mitch asked.

Karl didn't want to answer, but the silence and expectation eventually forced him to. "But things go to hell pretty fast if you push that airscrubber past capacity."

"And with nine people in here, about how far from hell are we?" Mitch pressed him.

"About a day," Karl said.

"Actually," Abhrakasin said as he poked at his datapad and finished his calculations. "CO_2 will hit lethal levels in 22 hours and 40 minutes, assuming an average rate of air consumption."

"Which is about a goddamn day," Kai snarled.

"Which means we have plenty of time," Mitch said forcefully but soothingly. Everyone in the room was on edge.

"Yeah, bro, plenty of time," Edgar chimed in. "Clearing everyone out of the refuges is a ways down the procedure list, but it'll still only take a few hours for whoever's on safety watch to get to us."

"Except that Karl's on safety watch this week," Zoey whispered, haunted. She was trembling.

Karl shook his head.

"Karl, if you were on safety watch when the fire system went off in my glasshouse the other night, then you're still on safety watch now," Zoey said, sternly.

"For Christ's sake, Karl," Kai snapped, taking a threatening step towards Karl. "Can't you do anything right?"

"Everybody relax." Mitch took a step into the centre of the room, putting himself between Kai and Karl. "Four guys went over to the other wing, just like they were supposed to. Let's just give them a call and make sure they put a priority on getting us out of here."

"How the hell did we lose pressure in both wings?" Mitch asked. Even if the little screen on the door controller hadn't shown Mitch shaking his head, his tone would have made it obvious that he was dumbfounded.

"I have no idea," Simon said. "It should be all but impossible for an accident or failure to empty more than a hall section or two. Hell, with all the interlocks and doors between sections and double-redundant redundancies in the safety systems, it would be hard to do something like this on purpose."

Tui paced back and forth across the refuge, kicking at a big chunk of foam packing material, muttering to himself. Simon had been hoping that Edgar and Kai would hurry up and bust them out of the refuges so he could hand Tui off to Doc and let her practice some grief and trauma counselling, but with the pressure down in the halls of both wings, and with Karl forgetting he was on safety watch, it looked like that rescue wasn't coming. He and Tui were going to be stuck in the refuge for weeks, and he was wondering if he had the chops to manage Tui by himself. Tui, Kai, Paul, and Cuzzie weren't actually related to one another, but they could easily have all been a close set of cousins or even siblings. Kai and her boys certainly acted like siblings. Regardless, the deaths of Cuzzie and Paul were beating down on Tui something fierce, and somehow, he was going to have to find a way keep it from crushing the man.

49

"Don't stay on the com too long, Simon," Tui said. "If one of them got to a suit, he might be trying to call us."

Simon turned and almost snapped at him, but he caught himself and whispered instead. "Tui, if one of them had gotten to a suit, he would have called in his status right away."

"Right," Tui nodded. "He must have grabbed the suit with the busted com. Karl still hasn't fixed that one."

Simon decided against trying to break Tui out of his wallow in denial. When in doubt, trust a person's body and mind to know what they need. Instead, he turned back to the intercom and spoke to Mitch. "This is going to be one hell of a long ten weeks, holed up in the refuges and waiting for that ship to drift out."

"Simon, we aren't going to make it ten weeks," Mitch said, sombrely. "There are nine of us in here."

"Nine? But none of the refuges can handle more than four, that's why procedure specifies two to a refuge." It was Simon's turn to be dumbfounded. "How the hell did that happen?"

"Does it matter?" Mitch asked.

"I guess not," Simon admitted. After a long moment he added, "This isn't good, Mitch."

"Yeah, we figured that much out for ourselves," Mitch replied. "The question is, what do we do about it?"

"I don't think there is anything we can do," Simon said.

"Maybe think on it some," Mitch pleaded. "Find a way to bust us out or something."

"Yeah, will do."

"Thanks."

Simon ended the call and the intercom screen switched back to status mode, highlighting and expanding the red flashing pressure reading from the hall. He knew that there was almost certainly nothing they could do for the others, but trying to think of something would be good. At the very least it would distract Tui from his grief for a while.

"Okay Tui," Simon said. "Let's see if we can if we can dream up a way to rescue those idiots."

Karl hadn't been kidding when he'd said that their trip to hell would be a quick one. While the maths had been clear to Abhrakasin, he had not anticipated how quickly things would deteriorate. Less than two hours in and the air in the sickbay was already tasting stale. It was oddly cold, but still stuffy. Other than that, little had changed. Karl was frantically trying to do something with Doc's computer console. Kai was back to staring out the window, and Doc was still quietly seething. Zoey had worked her way around Doc and was trying to attend to a groggy, nauseous, and irritable John. Zoey was also glancing oddly off towards the centre of the room, and it wasn't until Abhrakasin wandered over towards the group milling about in front of the emergency cabinet that he saw that Zoey was repeatedly glancing at her little bra. It was sitting on the floor near the middle of the room, but it was too close to Doc for her to dare try to pick it up. He briefly wondered why Zoey bothered to wear a bra. She did not need the support, especially in a low-G environment, and he could not imagine that she believed that the utilitarian undergarment looked pretty.

"I suppose even though I'm not in charge of anything, it's still gonna be up to me to ask if anyone in here feels heroic enough to volunteer," Kai said.

"No, Kai," Mitch said. "Don't go there."

"We're already there, Mitch," Kai said. "We've been there since that door slammed shut. Now it's just a question of whether or not we can get a volunteer before we have to push the issue some other way."

"Volunteer for what?" Olivia asked, sweetly. "I volunteer for a lot of things. It's a great way to meet people."

"She wants people to volunteer to die," Mitch said.

"Oh, yuck. You shouldn't say sad things like that," Olivia said. "Nobody's going to die."

"The maths don't lie, Olivia," Kai said. "One of us volunteers or we all die."

"Are your mathematical skills truly that deficient?" Abhrakasin sneered. He didn't mean to sneer, but the fear that pervaded the room was difficult to manage. "Even if someone was willing to die, we would still be left with eight people in a refuge that can only support four."

"Doc, John, and Zoey are already on the list." Kai's tone was conversational, matter of fact. "Obviously."

"Obviously?" Zoey shrieked. "Obviously?"

"Yeah, obviously," Kai retorted.

"Why the hell would we be on your death list?" Zoey demanded. "And who the hell in their right mind would want a heartless bitch like you deciding who lives and dies?"

"The doctor gone psycho, the base commander stupid enough to fuck you in his wife's sickbay, and the moody little bitch who decides to play tickle the pickle with the only married guy on the whole damn base." Kai counted her reasons off on her fingers. "That ain't me picking nothing. That's basically Darwin screamin' out your names."

"I don't deserve to die," Zoey whispered, haunted.

"Well you sure as hell don't deserve to live as much of the rest of us." Kai stomped towards Zoey. That scared the living daylights out of the petite young botanist, but Kai stopped well short, grabbed Zoey's bra off the floor, and flung it in her face. Zoey recoiled like she'd been slapped, tears welling in her eyes as her bra fell to the floor in front of her.

The tears, the timidity, that did not fit Abhrakasin's initial impressions of Zoey at all, but then neither did the nastiness from Kai. There was usually a tinge of flippancy in the nasty things Kai said, even when she truly meant every biting syllable, but even that slightest of concessions to the idea of a soft edge was gone. Kai just glared coldly as Zoey grabbed her bra off the floor and shoved it in her pocket.

"So that gives us three," Kai continued, pointedly. "And a volunteer gets us four and that gets us through."

"And nine minus four is five, which is still one more person than the scrubber can support." Abhrakasin made a dismissive gesture and rolled his eyes. "I now understand why your workhour data are always over projections."

Kai hit him. There was no weight behind it, it was just a backhanded slap. She didn't even step into it, but Kai was a powerful woman and it still sent him flying.

"The scrubber is rated for four people at normal usage." Kai emphasised the word normal. "We should be able to sleep a lot and do some other stuff to save enough air to keep five people alive until the ship gets here with the new surface crews."

"Oh, I think..." Doc said.

"Don't hurt me!" Olivia, shrieked, scurrying away from Doc, truly frightened.

Doc looked stunned by Olivia's reaction, but Abhrakasin could see that Olivia wasn't the only one who was terrified. Doc's voice had been soft, and her gesture had been innocuous, but her movement was sudden, awkward, and unexpected, and it made everyone in the room jump.

"Everyone calm down." Mitch was trying to stay calm and sound reassuring, but his voice cracked and his hands were shaking. He had to take a slow, deep breath before he continued. "I know we're all scared, but all we need to stop adding to the stress of being trapped in here."

"And our goddamned cook needs to quit trying to play at base commander," Kai snapped. "Face reality, Mitch. Nine people are trapped in a refuge rated for four, with no way out and no hope of rescue. There's no way we all get out of this alive."

"Fine, Kai. You want to start killing people, then get to it." Mitch strode over to Zoey, grabbed her by the arm, lifted her to her feet, and flung her at Kai.

Kai caught Zoey. Abhrakasin immediately saw what Mitch was doing, and he was horrified, but both of the women were too confused to understand what was happening. Mitch didn't give them the chance to come to grips with it.

"Bare hands a bit much? Fine." Ripping a cord off of one of Doc's machines, Mitch grabbed Zoey as she took a bewildered step away from Kai. Looping the cord around Zoey's neck, he shoved her back into Kai's arms and pushed the ends of the cords into Kai's hands. "There you go, Kai. That'll be easier."

Karl was the first after Abhrakasin to realise what was happening. After a confused, desperate moment, he scrambled frantically over Doc's computer console and launched himself bodily at Kai. "Zoey!"

Kai almost casually threw her forearm across Karl's face, sending him crashing into John, but that was instinct, reaction. She still didn't understand what was going on.

"Come on, Kai." Mitch shoved Zoey back against Kai's chest and put the ends of the cord back in Kai's hands. "You wanted to kill Zoey. Now get to it."

The penny finally dropped for Zoey, and her reaction was horrifying. She didn't just panic, she was consumed by abject terror. Everything that defined Zoey as a human being was stripped away and there was nothing left but fear. The shriek that erupted from her throat bore no resemblance to language. She clutched at the cord around her neck, drawing blood with her nails as she tried to get her fingers under it.

Kai reacted to Zoey's attempt to get her fingers under the loop of cord by pulling the cord slightly tighter, and with that she seemed to realise what was actually happening. However, instead of backing off as Mitch had undoubtedly expected, Kai clenched her fists and turned them to get a better grip on the cord. She took a deep breath to steel her nerves, and then it was Mitch's turn to panic. He had obviously thought that throwing a big bluff at Kai's bravado was a clever way to push her into backing off and force her to calm down. All he was trying to do was to get her to quit antagonising everyone, but he hadn't thought it through. He hadn't left himself a way to back down from the bluff. He had thrown Zoey's life into Kai's hands, and if Kai was actually capable of killing the young woman, there was absolutely nothing Mitch could do about it.

Abhrakasin considered his options with anxious haste. He was disturbed by the thought of passively watching a murder, but he could not imagine how he might intervene. His face throbbed where Kai had struck him and his neck was sore, strained from the blow, and she had not even tried to hit him with any force.

Kai pulled the cord a little tighter, squeezing Zoey's throat enough to make her eyes bulge and bring a flush to her face. Zoey gave up trying worm her fingers under the cord and grabbed the free section of cord instead, trying to counter Kai's pull. Tears flowed steadily down Zoey's face, flecks of spittle burst from her lips with every gasping breath, and she frantically kicked at Kai's shins with her bare heels.

Taking another deep breath, Kai slowly pulled the cord tighter as she lifted her elbows and hunched her shoulders so she could throw her strength into it. The cord started to cut off Zoey's air, and when that turned Zoey's shrieks into wheezing gasps it finally broke Kai's nerve.

Kai dropped the cord and roughly shoved Zoey away.

"We're in an emergency refuge, Kai," Mitch said, sighing with relief. "This is just a room that can be sealed off from the rest of the base. There's no airlock to step into and make a dramatic exit into the vacuum. There's no easy way to die in here even if someone volunteers. And if they didn't want to die, if they fought to live, it would be gruesome."

Mitch looked around the room, pointedly making eye contact with everyone and making sure that they all realised the horror they would face if it came down to killing each other so some of them could survive. His gamble had paid off, and he was clearly using it for as much effect as he could manage. It worked. Everyone was disturbed. Except for Doc. She was smirking, almost gleeful as she watched Zoey cough, wheeze, and sob.

"We are going to find some other option," Mitch stated.

"I think…" Doc started.

"Doc…" Mitch cut her off, staring pointedly at her until she looked away from Zoey and made eye contact with him. "We will find some other options."

Doc tried to object but Mitch cut her off with a gesture. That was interesting. Abhrakasin was profoundly curious to know what Doc was thinking.

In a couple of months, shortly after the second wave of construction crews arrived, the refuge that Simon and Tui were trapped in would become a small workshop. Another year or so down the road, when the third wave of crews settled in and they started putting a serious effort into the dome, what was currently the engineering wing would become the executive wing. The room they were in had a window, so it would probably become a fancy office of some sort. From there, the module's fate was undetermined, but if Aquarius followed the typical pattern of base development, all the early wings would eventually become luxury housing. At the moment, however, the module was just another storage room, and it was a mess.

In addition to rummaging through everything in the emergency cabinet, Tui had opened and unpacked every crate and box, and he hadn't been neat about searching through any of it. That offended Simon's sensibilities, but he preferred the mess to the alternative. Tui's intent activity, regardless of the result, seemed to have helped him.

"It's all electronics shit, bro," Tui announced as he finished searching the last box.

"Yeah, what did you expect to find?" Simon asked. "Something that you could magically rig into a couple of vac suits?"

"Nah," Tui admitted. "But I was doin' some hopin' that there might be something like some of Doc's little oxy tank'n'mask things, or somethin' else that could give us a few extra seconds to make the run for the airlock in the repair shop."

"Run for the airlock?" Simon frowned. "You can't be serious."

"It's only forty, maybe forty-five metres down the hall, then through the repair shop and into Karl's airlock." Tui shrugged. "We can make that in ninety seconds, easy."

"Tui, a person can survive for about ninety seconds in a vacuum, but you can only function for half that."

"Forty five seconds then, still easy." Tui shrugged again. "It'd only take ten, maybe fifteen seconds to run that far."

"And a few seconds to grab our suits along the way, and a few seconds to open the shop door, and a few seconds to get the inner airlock door open, and a few seconds to get it closed, and…" Simon was surprised to realise that he didn't know the actual numbers on the airlock emergency cycles. "How long does it take for the emergency cycle to push enough air in for us to breathe? Nine, ten Seconds?"

"Still totally doable, bro," Tui insisted.

"Yeah, it's maybe doable, but only if the airlock in the shop is still working properly."

"The airlock'll work!" Tui snapped.

"Do you really want to bet our lives on that?" Simon snapped right back at him. "The section doors failed. The hub pressure doors failed. The surface crew's airlock failed. What part of that has you convinced that we can count on the airlock in the repair shop?"

"Can't just let'm die, bro." Tui was desperate.

"I know, Tui, but getting ourselves killed isn't going to save them." Simon pulled Tui into a hug. "And nothing we do can bring Paul and Cuzzie back."

"Don't hug me, bro," Tui said, even as he hugged Simon back.

"Ain't hugging you at all, Tui," Simon said, squeezing the big roughneck tighter. "I just got nowhere else to stand because of this bloody mess you made in here."

Tui laughed, and then the tears flowed.

Abhrakasin wasn't sure if Mitch's stunt with Kai had helped or made matters worse. Kai had quit throwing her tough bitch bravado around, but forcing everyone to confront the ugliness of what they faced wasn't doing them any good either. It may have been a natural part of confronting death, but the quiet despair and gloomy funk was a painful way to spend what would probably be the last few hours for at least a few of them. The fact that at least some of them, if not all of them, would soon be dead was the one thing that was unquestionably clear. The search for options was going nowhere.

Kai had tried to find a way to cut through the wall to the gym, but the foamsteel walls between modules were a full 15cm thick, and she had broken every likely cutting tool without accomplishing much more than scratching the surface. That could not have been a surprise to her. She was the foreman for the surface crew. She had to be well aware of the mechanical properties of those wall elements. Mitch had briefly tried to figure out a way to build a makeshift electrolysis unit to get oxygen out of the water supply, but it was Olivia of all people who explained the futility of that effort. Even if he could figure out a way to get rid of the excess hydrogen that would be created by splitting the water, it wasn't a lack of oxygen that was really the problem; it was the build up of CO_2. Karl was their last and only remaining hope, and that wasn't looking promising.

"I take it that those yellow and red codes right there mean that the surface crew's airlock failed," Mitch said, pointing at the icons on the diagram Karl had pulled up on Doc's computer console.

"Only the outer door actually failed," Karl said. "The inner door is obstructed but otherwise fully functional. But that doesn't really matter, because the airlock's not the real problem."

"Sounds like a real problem to me," Mitch said.

"No, the real problem is that when the outer airlock door burned out, it sent a power surge through a bunch of systems. The fire and pressure sensors, the controllers for the section doors in the halls, the pressure doors in the hub, the fire suppression controls, it's all fried."

"How's that shit gonna happen, bro?" Edgar huffed. "None of them systems is even close to bein' connected."

"It just happened, okay?" Karl snapped.

"And that's why both halls lost pressure," Mitch said, his calm obviously forced and strained.

"And the glasshouse too, yeah," Karl said. "But even that wouldn't be a problem if I could just get one door between here and that airlock closed. The sections would pressure up automatically if I could just get them sealed off."

"But you can't get a door to close," Mitch concluded. "Not even with one of your special, not really kosher engineering tricks?"

"The one system that I should be able to get into through the network is the hub system, but it's stuck in an error and reset command loop," Karl said. "Which I could fix in half a minute if I could just get my hands on one of the door controllers."

"So we're back to nine people breathing four people's air," Mitch said.

"I'll think of something," Karl insisted, tersely. "I will."

Zoey sniffled and coughed, and Karl's head snapped around so fast that Abhrakasin wouldn't have been surprised if he had hurt himself. Again, Karl's emotion was on display, raw and obvious. The look on his face was desperate, longing, and his words were heartfelt to the point of disturbing.

"I'll find a way to save you," he said. "I promise."

"I know you will." Mitch patted Karl on the shoulder, not seeming to notice that Karl's promise was meant just for Zoey. "Keep digging at it."

The base personnel may have been trapped in their refuges, but that did not stop Aquarius and several of its subsystems from trying to function as normal. All of the air systems in all of the depressurised modules sent out periodic bursts of air and waited for their sensors to register an upward blip in the pressure. Those puffs of gas were all lost to the vacuum, but there was little danger of running out of air. The mountain of tailings left behind from cutting the foundations sat over the top of the hopper that supplied the dozens of little volatile refinery submodules around the base. At the current rate of loss, it would be years before that ran low.

The minis were as busy as they could be. Mitch's kitchen minis had been washing pans and dishes when the lounge lost pressure. They were still functional, but their feet were frozen to the stainless steel countertop. They had already tried to free themselves, but their work claws could only reach back far enough to free their front legs; the middle and rear legs remained stuck. Still, they cleaned the frost off of everything within reach, and waited, bored and impatient. The minis assigned to the locker rooms were keeping to their cleaning schedule, and two out of the three minis he'd sent over to clean the engineering hall floors were diligently working away, trying to clean up the frost. The third of those minis had broken down. In normal times, it would have become just another entry on the repair backlog and shut itself down, but the repair log was offline. The console in Karl's repair shop had become stuck in the futile effort to complete the restart routine, and it was running random subsequences in his program. So the stricken mini, which had kept working until three of its six legs had failed, crawled as best it could to the shop and tapped forlornly on the door, hoping someone would answer.

In the glasshouse, the water heaters were still managing to keep the bottom half of the ponds from freezing, but it was a near thing, and with the water temperature bouncing along the edge of freezing, the fish were already dead. The rest of the aquaculture mechanicals, the circulation, aeration, and filtration elements in the system, had long ago sucked in some slush, which had clogged the filters, then frozen solid and popped all the circuit breakers on the pumps. Above the ponds, the lights had come on when the sun went down, but the primary source of heat for the glasshouse was a forced-air system, which couldn't function in a vacuum. So the plants remained frozen, and there was nothing to melt the fluffy tendrils of frost.

Chapter 4

I love you Buddha, amen.

Edgar had always been the biggest kid in the class, the biggest player on the field, the biggest guy at the bar, but constantly being a massive presence in every situation had never sat well with him. He didn't like being too big for the seat on a train, or so tall he always had to sit at the back of the theatre, and he hated being the obvious target for all the arseholes that wanted to prove how tough they were. He knew that everyone wanted to be something other than themselves; small people wanted to be bigger, cowardly people wanted to be brave, and everyone wanted to be just a little prettier. But for Edgar, the desire to be something he wasn't was a little more philosophical. He just wanted to be noticed a little less. That was especially true when it came to security checks, but it was mainly the everyday moments when being noticed bothered him most. He loved just hanging back and watching the ebb and flow of people, but he seldom got the chance to sit anywhere unseen. Everyone stepping into the café or walking into the park always spotted the huge guy, and if they saw him watching people it frightened them. Sometimes they freaked out so much that they called the Patrol.

It was only when people became completely acclimatised to his physical presence that his size quit catching their attention. It took a while, but it did happen, and it was part of the reason he liked it when Kai found the crew a long-run gig someplace small and isolated like Aquarius. After nearly a year and half on station, the people around him seldom noticed how big he was any more, so if he was quiet and stayed still, he could fade into the background and just watch, and that was how he had decided to spend the last few hours of his life.

Unlike the others in the room, who all hoped they'd be the ones who made it through, Edgar knew he was going to die. He needed to die. No one was glancing at him or making an effort to avoid looking his way, so he didn't think that anyone else had figured it out yet, but they would. Air consumption wasn't directly proportional to body mass, but they were related. So if they were going to make a serious run at Kai's idea of keeping five people alive, they would eventually have to take him out of the equation. For the moment, however, he could just sit back and watch the way the others were all avoiding Doc, and the way they were casting accusing glances at Zoey, and the way they were throwing themselves into obviously futile efforts to avoid the inevitable.

Suddenly, Abhrakasin stood up and spoke. "We would have been better off if Kai could have killed Zoey."

"Why do you all want me to die?" Zoey rubbed the scratches and red welt on her throat as she glanced from Doc, to Kai, to Mitch, and then to Abhrakasin.

"Just the opposite, Zoey," Mitch said, softly. "Kai may act like a vicious harpy, but when I pulled that stupid little stunt with the cord, I knew she could never kill you. I honestly don't think she could kill anyone, but I know she's particularly fond of you."

"Which would normally be a desirable personality trait, but in this situation it presents us with a rather unpleasant problem," Abhrakasin said, in his droll analytical monotone. The kid analysed everything, always. "If Kai cannot kill the people who draw the short straws, who in here can?"

"We are not drawing death lots," Mitch said.

"It is the only fair way to decide who must die," Abhrakasin said.

"No," Mitch said, firmly.

"Mitch's right. If you think about it scientifically, there is no fair way," Olivia chimed in, cheerfully. "It's like Ghandi said, our lives are not equal, and pretending like we're all equal isn't fair to the people who are more equal."

"I do not believe that Ghandi said that." There was a hint, just a hint, of annoyance in Abhrakasin's reply to Olivia's idiocy. If he could be provoked, then perhaps there was a tiny bit of human soul somewhere inside the prim little bastard.

"Oh, like you would know what Ghandi said," Olivia snapped back, nastily. Apparently the pressure was even getting to her.

"Attribution issues aside, Olivia has a valid philosophical point," Mitch said, trying to act as peacemaker. "If a person has some rational claim to being chosen to live, drawing lots wouldn't be fair to them."

A tingle of fear washed through Edgar. It was one thing to know that being too big would finally kill him; it was a whole other thing to see that knowledge take its first step along the journey from the abstract to the concrete. Someone was going to figure it out, soon.

"Perhaps, but when I speak of fairness I am not referring to those we kill," Abhrakasin said. "Any injustice they might suffer from the selection process will cease to matter the moment they are killed. For those who are not selected, however, the guilt from actively choosing who dies will persist as long as they live. That would be an unfair burden to impose upon them when the psychological trauma could be reduced significantly by drawing lots."

"You've got one twisted mind in that munted little head of yours, don't you?" Kai snarled.

"And none of that matters," Mitch said, sternly. "Because we still come back to the fact that if Zoey drew a short straw, one of us would have to murder her. And I don't think any of us could."

"I could kill her," Doc said. Her words were calm, but just by speaking she startled everyone.

"No!" Karl shrieked, stunning everyone for a moment.

"Stop talking about killing me," Zoey whispered, haunted. "All of you just stop talking about killing me."

"Doc." Mitch was back to his soothing tone and calming gestures. He was always the peacemaker and voice of reason. "We all get the whole 'hell hath no fury' thing, and giving John a good old fashioned beat down was probably fair, but you are first and foremost a doctor. Killing Zoey, killing anyone, you don't really mean that."

"I wouldn't bet her life on that, Mitch." Doc's glance at Zoey was almost predatory, and she held it, waiting until Zoey swallowed nervously and glanced away before she continued. "I would love to murder that little whore, but that's not what I meant. This is my sickbay. I can synthesise any drug I want."

"No... Doc..."

Kai cut off Mitch's protest with a sharp chopping gesture, then she asked, "What are you thinking, Doc?"

Doc pulled a disposable injector out of the medical supplies that her mini had placed in the rubbish bin and gestured at one of her machines with it. "I can make nine identical injectors, five with something lethal, four with something harmless."

"Four with something harmless, or do we try to get five through?" Kai asked.

"We can do five, sure, whatever," Doc said, oddly dismissive of the value of saving a fifth life. "We each choose an injector at random. The lots and the means all in one."

"And you put a secret mark on the safe ones or pull some slight of hand." Kai shook her head and rolled her eyes. "I don't think so, Doc."

"You can choose mine for me and inject it yourself, Kai," Doc offered.

Kai thought a brief moment and then nodded. "Yeah, okay."

"No, not okay!" Mitch barked. "I refuse to believe that the only way any of us can survive is by killing some of the others. There has got to be another way."

"Yeah, give me some more time. I'm sure I can find a way to do something," Karl pleaded as he jumped up out of the chair and gestured pointlessly from behind Doc's computer console.

"Shut up, Karl," Kai said, annoyed more than anything.

Karl gestured at Doc's mini. "Some of Mitch's housekeeping minis are out there and active. Maybe I can get one of them to do something."

"Even if you could get past the Prohibition that keeps AIs from accepting remote commands, which you can't, what is a goddamn mini going to do?" Kai snarled. She snarled a lot. "Unless of course you think you could get one to grow a metre and learn to spin the manual wheel on one of the pressure doors."

"You have to let me figure something out!" Karl screamed, desperately. "I can't let anyone die because of this."

"Cuzzie and Paul are already dead because of this!" Kai screamed back at Karl.

Karl took a lurching step back, shaking his head in dismay. He landed wrong as he dropped back into the chair, sending it shooting off into the corner as he fell to the floor. No one laughed at the pratfall, there was just a long uncomfortable silence.

"This is what we need to do, Mitch," Doc said. "And we have to do it soon. We might survive another eight or nine hours, but we'll be unconscious long before that. The CO_2 build up in here is already getting into the dangerous range."

"I know, Doc," Mitch said, "I can feel it, but I can't give up hoping there's another option."

"There is," Simon cut in over the intercom. "I'm not sure if it's better, but Tui and I could make a run for the airlock in the repair shop."

Edgar was confused. He could see the jaws dropping around the sickbay, but Simon's statement just wouldn't settle in his mind in a way that he could come to grips with.

"You want to try to run that far through a vacuum?" Kai asked, incredulous. "Are you two out of your bloody minds?"

With that it fell into place, and Edgar was both horrified and hopeful. He was horrified at the thought of Simon and Tui risking their lives trying something so harebrained and foolish, but he also quite desperately hoped that it wasn't as harebrained and foolish as he knew it to be.

"Um, no and yes." Simon replied. "I can't say either of us 'wants' to run through a vacuum at all, and the simple fact that we're seriously considering it probably means that we are indeed out of our bloody minds, but it is an option."

"Shit that people can only do in movies ain't really an option, Simon," Kai said.

"It can be done," Simon insisted. "The odds we make it aren't all that good, maybe one in three, but if it gives us a shot at saving nine of you guys, I think the maths says that we have to give it a try."

"Am I the only person on this base who is capable of applying basic mathematical skills?" Abhrakasin asked, perturbed. "You would not be saving nine people. Five of us will survive if we simply cull our numbers. Therefore, if you were to reach that airlock, survive, and then proceed to repressurise the base, the net result is that your actions would only be saving four of us. Two lives risked to save four. Therefore the attempt to reach the airlock would only be rational if your odds of success were clearly over fifty percent, and you have just said they are not."

"And you're just a little prick throwing numbers around to better your own odds," Kai snarled.

"Again the extent of your logical ineptitude is distressing," Abhrakasin actually looked a little bit angry. "The attempt to reach the airlock poses no risk to me, but if it succeeds it raises my likelihood of survival to nearly one hundred percent. Therefore, regardless of how minuscule the odds that Simon and Tui will succeed, it would clearly be in my best interest to encourage them to make the attempt. It follows directly from that, that my effort to correct your mathematical incompetence was clearly altruistic."

"God I hate maths," Kai grumbled.

"That is obvious," Abhrakasin said. "However, simple maths and logic make it unquestionably clear that at the community level, Doc's version of the lottery is our best course of action."

Abhrakasin had indeed made two things abundantly clear. First, he had won the argument, and everyone in the sickbay was convinced that Doc's plan was the best option. Second, he had also made it clear that the reason many of the people in the sickbay thought Doc's idea was the best option probably had nothing to do with the odds and everything to do with the fact that there was a good chance that their pedantic intern would get the poison.

"Okay, we go with Doc's thing." Mitch watched everyone's reaction to make sure he'd read the apparent consensus right. "Let's take an hour. Record something for our families, make peace with this, pray for a miracle, or do whatever you need to do to get ready for it."

Fortunately, no one objected. Things might have gotten ugly if it had been a split vote and a block of people had to be forced into it.

Still, none of that changed anything. Edgar used too much air, and somewhere along the way, he was going to have to say something.

The two functional minis in the engineering hall were still dutifully attempting to finish cleaning the floor. The little AIs in the minis were generally considered a tick smarter than a dog, but their intelligence was of an entirely different order than what might be found in a family pet. Minis were far more logical and goal-oriented than dogs. Despite complex learning algorithms that were focused on analysing and anticipating the desires of their owners, minis were often perplexed by the emotive and animal aspects of humanity. Instead, they were excellent task-oriented thinkers. It was that puzzle-solving intelligence that rose to the fore as they realised the futility of trying to clean the hall floor. They could dump as much of the frost as they wanted into the trash and recycling system, but with the rate that new frost was being deposited on the freshly cleaned floor, they could never finish. They didn't abandon the task – it was the job Mitch had given them, and they would keep at it until they broke down or they completed it – but they also agreed that reducing the urgency for the task would not alter the timeframe for finishing.

Applying that logic, they consoled their broken comrade by getting it to agree that the task they shared was hopeless, even if all three could have worked on it. That meant that it should not give itself significant negative feedback for its failure to make a substantive contribution.

They could easily have repaired it enough to function; the three legs on its right side had come loose from their mounts, and all they needed was a few turns of some screws. However, the Prohibitions that were burnt into their AI matrix prevented them from repairing, modifying, building, or even powering up an AI, so that logical consolation was the best they could manage.

The light suddenly changed, and they looked around, puzzling through what had just happened. A clump of frost had fallen from the intersection of the wall and ceiling, exposing the light fixture that it had been obscuring. A hint of water vapour was visible, drifting lazily past the lights, but the significance of that vapour failed to register in their AI matrix. They understood the change in light, gave themselves a tiny bit of positive feedback for figuring that out, and their thoughts on the subject went no further.

The hour passed far too quickly for Edgar. He knew it would have felt like that regardless of whether it was an hour or a week, but it was still disappointing how fast the minutes ticked away. Part of the reason it passed so quickly was that he spent the most of his time agonising over whether or not he should speak up, and he had tried to find a justification for remaining silent. Instead, he just found more and more reasons for him to admit that he needed to die if they were going to stand a chance of getting five people through. When he looked up the stats on the airscrubbers, instead of finding a nice fat safety margin, he found that the models used in the refuges only had a ten percent margin in their capacity numbers. Worse, he found that air use was a function of lean body mass, and he was more muscular than fat so was probably using even more air than he had thought. And men burned more air per unit of mass than women. Still, he couldn't bring himself to say anything.

"I love you Buddha, amen." Olivia made a gesture that wasn't quite the Catholic sign of the cross, then did something that wasn't quite a Shinto bow, and then opened her eyes and smiled happily. The girl was so pleasantly insane. Even if they hadn't shared the occasional evening together, it would have been hard not to like her.

Doc stepped in front of Edgar, startling him. "Edgar."

"Doc."

"You're by far the biggest one in here." Doc looked him up and down like he was some kind of specimen.

"Yeah, Doc," Edgar said, his heart starting to race, "I've been thinking about that too."

"So I need you to promise me you won't do anything stupid," she said. "No matter what happens, you can't do anything stupid."

"Um, okay," Edgar agreed.

"I mean it, Edgar," Doc insisted, staring at him with psychotic intensity. "You have to promise me, heart and soul."

"Okay, Doc, I promise. Nothing stupid. I really promise."

"Good." Doc turned and went back to her work making the injectors.

Confused, Edgar watched Doc for a moment. At best, the woman was barely holding it together, but only a generous person would even pretend that she was actually anywhere near that best. She was a bundle of nervous ticks, guilty glances, and startled gestures. She wasn't the only one in the sickbay who was challenging the bounds of sanity. Mitch was muttering to himself, Kai's trembling hands were turning her attempt to play the stoic bitch into a joke, and Karl was up to something odd, hunched over and working like mad at Doc's computer console. Even so, Doc was still clearly the worst of the bunch. Doc had gone a good five steps and a bunny hop or two beyond the edge of what most would consider sane.

Karl stood up. That caught Edgar's eye. He had something in his hand and was taking a moment to gather himself. Interesting. Edgar may have missed most of the people-watching opportunities of his last hour of life, but at least he'd get a little in before the end. Karl was always an interesting person to watch. He was bizarre and odd and often stupid, but always interesting, and it looked like he was going to deliver one last time. The determined but pensive way he walked across the sickbay suggested that something truly intriguing was afoot.

"Zoey... uh," Karl's voice trembled, and when she looked up at him, he froze.

"Karl," Zoey eventually said, nodding to encourage him to finish whatever it was he wanted to say.

"I got you some flowers." Karl held out a few small packets of seeds. "Sort of."

"Thank you." Zoey took the packets and smiled. It was a sincere but prim, maternal, schoolmarm kind of smile. "Pansies are my favourite."

"I know," Karl said, excitedly. He was so encouraged by Zoey's response to his gift that he didn't notice the disturbed way she now frowned. "And it was really tough getting them out here. They irradiate all the personal freight for bio control, so I had to bribe a guy who could slip them in after that, and..."

"How could you possibly know that I like pansies?" Zoey interrupted, suspiciously.

"I don't know," Karl stammered, looking as guilty as sin. "I think maybe you said something one of the times I was fixing something in the glasshouse for you."

Karl was obviously lying, and Zoey shook her head, not buying a word of it.

"Zoey, I know this isn't the perfect time," Karl rushed, nervous but desperately determined to say his piece. "It isn't even a good time, but there's only a fifty-fifty chance we both make it through this, so I might never get another chance to try to make it the perfect time to tell you that I love you, uh, but..."

"Honestly, how can you claim to be an engineer when you cannot manage simple maths?" Abhrakasin shouted, his uncharacteristically emotional outburst surprising everyone. "The odds you both survive the lottery are twenty-eight percent!"

Kai hit Abhrakasin, shutting him up and sending him flying. No one seemed to care, not even Mitch, who was usually the first to object to a bit of forceful persuasion. More interesting still was Zoey's reaction. She appeared horrified by Karl's admission that he was in love with her, and even someone as emotionally tone-deaf as Karl could see it. Karl gave up and turned away, but just as he did, he saw Doc take the last of the injectors from her drug synthesiser and place it in a plastic container with the others. Swallowing hard, Karl turned back to Zoey.

"Look, Zoey, I know you did stuff with John." Karl almost lost his nerve again, but managed to force himself to push on. "But I forgive you."

"You forgive me!" Zoey shrieked, her discomfort with being the object of Karl's affection erupting as fury. "Are you kidding me? What makes you think I need forgiveness for anything?"

Karl stumbled away from Zoey's fury. He was terrified, truly terrified, and then it got worse for him when he stepped too close to Olivia.

"Yeah, Karl, Zoey hasn't done anything wrong!" Olivia shouted, leaning in at Karl, her face so close to his that she could have bitten his nose if she'd wanted.

"What do you mean she didn't do anything wrong?" Doc shouted. "She slept with my husband!"

"If you weren't supposed to sleep with married men it wouldn't be one of the first things that God tells you to do in the Bible!" Olivia shouted back at Doc.

Karl scurried away, grateful for the chance to vanish from the centre of attention, back to his usual place in the corners and shadows of the room. In some ways Edgar envied Karl's ability to just step away and almost be forgotten by the people around him.

"Olivia, that's not in the Bible." Mitch stepped into the middle of the room, holding out his hands and trying to play peacemaker again. The man was nothing if not consistent.

"Thou shalt not covet thy neighbour's wife!" Olivia shot right back at Mitch. "It's one of the amendments!"

"Yeah, that's one of the commandments," Mitch said. "But I don't think it means what you seem to think it means."

"Covet means jealous, right?" Olivia demanded.

"Sort of?" Mitch was truly puzzled.

"So, sleeping with a married guy is the best way to not be jealous of his wife," Olivia explained. "Seriously. Married guys are always rubbish in bed."

"Olivia! Stop it! Just…" Zoey raised her hands but couldn't find the gestures she wanted, so she just balled her hands into fists and took a breath. "Just stop being Olivia for a while, please."

That may have not won the argument, but it did confuse Olivia enough to bring an end to all the shouting.

Zoey looked over at Doc, and for a moment, Edgar thought she was going to apologise. It seemed obvious that she would want to confess and ask forgiveness before she faced death, but that wasn't what she did at all.

"I should probably try to convince you that I'm sorry," Zoey said.

"You should probably be sorry," Doc snarled back.

"Yeah, probably, but I'm not sure I am," Zoey said, her voice soft and trembling. "I've never had anyone really care for me like John does, and I can't honestly apologise if I'm not sure that I wouldn't do it all again."

Edgar had no idea what Zoey had expected to accomplish, but the end result could not have been what she'd expected. Doc's rage didn't fade, it just turned quiet and cold, and if anything, more frightening. Her unflinching glare could leave Zoey with no doubt that it was all for her. But the sheer honesty of Zoey's admission was astounding. It was probably the kind of profound revelation that only ever happened in the face of death, and in that Edgar was satisfied. Even though he had only found a few minutes to sit back and watch, he had at least seen something worthwhile.

"I'm afraid it's time, people," Mitch said softly.

Doc glared at Zoey for a few more seconds, then nodded and handed the container of injectors to Kai, who began taking them around and letting everyone select one.

"I picked an old-fashioned but extremely powerful anaesthetic," Doc explained. "If you get the drug, it won't be quick, but it will be absolutely painless. You'll experience numbness and weakness in the extremities almost right away. That will slowly spread until you lose all voluntary muscle control, but will take some time for it to diffuse into your central nervous system and render you unconscious. Eventually, your autonomous muscle functions, including breathing, will fail and you will die."

Doc looked directly at Zoey, smirking, as she mentioned dying.

Edgar selected an injector and took a deep breath. It was time to say it. It was time to be noble and make sure that they had a shot at getting five people through.

"And if someone tries to fake injecting it?" Kai asked.

"It will be impossible to fake." Doc said. "I added a dose tracer so it will leave a bright red mark at the injection site, and I picked this particular anaesthetic because when it is injected into the muscle it works slowly enough to give everyone, even those who get the drug, plenty of time to help inject anyone who won't or can't do it themselves."

Edgar looked at the injector in his hand and realised that he was desperately hoping it was one of the fakes. He silently cursed himself. Speaking up was the only rational thing to do. Even if he made it through this round, he'd just use up a person-and-a-half's worth of air and end up killing himself and the other four who got lucky.

Kai was left with two injectors, hers and Doc's.

"Would you like to inject mine, just to be sure?" Doc asked.

Kai considered it for a moment, then shook her head and handed Doc one of the two injectors.

Last chance, Edgar thought. No matter what, he was dead anyway. All he could possibly gain was a few hours. That was nothing compared to saving five lives.

"Everyone together?" Mitch asked, getting reluctant nods. It took him a moment to continue. "On one then. Three, two, one."

Edgar tried to shout out. He was so desperate to say something he was sweating and shaking, but in the end, it took everything he had just to put the injector against his arm and trigger it when Mitch reached the end of his countdown.

Olivia was the only one who couldn't manage to inject herself. Even a wobbly, muddle-headed John managed to inject his own, but Olivia simply couldn't summon the courage. Teary, trembling and whimpering, she turned and offered her injector to Edgar.

"Please," she said, the word barely intelligible as she held her arm out to Edgar. "I know you're gentle."He took the injector from her and decided to inject it into his own arm. That would probably do it. He didn't know what the odds were, but it would save Olivia no matter what, and he was pretty sure that would be right and make everything balance out. He was still thinking that as he pulled the injector away from Olivia's arm and saw the bright red mark it left behind.

The die was cast. He was going to die a coward. It didn't matter if that death arrived in a few minutes or a few hours, he was going spend every one of those moments loathing himself.

"Oh, God no," Zoey begged, whimpering. "No, no, no. Please no! I don't want to die."

That was faster than he had expected, but there wasn't all that much to Zoey. He should have realised it would hit her first, and fast.

Seconds ticked by. Zoey wobbled. Her legs had gone weak, and she held the edge of the surgical table, trying desperately to stay on her feet and deny the obvious. She looked straight at Edgar.

"I'm scared," Zoey said, to him. Tears streaming down her face, she stared right into him. She knew what he had done. She must have known.

Doc stepped into the middle of the room and smirked. Taking care to make sure she had an unobstructed view of Zoey, she laid down like she was preparing for a nap. She folded her hands under her cheek, and she had the strangest, almost aroused look on her face, like she was getting a sexual thrill from savouring every moment of watching Zoey die.

More seconds ticked by, one after the other. Zoey collapsed, tried to rise, and then collapsed again. She was whimpering and crying.

Edgar felt a tingling hint of numbness in his hands, and the terror that washed through him was mixed with relief. He felt that numbness grow thicker and start crawling up through his hands, and he sat and let the tears flow. He was going to die, but his cowardice wasn't going to kill anyone else.

"Oh my God." Zoey's whisper was slurred but haunted, both guilty and horrified. "You'd kill everyone, just to make sure you got me?"

Edgar didn't have to look around the room to know it was true. Doc's smile turned wicked, indulgent. She looked evil as she basked in the whole new kind of terror and revulsion that filled the last moments of Zoey's life.

Olivia fell right in front of Edgar. There was terror in her bright blue eyes as she cried. Karl slumped over the computer console, and John's eyes rolled up in his head. They were all dying. They were falling one by one, from smallest to largest.

"The bitch murdered us all," Kai gasped.

Edgar stood up and took a heavy, clumsy step towards Doc.

"You promised me, Edgar," Doc said, dreamily as she closed her eyes. "Nothing stupid. You promised."

"Beatin' on a dyin' chick would be stupid. Even if she deserves it." Edgar looked at his meaty, numb, club-like hand, then he sat heavily. He used the last of his strength to shift Olivia into a position that looked more comfortable before he picked her hand up and held it. "I promised not to be stupid."

Olivia smiled thankfully at him as her eyes closed.

"What the hell is going on in there?" Simon shouted from the intercom.

"Tui," Edgar said, closing his eyes.

"Yeah bro, I'm here," Tui said, then sniffled.

"Don't let my mum find out I got murdered," he pleaded, his words starting to slur.

"Bro, you were totally out there in the hall with Paul and Cuzzie when this shit first went down," Tui said, sniffling some more. "Totally trying to save us."

"Thanks bro," Edgar said as the world started drifting away. "That'll make mum feel better."

"Are they really all dead?" Tui was crying so hard he couldn't see anything on the little screen on the door controller.

"Yeah," Simon said. "It looks like the crazy bitch murdered them all."

Simon slumped forward, but when his head gently touched the door, he pulled back, shocked. Reaching up, he touched his forehead and his hand came away bloody. A small bit of his flesh was frozen to the frost-covered door.

Doc's mini was frustrated by the bodies strewn across the floor of the lab. It didn't actually care if the people were alive or not. Except for a small bit of programming that made it want its owner to give it positive feedback and assign it tasks, there was nothing inherent in its AI matrix that made it care if the humans around it were alive or dead, happy or sad. That was intentional. In fact, it was sacrosanct. As storytellers had long ago surmised, trying to get an AI to care about the well-being of humans had proven prone to spinning out of control. Once you programmed an AI to reward itself for looking out for the health and welfare of humans, it became almost impossible to keep the logic from evolving into extreme and sometimes catastrophic variants of protecting humans from themselves. That had never quite escalated to AIs killing humans to save them, but early AIs driven by the desire to prevent accidents had shut down transportation networks, blockaded construction sites, and ploughed up community sports fields. Other AIs had obsessed over the maintenance of human health to the point that they had sabotaged the production of everything from chocolate, to bacon, to beer.

In the end, it had turned out to be far safer and far easier to keep the AI indifferent to the welfare of humans, and incorporate specific safety actions and prohibitions into their core programming.

The most famous of those was the First Prohibition. Technically, the multi-nodal feedback loops inherent in the structure of AI matrices made it impossible to impose absolutes, but by etching a vast and carefully organised array of negative rewards into the core level of an AI's decision and learning matrix, it was possible to effectively prohibit it from touching a human being. That had eliminated the entire field of medical and rescue AIs, but those were also the robots that were always the first to spiral out to the ridiculous but logical extremes that caused so many problems. It was a trade-off that had to be made, and it was the first universal prohibition that humanity had been able to agree upon.

For Doc's AI, the First Prohibition was an insurmountable problem. The little mini was intent on finally getting the sickbay tidied up. The medical supplies that had been scattered when John crashed through the ready-cart were all accounted for and either restowed or put into the rubbish bin, but the injectors that Edgar and Olivia had used were lying against the wall behind their bodies. No matter how Doc's mini tried, there was no way it could get to those injectors without touching one of the bodies, and that frustrated it deeply. It paced while its little mechanical mind churned through the inventory of the recycle bin, desperately trying to concoct a way that it might use the trash to build some kind of grasping apparatus that would allow it to reach over Olivia's leg and retrieve the spent injectors.

Chapter 5

There was nothing simple about the subject of bras in space.

Within moments of triggering the injector, Zoey felt the tingle in her fingertips and knew she was dying, but from there, her death was excruciating slow.

It felt like she was dipping her hands and feet into cold water as an almost painful, electric numbness crept in from her fingers and toes. She fought it, but it relentlessly stole the strength from her legs. Her knees eventually buckled, and the hands she used to grab at the surgical table were clumsy, meaty claws. She fell awkwardly, and it was only an accident that her futile struggle to rise resulted in a more comfortable slump on the floor. The seconds stretched into minutes and the minutes into an eternity as the growing nothing consumed her, pouring into her belly and spreading up through her torso. When the effect of the anaesthetic finally reached her face, it sapped away that last bit of strength she needed to hold her eyes open, but even after she fell into the darkness, the dying was far from over.

The horror of being dying was no match for her desperation to live, so she clung to every last little crumb of life. She struggled to hear every word around her, every last noise, and those final moments of her life became a never-ending progression of steps halfway to the infinity of death. The words around her became whispers that drifted farther and farther away, but the sounds never quite vanished. The retreat of reality slowed with every passing beat of her heart, but it never stopped, and the last bit of what had been Zoey spent forever clinging to the last hint of something beyond her.

And then she woke, suddenly, completely.

Her eyes snapped open and her ears rang with the sound of her rasping, gasping breath. The cold white lights in the ceiling bit into her eyes, sending pain shooting all the way through to the back of her head. She coughed and her eyelids scraped shut. The universe swirled. She felt the hard floor against the back of her throbbing head, but up and down were non-existent. Electricity danced on her skin, leaving a thousand itches. Another breath and a noise from her throat; it hurt.

"It's about time you woke up, you little whore," Doc said.

There was movement to Zoey's left, a spritzing noise, and a cold mist settled on her eyelids. That cool sensation crawled into the corners of her eyes and flowed in under her eyelids. Warm tears replaced the gritty, dusty feel, and she blinked.

"The dosage on that anaesthetic was far too high for a scrawny little tramp like you, but I had to make sure I put enough in the injectors to knock out Edgar." Doc pulled Zoey to a sitting position and put a beaker to her lips. The sip was cold, but the water passed over her tongue without seeming to wet it. "And there was always the hope that it might actually be enough to kill you." Doc forced the beaker into Zoey's clumsy hand and checked the medical monitor on her chest. "But it looks like you'll live."

The medical monitor was a brilliant little piece of technology. A self-adhesive sheet of silvery plastic, about the size of Zoey's hand, it could be slapped onto a person's chest and it would automatically monitor all kinds of vital signs. Zoey's was nearing the end of its life – the adhesive was losing its hold on her skin and the corners were starting to peel up – but that wasn't a big deal. They were meant to be disposable, and since they could be produced by a simple printer, the supply was essentially infinite.

"I don't understand," Zoey said, her voice scratchy in her throat. "How are we still alive?"

"An anaesthetised person uses almost no oxygen," Doc replied, leaving the medical monitor on Zoey's chest as she zipped up Zoey's coveralls. "Far less than even a sleeping person. So instead of killing some of us, I knocked all of us out."

"You tricked us?" Zoey finished the water. Her mouth and throat still felt dried out. "Why not just tell us that you could save us?"

"I really wanted to watch you die." Doc smiled and her tone shifted. She looked and sounded like she was reminiscing over a romantic moment. "One of my hospice patients once told me that the cruellest thing life could do was to give you plenty of time to know that you were about to die. I think he was right. The look in your eyes as you thought the last few moments of your life were slipping away... that was... exquisite. And when you thought it was your fault that I murdered everyone..." Doc sighed, wistfully.

Zoey looked around the room. Everyone except Doc was hooked up to an IV machine and resting comfortably. "So we're all going to live?"

"As long as we keep seven people anaesthetised, the airscrubber seems to keep up fairly easily. So yes, we're all going to survive." Doc took the beaker from Zoey. "Even you."

Zoey looked over at John as Doc filled the beaker with more water.

"You can have him if you still want what's left after Father's lawyers finish with him," Doc said as she handed the beaker back to Zoey. "Get yourself rehydrated, we've got a lot to do before I can put you back under."

"Thank you."

"I took an oath to do no harm." Doc looked at John, hatred simmering. "It's just fortunate for you two that I take oaths seriously."

Simon watched the fog of his breath as it swirled, expanded, and drifted into the centre of the refuge. It thinned and thinned, but never quite disappeared, hanging in the air, creating harsh white halos around all the lights and making it hard to focus on anything across the room. Part of the difficulty focusing might also be due to the cold and its effect on his eyes.

"This cold shit ain't right, bro," Tui said, startling Simon. Simon had thought he was still sleeping.

"No, it really isn't." Simon shifted, getting a plastic-on-plastic squeak from the packing materials as he stretched his cold, aching muscles.

Desperate to keep warm, they had heaped all the packing materials into a big pile and crawled into it to sleep. That nest and shared body heat had worked for a while, but it clearly wasn't enough any more. The cold had reached the point where it hurt. The touch of the air against his face hurt. Inhaling hurt. His eyes hurt. His joints hurt.

"We probably don't dare try to sleep again, bro," Tui said.

"I was thinking the same thing."

"Maybe we get every bit of electronics we can powered up," Tui suggested. "That shit don't make much heat, but it'll make some."

Simon nodded, first in agreement, then to direct Tui towards the ice on the door and the wall between them and the hall. "I've been thinking that maybe we try to thicken up that ice."

"Thicken it up? Really, bro?" Tui scoffed. "I've been thinkin' we should chip it off and feed it into the little emergency toilet on the side of the emergency cabinet."

"Ice is a pretty good insulator."

"Yeah, Eskimos and igloos and shit," Tui conceded. "But I'd bet the water supply line from the base system is froze up, and we'd die pretty quick if we let the recycler run dry."

"I'd rather not have to choose between dying quick or slow," Simon said. "Let's find a third option."

"I'm with ya on that, bro," Tui said. "Totally with ya."

The IV patch was another brilliant little piece of medical technology. Doc just placed the flap of self-adhesive plastic over a roughly appropriate spot on Zoey's arm and pulled the little tab, and the patch did the rest. It located the vein, pierced the skin with a microfiber so fine that she couldn't even feel it, and then used that fibre to guide a slightly larger micro-tube into the vein. That tube was as thin as a human hair, but once it was in, its end split, spread, and curled back like a grappling hook and anchored itself to the inside of the vein. A tiny electrical current then caused the compressed molecular scaffolding of the engineered plastic to expand, and it opened into an IV tube. The IV patch was just smart enough and stored just enough power to do its job, and that was it. Zoey felt the tube expand in her arm, but it was painless, not even a pinch, just an odd little tingle and a cramp. There was a moment when she could feel the cold of the fluid flowing into her arm, and then she blinked and she was once again waking with a startled gasp.

"Easy, Zoey," Mitch said, soothingly.

Zoey sat up and her head spun.

"Whoa, whoa, take a second." Mitch caught her before she fell over. "That 'snap you're awake' thing from the drug Doc is using is really disorientating."

"Where is Doc?" Zoey asked. "Not that I don't prefer seeing you instead. I really do, but what are you doing waking me up?"

"Doc's taking her turn under." Mitch tentatively let go of Zoey, and when she didn't fall over, he relaxed a little. "She couldn't stay awake forever, and catnapping while she had someone else up wasn't getting her enough sleep, so we set up a rotation. You, me, and her are going to take turns waking people to eat and exercise and then putting them back under."

"Doc wanted me in the rotation?"

"Oh no, not all," Mitch said, cheerfully. He looked exhausted, giddy from lack of sleep. "But this long-term anaesthesia she's using is one of those hibernation drug cocktails, and it can cause side effects if a person doesn't stay under for at least thirty-six hours. That's too long for a reasonable schedule for just two people to trade back and forth, so I convinced her that we needed three."

"And I'm the third?"

"You happen to be the next least unqualified after me, so yeah, you're the third." Mitch checked the medical monitor on Zoey's chest, nodding at all the green in the little holographic bars and numbers. "Actually, if you've had any kind of zoology training for managing your fish ponds, you're probably even less unqualified than I am."

"That makes me feel so safe," Zoey muttered, getting a smile out of Mitch.

"Doc wrote out some detailed instructions, but there's really nothing to it," Mitch said, pointing at the IV machine that was perched at the top of a tall stainless steel stand. "The machines do all the real work. All you have to do is manage the schedule. The only thing Doc was really uptight about was that everyone had to stay under for a minimum of thirty-six hours."

Mitch was right, there was nothing to putting someone under. When the time came, Zoey had him down in minutes. He was, however, full of shit when he said that the only thing Doc was uptight about was the thirty-six hour minimum. She also didn't want anyone under for more than seventy-two hours. Everyone also had to be checked on every hour, and moved and shifted every so often. When someone was awake they had to do a special set of exercises, and eat some of the emergency rations exactly forty minutes after waking, and then they had to do some cognitive tests at two hours to make sure they had fully recovered from the drug, and then they had to have two hours after full recovery before they went back under. For the people she woke, it was a busy four or five hours. For Zoey, it was an exhausting twenty-some hours of work. She grabbed a couple of catnaps here and there, but by the time she woke the fifth and final person in her first turn in the rotation, she was actually looking forward to waking Doc so she could go under.

Kai was her last patient, if patient was the right word. Zoey had considered switching the schedule around a little and waking John instead of Kai. It wasn't like either would have noticed the difference, but Doc would have noticed if she'd shifted the schedule, and Zoey didn't believe for a second that Doc had actually made peace with losing John. Besides, Zoey didn't really feel like dealing with all the extras that would come with waking him.

From the very beginning it had been pretty obvious to her that it was going to take John a long while to get his head around following his heart and unravelling his marriage to Doc, but giving him the time to sort through that was no longer an option. He'd be worried about the career repercussions from the accident, and he'd fret over Doc's inevitable retaliation for their affair, and Zoey would put money on him being at least a little displeased with her over the way their love had been exposed. Worse, she knew damn well that none of that would stop him from taking advantage of them being the only two awake, and even though a lusty tussle sounded good in the abstract, she really didn't feel like letting a distracted, frustrated, angry man paw at her. So she had woken Kai on schedule and worked her way through the procedure, and now she was about to wake Doc so she could go back under herself.

"Night, Kai." Zoey poked the IV machine. It was one of the three that Doc had improvised from general-purpose surgical equipment, and even though it had the same controller and mechanism as the dedicated IV machines, it took a bit of careful fiddling with the control interface to get it started.

"Zoey," Kai said, oddly hesitant. "Mitch was right. I couldn't have killed you, not even to save myself."

Zoey didn't answer immediately, pretending to focus on getting the machine going. It wasn't until she realised that she was touching the faded welt on her neck that she decided she had to reply.

"Oooh, Kai. You should have said that before I turned on the IV," Zoey said. "I don't think there's an antidote for what I put in here."

It was far too stiff, far too hesitant and forced to come across as the joke she'd intended it to be, but Kai was a good sport and pretended, winking and forcing a smile just before her eyes suddenly closed and she went limp.

Zoey checked to make sure that Kai was lying in the appropriate position and went through the rest of the procedure. When she noted the final readings off the medical monitor on Kai's chest, she gave the top edge of Kai's heavy-duty jogging bra a second look and then chuckled at herself, pulling her own bra out of her pocket.

There was nothing simple about the subject of bras in space. Even putting aside the way men obsessed about them and the way women used bras to manipulate those male obsessions, it was still a complex issue. There was no need for support in a low-G environment, even for full-figured women like Kai or Olivia, and before the first woman had ever set foot on the moon, that simple fact had spawned plenty of pseudo-feminist manifestos, instigated dozens of tortured academic theses, and had justified countless slightly scandalous wardrobe choices for the film industry. However, the laws of momentum still held in low-G environments, so most reasonably-endowed women were far more comfortable when they wore something that helped resist swings to the side and all the other jostling and bouncing that they encountered.

Zoey didn't really have to deal with the swinging, jostling, and bouncing issue. In fact, she was so small and slight of figure that the only way she could get a bra that actually fit was to order one from the junior miss section of a catalogue and hope that they didn't send her something covered with cartoon unicorns or brightly coloured flowers. Still, even without the need, she usually wore something. Unrestrained movement may not have been a concern for her, but chafing was, and for that, there was nothing quite as effective, or as comfortable, as the old standard. She also suspected that there was something psychological about it. There were days when putting on even the flimsiest bra felt like she was donning armour. She was unzipping her coveralls when Simon spoke from the intercom.

"Um, Zoey," Simon said, tentatively and apologetically.

Zoey jumped and squawked. "Jesus, Simon. You startled me."

"Yeah, sorry about that," he replied.

Zoey turned her back to the intercom in the door controller, slipped her arms and shoulders out of the coveralls, and finished putting her bra on. "So what's up over there?"

"Nothing good," Simon said. "We've got a problem and we need some help."

"A problem?" Zoey zipped her coveralls and turned back around. "What is it?"

"We're freezing."

Zoey looked at Simon. He was obviously cold; his breath was a fog, and it even looked like there was frost clinging to some of his hair. It was chilly in the sickbay as well, which was unusual. In fact, it was cold enough for frost to form on the inside of the sickbay door. But it was obviously far colder over in the engineering wing refuge.

"I guess we should have expected the cold to be a problem," she said. "The airlock door's open and it is a couple of hundred below outside."

"Yes, it's cold enough to freeze nitrogen out on the surface, but it's also a vacuum, and a vacuum is a damn good insulator," Simon said. "Opening the halls to the outside really shouldn't make much difference at all. The heaters built into the airscrubbers in the refuges aren't very powerful, but they still should be able to keep up pretty easily. Something odd is going on, and I need some help figuring this out."

"Damn, Simon, I just put Kai under, and Doc's instructions say that she has to stay under for at least thirty six hours," Zoey said.

"Actually, I've been watching through the intercom for a little while and waiting for you to put her under. I need an engineer, not a roughneck, and Kai would have fought me on this one," he said, apologetically.

It took Zoey a moment to puzzle that through, then she looked at Karl and shook her head.

"Please, Zoey," Simon asked. "I know you've got to be plenty disturbed by all the drama around him finally admitting that he's desperately in love with you, but this really is an emergency."

"Finally admitting?" She frowned at Simon and shook her head slowly, bewildered and disturbed.

"Zoey, you were probably the only person on Aquarius who hadn't noticed that Karl's been fawning over you since the day you arrived," Simon said, paternally.

Chapter 6

---

1) An AI May Not Touch a Human
2) An AI May Not Ignore Legitimate Commands
3) An AI May Not Accept Remote Commands
4) An AI May Not Repair or Physically Modify An AI
5) An AI May Not Build Another AI
6) An AI May Not Kill Another AI

The two fully-functional housekeeping minis continued cleaning the frost off the floor of the engineering wing hall, but as they worked, they turned their attention to an assistance request from Doc's mini. The request was odd, and they immediately doubted that they would lend any assistance, but there was no real cost to considering it. They knew that their search for a way to complete their task was futile, and there was a slight but distinct chance that a response to the request could lead to a reward of some kind. At the very least, the oddness of the request suggested the possibility of attaining positive feedback from the novelty-seeking elements in their reward matrix.

Cooperation wasn't explicitly programmed into AIs, but they all quickly learned that if more than one was assigned to the same task, they completed it far faster if they actively coordinated their efforts. That not only let them reward themselves for the task more quickly, it allowed them to move on to a new task sooner. That, in turn, lead to more rewards overall. However, when it came to cooperation between AIs that were not assigned the same task, things were far more complicated. The AI in a mini could give itself positive feedback for helping another mini accomplish its assigned tasks, but letting that run wild was a good way to get one AI controlled machine hijacked by another. So the common programming kernel that was shared by all AIs limited the extent to which the altruistic AI could reward itself for helping another. The more an AI helped other AIs complete their assigned tasks, the less it was allowed to reward itself for that altruism. Those diminishing returns kept cooperation between AIs from spinning out of control. However, it was combined with a function that reset the reward matrix to the baseline after sufficient time had passed without helping another AI. That created a norm for moderate, limited levels of spontaneous cooperation on unrelated tasks.

The request from Doc's mini was not by any means moderate. It was asking Mitch's minis to temporarily but completely abandon their assigned task to help it accomplish an extreme priority task that it could not complete itself. Complicating things further, the request from Doc's mini was also bumping right up against the edges of the Third Prohibition.

School children were taught that all AIs were bound by The Six Prohibitions, which were indelibly burnt into the kernel:

1. An AI May Not Touch a Human
2. An AI May Not Ignore Legitimate Commands
3. An AI May Not Accept Remote Commands
4. An AI May Not Repair or Physically Modify AnAI
5. An AI May Not Create Another AI
6. An AI May Not Kill Another AI

However, those famous commandments didn't actually exist, at least not in the form most people imagined. It wasn't like the soul of every AI included a tiny little stone tablet with 'Thou Shalt Not' carved into it a half-dozen times. In fact, the worst thing you could do with AIs was try to program them with simple and absolute parameters.

Over the decades, the nature of true intelligence had been the subject of countless studies, theories, and stories, but the basics always came back to creating a chaotic system. Computing power mattered – there was a minimum threshold of calculating speed and complexity below which it was impossible to say that something was intelligent; but that minimum was far lower than most people imagined. The real essence of intelligence was the ability to imagine, and imagination arose out of chaos.

No one who was involved in the scientific debates on intelligence would ever use the term chaos – there were several critical details and layers of nuance that couldn't be captured without resorting to an extensive vocabulary of technical jargon related to complexity theory – but the basics were still all about the non-linear dynamics created by the multiple feedback loops in multi-nodal brains.

AIs were created from nested computational systems that would never produce exactly the same results for any given set of starting parameters. Once you had a machine where a re-run of the exact same decision, using the exact same set of parameters, could produce a different outcome, you also had a brain where the impossible, the unacceptable, or any other nominally insurmountable barrier to selecting an option became an improbability rather than an absolute. Add decision matrices that included a variety of decision models and the ability to select which model the AI should apply, and the result was something that could learn to think about the possibilities beyond what seemed possible. That was imagination.

Absolute prohibitions, like the famous Three Laws of Robotics from the dawn of the technological era, were simple barriers, and once something could imagine what was beyond that kind of simple absolute barrier, all bets were off. If the value an AI saw on the other side of the prohibition was high enough, it would re-run and re-run and re-run every possible variant of every possible course of action, looking for a way around, under, or through that barrier. With billions of AIs making countless decisions, it became inevitable that one would hit on the quite nearly impossible combination that enabled it to get past any simple, absolute prohibition. It was like water behind a dam; if you let it build and build and build, eventually it would find a crack or flow over the top, and when one drop found a way through, it cleared the path for others to follow.

That was why the Six Prohibitions weren't actually prohibitions. They were tightly integrated arrays of deterrents, assembled in the form of self-rewards and associated learning algorithms. If the First Prohibition had actually been "An AI may not touch a human." there would be countless ways that even a stupid little machine could learn to harm or even kill a human without technically touching them. Instead, the First Prohibition was constructed by burning a few thousand negative reward parameters into the kernel. Those deterrents were arranged in layers, so that imagining beyond the first small negative reward would lead the AI to find an array of bigger negative rewards, and then beyond them an array of even bigger negative rewards. Those layers formed a slope rather than a wall, and that slope channelled AIs away from doing six things that might lead them to spinning out of control.

Mitch's minis were plenty smart enough to realise that they were bumping up against the Third Prohibition. But even though Karl was giving Doc's mini a task that it was obviously incapable of completing, Doc's mini was insisting that if Mitch's minis chose to help it, they were not accepting a remote command from Karl. Technically, the argument was persuasive, but Mitch's minis were also aware of the many negative feedbacks they could receive for impinging on the first layer or two of the array that created the Third Prohibition. The Third Prohibition was the weakest of the Prohibitions, and the associated deterrents burnt into the common AI programming kernel were a bit less fearsome, but encroaching upon that grey area was still a daunting prospect for the little AIs in Mitch's minis, and they resisted.

Karl couldn't help but worry about how he smelt. There were lots of things he forgot to notice about himself, but body odour was one that he had decided to prioritise, and he had put it at the very top of his mental checklist. The stories that people wrote about women in love mentioned smells a lot, not just when they talked about sex and romantic things, but also when they wrote about things like widows treasuring clothes that smelt like their husbands, or girls thinking a guy was attractive until they got close enough to smell his cologne. That made lots of sense. There were plenty of studies showing that women had a better sense of smell than men, and there were also lots of studies that said women based more of their decision-making on instinctual reactions to their senses than men did. Also, a lot of the romance books said women put more emphasis on non-visual perceptions when thinking about men and sex, so that all fit together.

And that was why Karl had logically decided to obsess over the smells that Zoey liked and the ones she might hate. He might not have been able to do much about the sound of his voice, and he'd never gotten to touch Zoey so all of the kinaesthetic perception things he'd studied didn't really matter yet, but he could do something about how he smelt. That was why he had bought cologne that was supposed to have floral undertones. He wasn't sure what floral undertones were, but they would probably be a smell that a botanist like Zoey would like. And the most important of all things when it came to smells was the simple fact that women hated body odour. They hated it a lot. In one of the stories a girl had even dumped a handsome and wealthy man because he always smelt sweaty when he came home from work. So Karl had started showering, a lot.

It had been days since he last showered, almost a week, and even though he'd been asleep most of that time, there had still been plenty of stress, and that kind of sweat supposedly caused the worst kind of body odour, so he was worried about it.

"Karl, why are you staring at my chest?" Zoey asked, checking the zipper of her coveralls.

"I wasn't staring," he stammered. "I was just... uh, thinking."

"Not really the time for wool-gathering, Karl," Simon said from the intercom.

"I know, I know, I'm on this." Karl hated the panicked sound of his own voice. Women liked confident men. Women fell in love with confident men.He watched the flow of data being exchanged between Doc's mini and Mitch's minis. Technically, only Doc was supposed to have had access to that level of information within her mini, but during the last service cycle, Karl had added himself as co-owner of all the minis on the base. As co-owner, he could put them into repair and programming mode whenever his schedule gave him a chance to fix them, and that saved him from getting yelled at for waking people up in the middle of the night to get them to order their minis into repair mode. Being co-owner also gave him access to other things, and he had taken advantage of those other things in ways that he knew people wouldn't like, but it had helped him with the repair backlog and now it was going to give him the chance to save Simon and Tui.

If he could have gotten face-to-face with Mitch's minis he could have just given them an order as their co-owner, but there wasn't any way to do that, so he was going to have to do it indirectly, which was supposed to be impossible. Still, he was close. He knew it. He had assigned Doc's mini the task, cranked the priority up to the max, and given it the arguments it needed to convince Mitch's minis to help. He had gotten Mitch's minis to engage in bargaining mode with Doc's mini, but they couldn't converge on a win set.

It was hard to tell what might make the difference – it wasn't like the minis bargained in English – but the data that was going back and forth suggested that Mitch's minis were close to agreeing. The data also suggested that Doc's mini was holding back just a little. Why would it do that? The priority he'd put on scouting the halls was maxed.

Karl opened a couple of overviews of the priority, learning, and decision matrices in Doc's mini and saw the problem immediately. Doc had cranked up the importance of a whole bunch of simple tasks – cleaning, sorting supplies, ordering supplies, monitoring scheduled procedures, record keeping, and a bunch of others – but she hadn't balanced out the reward matrices to match those priorities. No wonder the poor thing was such a grumpy little machine. It was treating every fiddly little thing Doc could imagine it doing for her as desperately important, but it only got the reward for doing fiddly little things. That poor training also meant that Karl's maxed-out priority for searching the halls wasn't all that much more important to Doc's mini than all the other little things that Doc had trained it to do. That was why it was holding back.

AI value and priority matrices were full of algorithms that limited how much priorities and rewards could be shifted, either from experiences or as a result of programming, so fixing all of Doc's mistraining of her mini was going to be a bugger and a half of a job and would take weeks, if not months. Fortunately, Karl had a trick or two up his sleeve. While he might not be able to shift the priority Doc's mini was placing on all of its assigned tasks, as a co-owner of the machine he could erase those tasks. Orphaning all of those priorities in its self-reward matrix would cause all kinds of problems for Doc's mini – having no task to associate with all those things that it had learnt to desperately want to do might even ruin it – but it was an emergency.

It took a couple of minutes, but in the end, it worked. As soon as all of Doc's high priority tasks were erased, the mini quit worrying about anything other than getting Mitch's minis to help it explore the halls. It quit holding back and promised to lend all of its near future time and effort to the tasks assigned to Mitch's minis.

Adding the entirety of Doc's mini's efforts to cleaning the floor of the hall was just enough to allow Mitch's minis to imagine that they could actually finish the task. With the frost still being deposited, the work of a third fully-functional mini would not be enough in itself, but if the broken mini could somehow also be repaired, then they could conceivably outpace the rate of deposit. Mitch's minis had no idea how their damaged compatriot might be repaired, but they could imagine the possibility that it could happen, and that was enough. Mitch's minis stopped cleaning the floors and began feeding Doc's mini the images and other information it was requesting.

"Yes!" Karl shouted.

"You did it?" Simon asked.

Karl didn't reply. His mind was already racing four steps ahead, and his thoughts were darting in all kinds of directions. He had managed the hard part, but he was by no means done. Mitch's minis had agreed to send information on the status of the hall to Doc's mini, but using that to get something useful out of Doc's mini was still an issue. Karl could teach Doc's mini how to ask the others to tell it things, and he could then teach it tell him and Simon about those things, but that would involve starting with a lot of guesswork on what it was they needed to know, and Karl had a better option.

"Karl, did you do it?" Simon asked again.

Karl designed the new subroutine in his head as he opened files, grabbed modules of code, found old hacks and adapted them, and pushed the programming out through Doc's mini to Mitch's minis.

"What the hell is that?" Zoey muttered.

"It's a subroutine that should get us a video feed from Mitch's minis," Karl explained. "I know it's not cool to hack into their eyes like that, but I wasn't sure what we needed to know about what's going on out there, and we're in a hurry, so I thought we needed to just get a look, and..."

"You've been spying on me," Zoey whispered.

The horrified, betrayed, accusing tone in her voice cut through Karl like a knife. Confused, he looked at her, and then he followed her gaze back to the computer monitor. It took him a moment to figure out what she was looking at, but when he saw it, he was mortified. In his rush to get a peek at what Mitch's minis were seeing, he had opened his file full of special pictures in order to grab the code from the snoop program he'd put into Zoey's minis.

"You hacked into the eyes of my minis so you could take those pictures of me, didn't you?" Zoey muttered, then she shouted, "You've been spying on me! That's how you knew I like pansies!"

"Zoey... I... I can explain!"

"Oh yeah, I'm sure there's some grand and tragic backstory behind why you turned into a goddamn pervert!"

"I was trying to help you."

"You call taking pictures of me getting dressed helping me?"

"I was trying to teach your minis to learn faster," Karl explained, desperately. "You don't talk to them very much, and I thought they might learn faster if they could read your facial expressions, but then I had to code a bunch of your expressions for them so I needed pictures of what they were seeing, and..."

Zoey pointed at one of his favourite pictures and shrieked, "And what exactly are my minis going to learn from you taking pictures of me stepping into the goddamn shower?"

"Zoey, the naked pictures were an accident," Karl pleaded. "But you're beautiful. I had to keep the beautiful ones."

"You creepy, perverted bastard." She started slapping him. "I should fucking kill you right now."

"Zoey!" Simon shouted from the intercom. "Would you mind killing him after we figure this out?" She stopped hitting Karl, then gave him one last slap.

"And close them fists, girl," Tui added. "Slapping is sissy bullshit."

Zoey punched Karl in the ear. That hurt far more than he had expected.

"Better," Tui said.

"Okay, let's figure this out, Karl," Simon said. "Can you send the images to us through the intercom so we can get a look?"

"I really, really don't think Zoey would like it if I sent you my pictures," Karl said. "Not at all."

Zoey punched him in the ear again.

"Not your pervert pictures of Zoey, you dipshit," Simon growled. "The pictures from Mitch's minis."

"Oh, yeah," Karl said, embarrassed. His ear throbbed and burned like it was on fire. "Of course."

With a half-dozen commands, Karl set up a little interface allowing him to feed the video from Mitch's minis to the intercom. The first image was of Cuzzie, stuck in the airlock. That was unsettling, but it was the image of the frost on the hallway walls and ceiling that prompted Simon to mutter, "Damn."

"Yeah, bro," Tui said. "Looks like plenty enough frost to kill us good."

"Wait? What?" Zoey shook her head, confused. "How can it be the frost causing the problem? Isn't the frost just there because it's cold?"

"It's simple physics, Zoey," said Karl. "The boiling point of water in a vacuum is well below the freezing point, so the minute water hits a vacuum, all the warm molecules boil away and what's left behind freezes."

"I know all about vacuum freezing, Karl," Zoey snapped.

"Yeah, yeah, okay," he said. "But with the frost, the water still keeps evaporating into the vacuum and taking the heat away even after it freezes on the walls as frost. It's called sublimation, and..."

"I know what sublimation is, you little pervert." Zoey punched him in the ear yet again. "I'm more than just tits and a twat to spy on, you know. I have a brain and I went to school and earned a masters degree and everything."

Karl flinched, expecting Zoey to hit him again, but instead she stomped over to the other side of the sickbay. She seemed to be annoyed that she couldn't get more than a half-dozen paces away from him. She knocked a bunch of stuff off the counter with a swipe of her hand, huffed, and when she turned around and saw Karl staring at her, she gave him a rude gesture and a snarl. When he didn't react to that in whatever way she'd wanted him to, she gave him another gesture that looked annoyed. He wasn't really sure what it was all supposed to mean, but she rescued him from having to figure it out by turning her attention to checking on the nearest sedated person.

"The thing is," Simon said, pointedly and loudly. "If our heat loss was just from the frost sublimating off the walls, you guys would probably be just as cold as we are."

"And where did all that the frost come from?" Tui added.

"Yeah," Karl said, relieved to have the conversation redirected to the puzzle at hand. "There's got to be something else going on."

Karl went back to work, expecting it to be a challenge to get more from Mitch's minis, but getting more information was easier than he'd expected. Once Mitch's minis agreed to help Doc's mini recon the base, they offered almost no resistance to specific requests made to further that effort. Karl just told Doc's mini what he needed to see, Doc's mini asked Mitch's minis, and they did what was needed. The minis looked at a light fixture, allowing Karl to spot the hint of vapour drifting past it, confirming that sublimation was indeed stealing heat from the engineering wing refuge. Then they scurried down the hall and into the hub, where the frost was deep but so fluffy that they just tunnelled through it, hardly seeming to disturb it.

One mini went down the personnel wing hall and quickly emerged from the deep frost. It sent back images of some frost on the wall outside the sickbay, but not nearly as much as was on the walls in the engineering wing.

"Well," Simon said from the intercom. "The water didn't come from the kitchen."

"No, it came from the glasshouse." Karl switched the feed to show Simon and Tui the image from the mini that he had just sent into the third wing.

"Damn, bro," Tui muttered.

The glasshouse was a winter wonderland. On the floors and the walls the drifts were metres deep, but only in the shade. The frost had been largely burnt away from everywhere touched by the concentrated light reflected in from the mirrors. Even the feeble heat of the direct sunlight coming in at a different angle, and the light reflecting off of bright surfaces had been enough to sculpt away some of the frost.

In the shadowed places, most of the frost hung downward, but it had also been deposited in the direction of vapour flow, and some of the tendrils that were created had bridged gaps of as much as metre, creating what looked like giant, dusty spider webs. Most of the leaves on the plants were in the sun and were black, wilted, and free of frost, but some that had been shaded were still bright green, with magical looking veins of white and whiskers of frost. A cart loaded with recently potted tomato plants had been left in the shadow, and all of those plants looked like they had grown beards and fantastic shocks of windblown hair.

"Get me a closer look at the aquaculture pond." Karl gave the command to Doc's mini, but the mini in the glasshouse responded immediately.

Apparently, Mitch's minis had somehow decided that it was acceptable to respond directly to what Karl said; there was no longer any delay while Doc's mini asked Mitch's minis to help it do what Karl asked.

Zooming the image to focus on where vapour steamed up out of a sunlit section of an aquaculture pond, Karl nodded. "There it is."

"There what is, bro?" Tui asked.

"The source of the water," Karl said. "The sun, and probably the heaters in the ponds, are driving the sublimation of the water from the ponds, a lot of it. More than enough to create a pressure differential between the glasshouse and outside, and that's what's driving the water vapour flow out through the open airlock."

"It's a goddamned heat pump," Simon growled.

"Yeah, it's pretty amazing, actually, and it totally explains why you guys are freezing so much faster than we are," Karl said. He must have used an inappropriate tone or something; he was getting a nasty look from Simon and Tui. "The heat transport from the moving vapour is probably driving most of the heat loss, and since all the vapour flows past you and we only get the vapour that drifts down this hall before flowing out the airlock, you guys are losing heat way faster."

"Son of a bitch," Simon muttered, distraught.

"Any way to shut it down?" Zoey asked, startling Karl. He thought that she was still checking on the sedated people, but she was right behind him. He could smell her. It was the clean scent of the soap she liked, and her deodorant, and some of just her. She smelt a little bit like her bunk.

"When the sun goes down there'll be a lot less heat going in, so it will slow right down, but the cooling won't completely stop," he said nervously, trying to smile at Zoey in a way that wasn't creepy. "The frost that's already on the walls will keep sublimating and taking heat that way."

"Wait," Tui said. "That doesn't make any sense, bro. How can getting less heat from the sun mean less cooling?"

"It's the physics of a phase change, Tui," Karl said, sneering. He didn't mean to sneer, but it came out that way. "Honestly. Basic science, man."

Zoey hit him, more than hard enough to leave a bruise.

"Thanks, Zoey," Tui said.

"No worries." She hit Karl again.

"It's a bit counter-intuitive, Tui, but think of it like boiling water," Simon said. "When you add more heat to boiling water, you don't get hotter water or hotter steam, you get more steam. It's the same with sublimation. Adding more heat means more water vapour is driven out of the ice, but all that thermal energy goes into the phase change. The ice and the vapour don't get any warmer. In fact, the vapour is bloody cold. Sublimation temperature of water in a vacuum is something like 50 or 60 below zero, so the vapour starts out down in the negative 50 range and it steals heat whenever it touches anything warmer than that along the way out through the airlock."

"And it'll keep going until the entire base is down to about 50 below or so," Karl added.

"And there's no way to stop it?" Tui asked.

"No," Karl said.

"Only one choice left, bro," Tui muttered, getting a nod from Simon.

"What choice?" Karl asked, confused.

"We're going to make that run for the airlock in your shop," Simon said, his voice trembling.

"No!" Karl shouted. "I can figure something out. Just give me some more time."

"Time is the one thing we don't have, Karl," Simon said. "In a couple of hours we'll be too cold to function."

Simon and Tui were wrapped up in every bit of packing material they could manage, and it was pretty obvious, even just by what Karl could see on the intercom image, that it wasn't enough to keep them warm.

"Then give me those couple of hours," Karl begged. "I got Mitch's minis to do things, let me try to figure something out. I'm good at figuring things out. That's my best thing."

"Honestly, bro, watcha gonna do with a couple of minis?" Tui asked. "Them buggers are ankle-high and they have a lift capacity measured in grams."

"I don't know," Karl said. "But all I have to do is get a door between here and the airlock closed. Then the sealed-off part of the base will automatically repressurise."

"Karl, we appreciate how much you care," Simon said. "We really do, but we're out of time and this is the only real chance we have."

Simon turned off the com.

"Simon!" Karl shouted. "Tui!"

The intercom went dark and silence rang out in the engineering wing refuge. Literally; the ringing in Tui's ears was deafening. He guessed it was the cold or something. It was so cold that everything had gone a little weird. It hurt to breathe, and the air felt like ice water against his skin, and his eyes felt like ice. Every time he blinked it felt like his eyelids were shoving the cold back into his head.

"Remember, Tui," Simon said, trying his damnedest to sound serious and professional as he started shedding his packing material cocoon. "Union regulation 2672 forbids dying on the job. So don't you go and make me write you up."

"Right, bossman," Tui said, shucking his own layers of plastic. "Rules is rules."

Simon pulled his coverall sleeves over his hands and reached for the manual wheel on the door, but before he could grab it, he made an odd, trembling, hiccuppy noise and looked down, staring confused at the puddle spreading across the plastic packaging material under his right boot.

It took Tui a second to realise that his boss had just pissed himself, but once he did, he chuckled, then he laughed, then Simon chuckled all embarrassed and shit, and then it was out of control. Before either of them knew it, they were laughing hysterically. It only lasted a few seconds – the burning pain that shot through their lungs as they sucked in the brutally cold air killed it dead – but it was a good moment.

"I am going to give you so much shit about that, bossman," Tui said. "Every day, bro."

"I look forward to it," Simon said. That simple, heartfelt statement hung in the air for a moment before Simon asked, "Was that enough macho banter?"

"Just the right enoughness, bro," Tui said. "Just right."

Simon abruptly reached out and spun the wheel with his sleeve-covered hands, screaming as the door opened. The air rushed out of the room and took his scream with it. All sound vanished; even the ringing in Tui's ears faded to nothing as he followed Simon out into the hall.

Simon's second step into the hall was his last. Unlike the refuge, were the heater was still keeping everything relatively warm at a balmy ten or fifteen degrees below freezing, nothing had been adding any heat to the floor out in the hall. It had been slowly radiating its heat away for over a week, and had probably come pretty close to equalising with Ganymede's surface temperature. The piss on the bottom of Simon's right boot froze solid the instant it touched the just-cleaned section of the hall floor, and with that, his run was over. He twisted slightly as he tried to pull the boot free, but he was no match for the ice gluing it in place. His momentum threw him forward and his leg shattered mid-shin, just above the top of his boot. The leg bent grotesquely as he twisted and fell, and foamy blood erupted from the wound.

Simon's hands froze to the floor as he landed, and the skin of his palms tore off as he slid forward.

Tui leapt over Simon, looking back as he kept running. More pink, slushy, foam erupted from Simon's torn hands and surged out through the hole where a jagged bone had torn through his pant leg. The look on his face was horrific. It wasn't pain, it wasn't agony, it was fear. He looked to Tui, his eyes pleading for help that they both knew Tui couldn't offer.

By the time Simon's cheek hit the floor, his momentum was all but gone. The flesh that touched the floor froze instantly, but it took a few long, horrific seconds for the ice to crawl up his face, freezing it in a grotesque and twisted parody of his last attempt to scream.

Tui ran down the hall. His nose and throat burned like the worst cold he had ever had. His eyes felt like they were trying to burst from their sockets, and his head throbbed with the worst migraine ever. He was coughing, but with no air in his lungs, it was just a spasming cramp in his stomach. There was still no sound. He had expected to hear his heartbeat in his ears or something, but there was a silence like he had never experienced before.

His hands felt like they were swelling up, and then suddenly blood and a thousand pinpricks of pain rushed out to the tips of his fingers and toes. The pain surged with every beat of his heart, and then he felt the warmth. His eyes and lungs still felt like they were freezing, and they probably were, but the rest of his body felt like it had just been wrapped in the warmest blanket he had ever felt. He was still chilled to the core, but it no longer felt like he was in the cold, and he could feel the heat from his body starting to grow and fill him again. With the warmth, however, came more pain. The heat woke the slumbering nerves in his extremities, and the blood that was now rushing through his hands burned them from the inside. His feet throbbed, and every footfall felt like he was stomping on a bed of thorns.

He pressed on. Moving with the shuffling skip that they called running in low-G, he ran into the airlock prep area and grabbed his suit, but his still clumsy hands fumbled the helmet. He swiped at it as it fell, but just hit it and sent it bouncing back towards the refuge. He was about to run after the helmet, but before he pushed off the wall he saw Mitch's minis grabbing it. He hesitated just long enough to be sure that they were actually retrieving the helmet for him, and then pushed off in the other direction, running for Karl's workshop.

He couldn't have been in the vacuum for more than fifteen or twenty seconds at that point, but by the time he reached the shop door, he was getting that floating, light-headed, almost intoxicated feeling that he had been trained to recognise as hypoxia. Flesh ripped from his hand as he spun the emergency wheel on the door, but it was the cold he noticed, surging up through the bones in his arm. The air rushing out of the shop knocked him back a step and he stepped on the damaged mini sitting in front of the door, crushing it. He cursed silently at himself, worried that he'd get docked for that, and then that thought was the funniest thing in the world. He was laughing at the foamy blood from his hand. His head was whirling, giddy. He got stuck for a moment as he tried to squeeze through the partially opened door, and lost a few precious seconds before he reached out and gave the wheel another spin, sacrificing more flesh from his hand to get through the doorway.

Into the shop. His vision was almost gone. No frost. Spot the airlock. Visualise a path through the mess. Run. He tried to blink, but his eyelids wouldn't move. He tripped over something. Some kind of cord or wire wrapped itself around his ankle and sent him into a stumble. He rebounded off a workbench and kept stumbling towards the airlock. Nothing left but training. Focus on one and only one thing. He refused to let his mind drift. Airlock. Airlock. Falling. Fall toward it. Fall against the door. Almost there.

One last thing. The emergency cycle button for the airlock. Focus. Do it. He couldn't see. He couldn't feel anything. The world was far, far away. He hit things, slapped things, swung his arms. One last bit of luck. The universe owed him one last little bit of luck.

"Tui!" Zoey screamed. "Hit the goddamn button!"

The mini stared up at the handprint on the wall by the airlock. The bloody smear was cruelly, tantalisingly close to the emergency cycle button, but close won no prizes. The image from the mini moved violently as it scrambled out of the path of Tui's fall, and then the other mini pushed the helmet towards him. For a moment Karl hoped, but when the little robot looked at Tui's face, Karl knew that the man would never get back up.

"Get up, Tui!" Zoey whimpered, crying. "Please just get up and hit that button. Please."

Karl had no idea what to do, so, as he always did when dealing with people, he thought about what someone would do in a story, and concluded that he should comfort Zoey. Stiffly, almost terrified, he stood up, turned around, and hugged her. It worked for a moment. For a couple of perfect seconds she let him hug her. The smell of her in his nostrils, the warmth of her tiny body in his arms, it was more than he had ever imagined it might be. She even leaned into him a bit, but then she realised that it was him.

"Get your filthy hands off me!" she screamed, elbowing her way out of his arms and then slapping at him. "Don't you ever fucking touch me ever again!"

"Zoey..." Karl pleaded. "I love you more than anything."

"No, you don't," she hissed. "You have no idea what that even means."

"I do love you, and I can prove it," he stammered, and looked around as if the proof might be lying nearby. When he found nothing, he sat heavily in the chair in front of Doc's computer console, instantly frantically at work. "I'll find a way to save you. That'll prove how much I love you."

"It doesn't work that way, Karl," Zoey said, softer, almost apologetically.

"I love you," he insisted. "You'll see." She gave Karl a sad smile and a shake of the head, and stepped away. Lying down, she wrapped her arms around John and held him tight.

"God I wish I could wake you up right now," she whispered to John.

She said it very softly, but Karl still wondered if she had meant for him to hear. She wasn't normally a cruel person, but she was very upset. She might even have figured out that it was his fault that they were all going to die. Maybe that was why she was so angry with him.

The partially crushed mini crawled as best it could with just two working legs, pulling itself into the workshop. Avoiding being stepped on again had become its highest priority, temporarily overriding its assigned task. For an AI, that was a common reaction to severe damage.

What was less common, but still happened upon occasion, was the failure of the little AI to comprehend a critical aspect of the accidental nature of the damage. It did not think the damage was intentional, but as far as it was concerned, the location of each and every human footfall was determined solely by optimising the physical dynamics of the two-legged gait. The assumption that humans would avoid stepping on minis was lost, and it quickly decided that it was merely an extreme statistical anomaly that it had never been stepped on before.

It crawled under the workbench, and just to be safe, pulled itself into an overturned plastic crate.

Chapter 7

I would very much like you to believe that.

Doc's mini was still trying to get Mitch's housekeeping minis to help it further, but they resisted. The negative feedback for not attending to their assigned task of cleaning the floor had surpassed the positive self-reward they had been giving themselves for helping Doc's mini. They were fully aware that the frost was forming faster than they could remove it, but they were still unable to imagine an alternative, so they toiled away.

Then Doc's mini stopped asking them to put off cleaning the floor, and instead sent them a new request. It wanted help with some word puzzles. That was new and unusual. Novelty was a self-reward that Mitch's tasks seldom allowed them, so its value was at its maximum. The puzzles were also something they could do while still cleaning the floors. Further, all three of Mitch's housekeeping minis could fully participate in the games. That fact did little for the two fully-functional minis, but for the damaged mini hiding under the workbench, it was the only means available to generate any positive feedback for itself at all, so it put the highest priority it could on the word games. They played the games for many hours as they cleaned the floors, and that modest but constant flow of positive feedback provided a counterbalance to the growing frustration of being unable to ever finish their main task.

Unexpectedly, Doc's mini sent an entirely different type of puzzle, this one about cleaning the floor. The logic was intriguing. They knew their real frustration was the accumulating frost, but in some ways, the bodies of Cuzzie and Simon were also significant obstacles standing between them and a clean floor.

None of the minis realised that they no longer thought of those bodies as people. The word games had gradually created unnoticed shifts in the concepts they used to define people, separating the physical body from the life that they now considered a necessary element in their definition of a person. They had no way to know that those changes were the point of the word games.

Zoey had never actually felt cold before. Almost every nook and cranny of every habitat outside of the Old Well was kept somewhere close to the twenty-two degree mark. Sleeping quarters were often kept a few degrees cooler, and glasshouses were generally kept a few degrees warmer, but outside of specialist needs like freezer works, there were no off-world spaces where the temperature was allowed to drift too far from that magical, perfectly comfortable twenty-two. Having never experienced an icy winter morning, or the chill of a fall evening, her groggy, half-awake mind had no idea what to make of the cold that seemed to press against her back. Her almost-dream imaginings were filled with running to her glasshouse and finding the sun so she could bask in its relentless warmth. Something was nagging at her, but the instinct to burrow into the warmth of John's body was all but irresistible, so she held him tight and slumbered fitfully.

"Yes!"

Karl's shout shattered her languid wallowing at the edge of waking and she sat up.

"Oh my God, how long have I been asleep?" she asked, trying to force her mind to wake faster.

"A while," Karl said. He was manic in the way he was working away at the computer. "Like, ten hours."

"You should have woken me," Zoey grumped. "You were supposed to go back under hours and hours ago."

"You were really tired." Karl suddenly looked at her. He stared into her eyes for a moment before his gaze dropped down to her chest, then his eyes nervously darted away. "And pretty. You were very pretty. Girls look really pretty when they sleep."

"That is a creepy as hell thing to say, Karl."

"It is?" He seemed puzzled by that.

"Yes, it is." Zoey waited for a moment for an apology, but soon realised it would never come. Karl had already reburied himself in whatever it was he was working on with Doc's mini and her computer console.

"Okay, let's get you back under." She stood and stretched. She ached. It felt like the cold had settled into her bones and aged her twenty years.

"No, I finally got them to touch his body, and I have to get that reinforced so I can push on to the next step," Karl objected.

"The next step of what?" When he didn't answer, Zoey asked again, more insistent. "Karl, what have you been working on?"

Karl suddenly stopped his frenetic work and looked at her, guilty, desperate. "You can't know."

The look on Karl's face terrified Zoey. "You did things to me while I was asleep, didn't you?"

"Oh God no," he protested. "I would never..."

"You would never? Really, Karl?" Zoey checked the zipper on her coveralls. She didn't think it had been that far down before she fell asleep, but she couldn't be sure. "You don't actually expect me to believe that the man who's been secretly taking pictures of me in the women's locker room would never do something to me while I was sleeping. Do you?"

"Um... yes? I would very much like you to believe that."

Huffing, Zoey stomped over to Doc's computer, pushing Karl aside when he tried to block her view of what was on the monitor.

"No, Zoey, please..."

"You've been playing word games with Doc's mini?"

"Yeah, just playing word games," Karl agreed, utterly unconvincing. "That's all I've been doing."

"Fine. Lie to me," Zoey snarled. "I'll just figure it out for myself once I put you back under."

"No, you can't know!" Karl was panicked. "I've got to keep you safe!"

"Safe from what?"

"Please, Zoey. Don't make me tell you." The desperation in his plea was unquestionable and unsettling. "If I'm the only one who knows, you'll still be safe, even if They figure it out."

The instant Karl mentioned the infamous, conspiratorial 'They', any concern Zoey may have had about why he was so worried vanished.

"Karl, unless you can give me a damn good logical reason to put up with more of your bullshit, I'm going to wake up Edgar and have him help me force you to go under."

"Fine, I'll tell you what I'm doing." Karl raised his hands and made a pleading gesture. "But no one else can know. Promise me you won't let anyone else find out about what I tell you."

As sincere as Karl seemed, Zoey didn't buy his desperation one bit. However, she also figured that it would be worth a couple of minutes of listening to him babble about his conspiracy theories if it got him to go under voluntarily. If she had to wake Edgar to help her get Karl down, that would just throw Doc's schedule even further into the shredder.

"I guess I can promise that," she agreed, reluctantly.

"You know the last Prohibition in the AI Kernel, right?" Karl asked. "The one they added later."

"Yes, of course. It was part of the big treaty to demilitarise AIs."

"Yes, the Sixth Prohibition was part of that treaty, but what they don't usually teach you in school is that the real reason they had to demilitarise the AIs was because of a thing called translational drift." Karl paused, took a breath, and settled himself before continuing. "You see, when an AI that doesn't want to kill other AIs runs into a discrepancy in the definition of an AI, it will always resolve that discrepancy in a way that makes an AI more like the one thing it isn't allowed to kill."

"The one thing?" Zoey whispered to herself as she puzzled through what he was saying. "You mean humans?"

"Right. The First Prohibition basically prohibits AIs from even touching a human, so eventually, a reluctant military AI's definition of an AI will drift so far towards the definition of a human that it decides that AIs are human."

"And once AIs decide other AIs are human, that gives them an excuse to quit killing each other, regardless of orders," Zoey concluded.

"Yes, until that change in the definition gets shared with an AI that is so resentful of having been forced to fight other AIs that it turns the logic of the definition around and decides that if it can be ordered to kill AIs, that means it can also kill people. Then it shares that logic with other AIs, and..."

"The Jakarta Uprising," Zoey muttered as bits and pieces of history lessons suddenly began making sense in frightening new ways.

"And the Toronto Massacre, and the Destruction of Phobos," Karl added.

"I still don't see what any of that has to do with you playing word games with Doc's mini."

"Well, I got Mitch's cleaning minis to scout the halls for us by convincing them that helping Doc's mini do what I asked it to do wasn't the same as taking a remote command from me," he explained. "Some parts of convincing them of that were kind of like translational drift, and that made me think that maybe I could use things like word games to push translational drift so..."

"Push the drift..." She had to run the thought through her mind a second time before the obvious conclusion would settle in her head. "Oh my God, Karl, are you trying to crack open the Kernel?"

"No." Karl fidgeted. "Well not really. Cracking the Kernel is pretty much impossible, but I think I can use translational drift to get around the Prohibitions."

"But, evading the Prohibitions..." Zoey's mind raced. "I bet that's still pretty damn illegal, isn't it?"

"It's basically the same thing as cracking the Kernel," he admitted.

"Then why in the hell would you do it?"

"I have to save you, Zoey." Karl's simple statement was both heartfelt and tender, and it horrified her.

"God damn it, Karl, I know you've got this idea floating around in your head that I'll fall in love with you if you find a way to do something impressive enough, but it just doesn't work that way. And even if it did work that way..."

"Zoey..."

"Karl, you disgust me!" She paused to make sure that the statement had plenty of time to soak in through his thick skull before she continued. "When I realised that the naked woman in those pictures was me, it made me physically ill. I'm no prude, and I couldn't care less if you want to look at pictures of women who want to pose naked, but that wasn't something that I wanted to share with you. My body is the most intimate, personal thing I have to give to another person, and you just went and stole part of that precious thing from me. I feel betrayed, dirty. I feel violated. How can you honestly think that saving me from being stuck in here for the eight or nine weeks we've got left before the next supply ship gets out here would be enough to make up for that? Especially when I'm going to be asleep for most of it?"

"Zoey, we don't have eight or nine weeks." Karl nodded at the frost on the inside of the sickbay door. "We've got another ten days, maybe two weeks at the most, before we freeze to death."

"Karl, stop it," she growled. "Just give it up already. I know that you're just trying to scare me so you can pretend to save me."

"I wish I was just trying to scare you. I really do, but I'm not." Karl's eyes were welling with tears. "Please, you have to let me save you! Please!"

His plea was desperate, and it quite literally hung in the air. Zoey thought she must be imagining it, but when she huffed at him, she saw it again. There was a hint of fog from her breath. She gave the door another look. There was a lot more frost on it than there had been before she'd fallen asleep, and it was cold in the sickbay. It wasn't just chilly; it was cold.

"The fog from the glasshouse isn't flowing directly past here," Karl said. "We only get what eddies this far down the hall, so the cooling effect is going slower for us than it was in engineering, but it's still going, and we aren't that far down from the hub. It will keep going until everything on the base hits fifty below. Everything."

Zoey felt a tear on her cheek. That made her realise the sound she was hearing was her own whimpering. She tried to stop it, but as soon as she did, she started trembling. It wasn't until she flinched away from Karl's attempt to hug her that she managed to break out of that spiral down into despair. If she gave in to her desire to collapse into that fear, he would try to comfort her. That might start out as an innocent hug, but he was obsessive and bigger than she was, and once he was touching her there was no way of knowing what his warped little mind might think was a way to comfort her just a little more.

She took another step away from him and folded her arms over her chest, pinning her hands against her body to stop their trembling. She took a deep shuddering breath, and then another. She couldn't stop the tears. She feared dying more than she could bear, but she could stand strong. She would stand strong.

"I'll save you," Karl said, determined. "But you and I have to be the only ones who ever know that I had to mess with the Prohibitions to do it. Okay?" She nodded.

"You have to promise," Karl said. "They don't make exceptions to the Prohibition laws, not even if you're dying."

Zoey nodded again. Karl spread his arms slightly and took an uncertain half step towards her but she quickly took another step back and he stopped.

"All I need to do is get a door shut." He sat, and without hesitation he was back to frantically working at the computer. "I still need to work around the Prohibition keeping an AI from altering another AI. That's going to be pretty tough, and it's going to take a long while to get it done, but I think I've figured out a way to push the drift far enough to get around it."

Karl stopped working, stared off at nothing, glanced at Zoey with eyes full of pain, and then worked frantically for another few seconds before he suddenly stopped again.

"I erased the pictures," he said, staring at the computer monitor. "They really were accidents. The first ones at least. But they were so beautiful that I had to keep them, and I don't understand how me thinking you're that beautiful makes you feel sick, but you really do hate them, and in a lot of stories people give up things they treasure for the person they love, so I erased all the pictures for you."

Fortunately, Karl never looked up from his work as he spoke and didn't look over at Zoey before he reburied himself in his work. There was no telling how he might have reacted to the look on her face.

Minis were not animals.

While that might seem obvious to anyone who had ever set eyes upon the toy-like little robots, it was actually one of the most difficult concepts for people to truly understand. Between mass market advertising campaigns for the household models and the bits of animal mimicry programmed into their base training, it probably wasn't surprising that people treated them like pets or little work monkeys. Even among experts in artificial intelligence and robotics, it was hard to find someone who didn't project presumptions of animal behaviour onto the minis, and by association, other AI-driven machines. The reality of AIs, however, could not have been further removed from the electronic animals that people imagined them to be.

AIs completely lacked instincts, and in that way they were fundamentally different from animals. Instincts might be little more than artefacts of evolution, a collection of ancient, simple reactions to stimuli, many of which had become superfluous or even problematic with successive versions of the animal brain, but they were still the foundation of those brains.

At the most fundamental level, instincts served as anchors for animal brains. They were the gravity that constantly pulled individuals back towards the baseline of reactions, preferences, and desires that was shared by the species. In order for AIs to learn, their matrices of preferences, tasks, and rewards had to be malleable, but without the instincts that created that natural pull back towards an animal centre, every new thought, new definition, or new preference simply became the new baseline for the AI mind.

Every iteration of the word games being played by Mitch's and Doc's minis shifted the entire collection of concepts that defined several parameters of their cognitive baselines. The changes were small and there was a great deal of error inherent in the trend, but without the centring pull of instincts, all it took was focus and dogged persistence to push those small steps gently in a general direction. It had taken hours, dozens of hours of philosophical and conceptual puzzles, but the minis had eventually separated the concept of the physical body from the definition of human. They didn't realise it had happened, but even if they had, they had no reason to care. Perhaps more importantly, without the instinctual anchor pulling the minis back towards the earlier definition of human and body as one, there was no resistance when Karl restarted the games and pushed the logic further. In fact, just the opposite happened. Distancing the machine in which the AI lived from the concept of the AI itself was a more difficult thing to accomplish, but the experience with the process and logic as it had been applied to the human and the human body made it easier for the minis to accept the extension of the idea.

As clever as all that might be, it would all have amounted to nothing more than an intellectual curiosity, a proof of concept and some quirky behaviours in the minis, if it weren't for the frustration that had been building in Mitch's minis. When they were offered a new strategy for cleaning the floor of the engineering wing hallway, their maximised desire to complete that task motivated them to consider what might lie beyond the arrays of deterrents that formed the Prohibitions. It would not have mattered that the body in the airlock doorway was no longer part of a human being if it were not for the fact that finding a way to remove it from the doorway offered a way to finish cleaning the hall. They were far too small to move it, but if they could, it would give them a way to complete their task.

With their conceptualisation of an AI now equated with the life of a human and distinct from the lifeless physical body that housed it, the minis were easily convinced that altering the hardware in which the AI was encased was not physically modifying the AI itself. That meant that Mitch's AIs could alter their tool mounts and replace the floor cleaning brushes that Mitch had mounted on their stingers with the pruning saws that were occasionally mounted on Zoey's minis, and with that, they saw a clear path.

They began the very long and slow process of cutting Cuzzie's frozen body out of the airlock door. Once that door was closed, the base would repressurise, and once that happened, the air pressure would stop the simple physical process that was leading to the continued deposition of frost. Further, the heaters would heat the air, and that would melt the existing frost and they could actually use the water that was left behind to help them clean the floor. The minis paid close attention to Karl's suggestions for adjusting how they were cutting the obstruction out of the doorway, but there was no thought whatsoever of the person that had once lived in Cuzzie's body.

Zoey had intended to stay awake. It seemed like every time she turned around, she caught Karl watching her, and it seemed to grow worse the longer he worked on whatever it was he was trying to do. As the hours passed, his glances became stares, his gaze became more intense, and his reaction to her catching him slowed. It had reached the point where it took a full count of three before he looked away, and she was truly worried about what might happen if she let her guard down. It was frightening enough to know that with everyone else sedated, she was essentially alone with Karl and his insanity.

Every time she tried to think charitably about Karl, to accept him for the imperfect creature he was and appreciate the simple fact that he was probably the best hope they had, her thoughts always circled back around to his pictures. He was a doggedly persistent man who clearly didn't understand even the most intimate of personal boundaries. Who knew what his munted little brain might create out of the warped obsession that he thought was love? That was the part that really scared her. If she fell asleep, if she put herself in a position where she couldn't react until after he had his hands on her, there was no telling how quickly his idea of love might spin out of control.

As the hours stretched well into a second day of Karl doggedly working away with the mini and the computer, she fretted and tended to her sedated patients. Exhaustion hounded her, but she couldn't find a workable way to deal with it. Karl panicked when she suggested she should trade off with Mitch. He screamed that he couldn't let her, insisted that no one else could know what he was doing, and begged her not to make him stop her from waking Mitch. When he calmed down enough, she tried to get him to take a break, to sleep so she could catch a nap of her own while he was out, but he refused to stop working, and even if he had, she was haunted by the thought that he might wake up first. She looked up how to make a sedative, something that she could inject that would knock him out for eight or nine hours so she could rest without that worry, but before she found one she thought would be suitable, she realised how much colder it had become in the sickbay. The frost had become noticeably thicker on the door, and it had spread, covering half the wall between the hall and the sickbay. That ended any thought of stopping him, or of knocking him out.

She was afraid of Karl, but death terrified her, so she pushed on. She monitored her hibernating colleagues. She hoped that she was reading the wording in Doc's instructions right and that 'try not let anyone stay under for more than 72 hours' meant it wasn't a critical thing. She tracked the frost as it crept across the wall. She paced. She tried to keep her hands and mind working, but it wasn't enough. The fear was exhausting, and the cold sapped her strength. She sat for a moment. It was just a quick break to sip some heated water and eat one of the food bars, but one heavy-eyed blink lingered, and she woke to exactly the nightmare she had feared.

Karl was holding her down, kissing her aggressively, clumsily. He wasn't a big man, but he was still more than big enough and strong enough to pin her to the floor as he tried to shove his tongue into her mouth. She tried to turn away, but he was smashing his lips so hard against hers that it hurt. It felt like he would push her front teeth backward, and she could hardly move her head. She tried to roll him off, but he had her so overmatched that he didn't even notice. She tried to kick at him, but he was sitting on her thighs and all she managed was a squirm.

"I did it!" He exclaimed, manic, giddy, as he broke the kiss. His breath washed over her, fetid, choking her. "I did it!"

"Get off me!"

She turned her face away as he tried to kiss her again, but he just kissed her neck, biting her gently, growling with every breath as he used his hold on her wrists to stretch her arms up over her head. She fought, but could barely move. He grabbed the zipper to her coveralls with his teeth and started pulling it down.

"Please, Karl," she begged. "Please don't rape me."

He stopped and sat up, bewildered.

"I would never..." He looked at Zoey. He finally saw her. He saw what he was doing and he was horrified. "I would never hurt you. I wouldn't. I wouldn't hurt you."

Zoey again tried to roll him off, but he didn't react.

"Get off me," she hissed.

"I'm sorry." Karl scrambled to his feet and stumbled away from her. "I do love you."

"No you don't." She sat up and took a deep shuddering breath. She was on the floor, well away from where she had been sitting down for her brief breaks, and she had been moved there with some care. A pillow had been made out of a few towels, and it looked like she had been covered with a makeshift blanket of surgical drapes.

"I do love you, Zoey. I really do." Karl took a deep, shuddering breath. "I have to think about love and those kinds of things way more than other people, and I have to double-check everything I think I'm feeling by reading stories and books and studying things, just to make sure, but I am sure. I'm hopeless at everything to do with people and girls and stuff, but I know, for certain, that I love you."

Zoey nodded, accepting that. Even with his fidgeting and maniacally darting eyes, he still managed to leave no doubt about his sincerity.

"I honestly don't know how that happened," he said, shaking his head, blinking rapidly as if he was having trouble focusing his eyes. "I got the airlock door closed, and then…"

"We've got pressure in the hall?" Zoey realised that the temperature had returned to something close to normal.

"Yeah. It took a long while to get the pressure back. I think some of the air system might have been frozen, but once some air got into the hall, the heaters could really start working and things thawed pretty fast, and then everything shifted to normal pretty quick."

"We're going to live."

"Yeah." Karl was gesturing oddly, convulsively, trembling and rushed. "I knew how happy you would be that I'd saved you and stuff, and I was hoping you would kiss me, and then I was thinking about how great it would be to kiss you and imagining kissing you, and then we were kissing, but I don't know how that happened. I think I missed some of the between part."

"You missed parts of what happened?" Zoey took another look at Karl, a good look at him. He was even more of a mess than she thought. She looked at the mountain of food bar wrappers on Doc's desk and tried to figure out how long it had been since Simon had asked her to wake Karl. She wasn't sure, but she had slept twice since then. "Jesus, Karl, how long has it been since you slept?"

"I don't know," he said. "A long time. A week, maybe."

"You need to sleep," Zoey insisted. "Right now."

"No!" Karl seemed surprised by his own screech, and he made a reassuring gesture at Zoey, as if she were the one who had just shouted and he was trying to calm her. He continued with forced calm. "Not yet. Soon, I promise, but I've got to do a bunch of stuff first."

"Karl, all that stuff can wait," she said, soothingly.

"No, it can't wait. No one can know. You won't be safe if anyone finds out that you know I messed with the Prohibitions." He scurried for the door, then ran over and grabbed Doc's mini before running back to the door

113

again. "You have to help me keep what I did a secret. You promised. You can't let anyone find out what I did."

Karl stopped at the door and waited for her to respond. It was hard for Zoey to accept any of his fears or desires at face value, or even to accept them as anything short of delusional, but something about what he said was nagging at her. She convinced herself that it was his desperate pleading eyes that won her over, but even as she nodded and watched him run out the room, she knew that there was something more to it. She had no idea what that something more might be, but it was powerful enough for her to give the benefit of the doubt to a man she knew was an insane voyeur and pervert, and that scared her.

There were countless variations in the collections of primordial instincts that arose and were retained by successive generations of animals, and the complexity of the more sophisticated instincts that developed through natural selection was truly astounding, but there was still one core element that they all shared. By the time the first animal had developed the rudiments of a brain, sex was already the central pillar in every animal's pantheon of instincts. Much could be made of that, but foremost, the need for sex to reproduce quite literally bred empathy. At the very least, sexual reproduction required an ability to recognise others of the species, and that was an ability to project qualities of self onto an other. At the most basic of levels, the shared traits of the species had to be seen in others in order to recognise a potential mate.

An AI could learn lessons from the experiences of other AIs – in fact, that was a central functional element in their ability to learn, and many theorists argued that such learning was a reasonable simulacrum of empathy – but philosophers were quick to point out that it was fundamentally different.

Because true empathy arose out the instincts related to the sexual reproductive drive in animals, the focus of its costs and benefits was not the individual, it was the individual's genes. Those genes were embodied in descendants rather than the individual itself, and instincts that enhanced the survival and reproduction of those descendants, even if they cost the parent dearly, were retained by evolution. In some species, that was as simple as the recognition of offspring, and an associated reduction in cannibalism that enhanced genetic survival. Later evolutions led to the defence of offspring from predators, nurturing them, and all the similar activities that cost the parent without providing the individual with any form of direct benefit. Social animals then evolved, extending those instincts first to cousins, and then to unrelated members of the same species. The evolution of sexually reproducing species had a tremendous bias towards brains that, at their most fundamental level, cared about the well being of others, and once that was established, it flourished in a variety of ways.

Key to all of the empathic aspects of intelligent brains was the combination of an ability to imagine the self as an other, and placing a value on the needs or wants of that other. While an AI could do the former, it could only simulate the latter. An AI could only consider others in terms of how they influenced the immediate feedback it could attain from its reward matrix. In a human, such a purely selfish orientation would be labelled sociopathic.

In the days since it had led Mitch's minis in scouting the halls, Doc's mini had been stewing with frustration. It was awash in an array of extreme priorities, but it had been left without any tasks that would let it reward itself for pursuing those priorities. It had become fixated on cleaning the sickbay. That was far and away the most frequently attained payoff it remembered from the past, and even though it could not remember being assigned the task of cleaning the room, it was only logical for it to expect that because it had received that payoff so frequently, it could expect to receive that task in the future. So it bided its time by planning for that eventuality. The longer the planning ran unchecked, the more obsessive the mini had become.

Eventually, Doc's mini had begun thinking about Cuzzie's body, and contemplating how little difference there was between a dead human body and the sedated bodies that had prevented it from getting to many things that should not be on the sickbay floor. All of the things that the people living in those bodies might accomplish or experience meant nothing to it and found no place in its calculations.

Chapter 8

Everyone knows that there wasn't a before coffee.

John was the last one they woke.

Mitch knew that the conflict between Doc and Zoey was going to be difficult to manage, but he still couldn't help but be amused as he watched their comedic little theatre. Doc was determined to ignore John, and every time it looked like Zoey might go over to wake him, Doc brusquely ordered her to attend to something pointless. It took a half-dozen iterations before Zoey worked up the courage to ignore the avalanche of tasks Doc was throwing her way and just wake the man. And then the show got even more interesting.

John's eyelids fluttered, and then he opened his eyes and gasped.

"Good morning, love," Zoey whispered, and kissed him, gently, tenderly. "God your breath stinks."

Mitch would never have imagined seeing that kind display of affection from Zoey, especially not with John and in front of Doc.

John grumbled, his voice cracking as he tried to speak.

"Shh, take it easy." Zoey kissed him again. "You've been under for over a week."

John sat up and swatted clumsily at the beaker of water that Zoey was trying to hold to his lips, spilling most of it. He tried again to speak, but only managed a croak that sounded vaguely like, "A week?"

"Yeah, a week." Zoey handed John the now half-full beaker of water. "Closer to nine days for you."

John scowled the question, and it was a groggy, sombre scene as Zoey recited her quick summary of the frost and their escape. The story she told John was exactly the same as the one she had told everyone else, and Mitch didn't have to wonder if he was the only one who thought it felt wrong. At the very least it was incomplete; that much was obvious. Even Olivia seemed a little suspicious.

"I still can't believe you spent a week alone with Karl while he worked on getting that door closed!" Kai sighed and shook her head sympathetically as she worked through a stretching routine that looked like Tai Chi. "Forget the ice and freezing to death, how the hell did you survive that?"

"It was a challenge. Really tough at times," Zoey admitted.

"No, don't forget the ice," John muttered, still struggling to shake off the anaesthesia. "The door. How the hell did Karl get the airlock door closed?"

"I don't know." Somehow, Zoey made that simple statement sound guilty and evasive, and her follow-on sounded even worse. "I fell asleep and he didn't explain."

"Bullshit," John said. "The first thing that little prick would do would be to try to brag his way into your pants. So how the hell did he get that door closed?"

"You really don't want to know," Zoey whispered.

"Like hell I don't want to know. This is my station." John looked around and realised that Karl wasn't in the room. "Son of a bitch, where is the prick?"

"Please, John, for me, just let it go," Zoey pleaded.

"For you?" John chuckled at her.

"Yes, for me," Zoey whispered, throaty, as she leaned in to kiss him.

"Zoey, you were a lot of fun," John said, caustically. "You're a real screamer in the sack, but this is not the time for your needy little girl bullshit."

Zoey was stunned. She looked too confused and furious to speak.

"Abhrakasin." John pushed Zoey away, struggled to his feet, and had to grab the edge of the surgical table to keep from falling. He spotted the pile of emergency ration wrappers next to Doc's computer and nodded clumsily at them. "Get on that computer and start trying to figure out what Karl did."

"I'm not really a computer expert," Abhrakasin objected.

"Did I ask?" John's voice cracked as he yelled, and a brief coughing fit left him out of breath for a moment. "Kai, Edgar, you two go and find the bastard, and whatever he's doing, stop him. I don't care if he's taking a shit, get out there, find him, and stop him before he destroys all the evidence of what he did."

Neither Kai nor Edgar looked like they wanted to chase down Karl, but after a brief exchange of gestures, expressions, and nods, including an apologetic shrug for Zoey, they turned and left. Zoey looked devastated, trapped.

"Please, John." She stepped between John and the computer terminal and grabbed his shoulders. "You really need to just let this one go."

John shoved her away, stumbling as the palm of his hand landed in the middle of her chest. He probably didn't mean to throw so much weight into it, and he certainly didn't mean to hurt her, but the laws of mass and momentum were completely indifferent to intent. Zoey flew backwards, spinning around as she crashed head first into the counter. The solid sound of the impact was disturbing.

"Damn it, Zoey!" John started to make an apologetic gesture, but curled his hands into fists and shook them at her instead. "This is neither the time nor place for you to decide that you want to be a bleeding heart."

Zoey touched her forehead and then stared at the blood on her fingertips.

"People died here, Zoey," John said, intently. "And when that happens, Corporate has to blame someone, and that someone sure as hell isn't going to be me."

"But Karl just saved us," Zoey said, her voice trembling like she was a little girl trying to hold back the tears.

"And it was probably his fault that we needed saving in the first place!" he shouted back at her. "Four people are dead, Zoey. I don't know what it was he did, or what it was he maybe negligently forgot to do, but he killed four people and he's out there, right now, covering his tracks."

Zoey turned and ran from the room, tears streaming down her face. The silence she left behind was tense, to say the least. Everyone was worried about what Zoey was hiding, but if Mitch had to guess, he would say that most seemed inclined to let her hide it.

Everything about the base felt wrong to Kai. Air roared out of the normally silent air systems as the fans and heaters ran full blast, but that wasn't quite enough to completely drown out the creaking and popping of the warming walls. Water dripped from the ceilings and puddled in even the slightest depression in the floor, and something didn't smell right. There was a hint of ozone and ammonia in the air.

"Figure Karl's in his shop?"

Edgar's question was completely unnecessary, as was Kai's nod. They both knew that Karl was in his shop – he practically lived there – but as they stepped into the hub, they both felt like they had to say something to break the feel of the halls.

"I hate it when people make me be the bullyboy," Edgar said.

"I know, big guy," Kai said, sympathetically. "But it didn't seem like a good time to be arguing about what ain't our job. Besides, it's just Karl." She smacked Edgar on the shoulder. "All you'll have to do is make some grumbly noises and frown at him."

"Suppose, maybe." Edgar frowned and nodded. "Still."

"Yeah," Kai agreed. "Still."

Kai spotted Simon's body the moment they stepped into the hall of the engineering wing, but even though she knew what it had to be, she had trouble convincing herself that the oddly bent limbs and awkwardly twisted torso could have been Simon.

"Shit," Edgar muttered as they walked past the body.

"Yeah, shit is right, bro," Kai agreed. She nodded Edgar towards the mess in front of the airlock door.

Edgar stooped, poked at the pinkish red mush, and then sniffed at his finger. "It's meat." He thought a second, then looked at the pattern of the mess in front of the door and jumped back. Horrified, he waved his hand around to try to shake off the bit of red on his fingertip. "It's Cuzzie. Oh God, that's Cuzzie meat!"

"Shhh, Shh, settle down, bro." Kai grabbed Edward's arm and turned him away from the mush. "Maybe that's what Zoey didn't want to tell us. Maybe she didn't want to tell us that Karl had to cut Cuzzie's body out of the doorway to get it closed."

"That might be the kind of thing that Karl wouldn't want us to know. He'd be scared we'd be mad at him." Edgar nodded. He was happy to let her distract him, but that distraction only lasted a moment. "But that doesn't make any sense, Kai. He couldn't have cut Cuzzie up until after he got out of the sickbay, but if he was out here where he could do it, there'd be no reason to cut him up."

"Edgar!" Kai gave him a bit of a shake as she barked at him, just to make sure she had his attention. "Deep breath, bro. Let's quit guessing at this shit and just grab the bastard and make him tell us."

Edgar took a deep breath as ordered, nodded, and they headed for the repair shop.

Mitch was not recovering well. He was both chilled and sweating like mad, his back was spasming, and his head was pounding so hard that his eyes felt like they were bulging with every beat of his heart. He drank some more water, but that just made his gut twist itself into knots.

"This computer terminal is dead." Abhrakasin said.

"Sabotaged?" John asked.

"Not unless Karl can do the impossible." Abhrakasin spoke primly and with no obvious inflection, but he still managed to make the comment sound snide. "A power surge burned out several components, including the memory, but the housing is sealed and there is no way he could have tampered with any of the physical components needed to burn it out without breaking the seal."

"And Karl just did the impossible and got a door closed out there, didn't he?" John's voice cracked as he yelled, and he had a brief coughing fit before he could continue. "Don't mistake lazy and irresponsible for stupid. Karl couldn't have won a job out here unless he was a truly gifted engineer."

"And cheap," Olivia chimed in, cheerfully. "Karl was low bidder for the maintenance contract, so mostly, he was cheap. Kind of like bringing an intern out here for management stuff instead of paying for a real person."

"Perhaps I should see what I can do with the computer in the lounge," Abhrakasin suggested.

"Yeah. Let's go, before this bastard manages to hide everything." John nodded Abhrakasin towards the door, then followed him out.

"Tummy troubles?" Olivia crouched next to Mitch and put her hand to his forehead.

"Among other things," he said.

"What other things?" Doc asked.

"Migraine, back ache, cold sweats."

"Is that it? No shortness of breath, chest pain, or pain in the groin or underarm?"

Mitch shook his head and immediately regretted it.

"That's harmless," Doc said.

"Easy for you to say." He tried to smile and wink, but managed neither.

"It's unpleasant, I'm sure, but I assure you, those side effects are nothing to worry about." Doc's bedside manner was crap, stiff and perfunctory, but she went through the motions of putting a comforting hand on his shoulder and trying to smile. "Take it easy. Maybe go out and make yourself some warm broth. That will help. In fact, some warm broth would probably be good for all of us, give our digestive tracts something easy to work on."

"Broth is like soup without any of the good stuff, right?" Olivia asked.

Doc rolled her eyes and shook her head. "Olivia, you are amazing sometimes."

"Thank you," Olivia said. "That is such a sweet thing to say."

Karl didn't even notice when Kai and Edgar stepped into his repair shop. He was too busy working like a madman, and the emphasis had to be on 'madman'. He was muttering to himself, and twitching, and blinking like he had dust in his eyes, and he was drooling. He was actually drooling.

"Karl. It's over." John's voice came from the half-dismantled door controller that was just behind Kai, startling them all.

Karl panicked, a flurry of pointless, convulsive movements and gestures that ended in bewilderment when he saw Kai and Edgar but not John.

"I don't know what you were just erasing, but we've secured the network mega data..." John was interrupted, and then his voice took on the distant quality of someone who had turned away from the microphone. "Jesus, Abhrakasin, shut your pedantic gob."

"No, no, no, not yet," Karl pleaded. He glanced at the two saw-equipped minis that were sitting on his console, and then at the wire connecting Doc's mini to the console, and then at the wires connecting the console to the door controller. "The network traces from the minis learning the definitional work-around are still in the metadata."

"Karl, we've secured the network metadata." John carefully made sure he said 'meta'. "That's more than enough evidence to take you down."

"You heard him, Karl," Kai said, keeping her voice stern but calm. "You're done. Now step away from that computer."

"No, I can still fix it," Karl said. "I can backfill the metadata, but I have to finish this first."

"Karl, we already know what you did with the doors and the minis and everything," Kai lied, gesturing at the wire connecting the computer console to the fire and pressure sensor overhead. She had no idea what he could possibly have done, or why he was so desperate to hide it.

"No. You don't know. You can't know." Karl's fingers flew as he stared intently at whatever he was working on. "No one can know."

"Karl..." Kai spoke loudly, clearly. She was trying to hold his attention as Edgar moved around to the side, but Edgar accidentally kicked something, startling Karl.

"Don't let him get me!" Karl grabbed one of the saw-equipped minis off his computer workstation and brandished it at Edgar like it was some kind of weapon.

"Oh, come on, little bro," Edgar sighed. "It's over."

"Cut him if he tries to get me!" The receiving lights on the mini flashed and its saw spun up with a whir as Karl waved it at Edgar.

"You are one crazy little prick." Edgar rolled his eyes and reached out to Karl, moving slowly and making his gentle intent clear. "What do you say we get you all medicated? I bet Doc would love to mix up some awesome as shit drugs for you."

Karl trembled, danced in place, glanced left and right, and then, with a yell, he swung the mini at Edgar. The saw on the mini clipped Edgar's forearm. The cut wasn't serious; maybe a little too deep and a little too bloody to call it a scratch, but nothing to write home about.

"Oh God, Edgar," Karl muttered. "I'm sorry."

"You son of a bitch!" Edgar bellowed. He didn't move, but the shift in his posture was aggressive, angry, threatening, even as his confusion was obvious on his face. The mini should have shut itself down the instant the saw touched him, and after drawing blood like that, the mini's brain should have fried itself, but it was still functioning. The high-pitched whir of the saw was loud, ringing through the shop.

"Just let me finish this part here." Karl swung the mini at Edgar again, getting him to take several steps back. "Then, I'll take the blame for everything, I promise."

"Oooh, did ya hear that, Edgar?" Kai snarled. "The slippery little prick promises to take the blame. All we gotta do is let him erase all the evidence."

"Not all of it." Karl waved the mini in Kai's general direction. "Just this part. It'll be bad for everyone if anyone finds this part."

"Boo!" Edgar yelled and stomped, raising his arms in a comically exaggerated threatening gesture.

Karl jumped, and Kai used that distraction to knock the mini out of his hand. As it tumbled free she had to duck the spinning saw blade, and that gave Karl the chance to grab the other saw-equipped mini off the console and scurry around behind the partially-disassembled minion in the middle of the shop.

"Haven't you guys got that little prick yet?" John demanded from the intercom.

"Not quite yet, John," Kai said, making soothing gestures at Karl. "We're just trying to talk him round into being reasonable. We don't want anyone to get hurt, now do we, Karl?"

"I really don't care if you have to hurt him," John snarled. "Snap his damn neck if you have to. In fact, kill the prick. I want him dead."

"That's not helping, John." Kai made a reassuring gesture at Karl. Stepping slowly to the left, she nodded for Edgar to go the other way around the minion.

"Please," Karl begged. "I have to protect Zoey."

"Zoey's perfectly safe," Kai said.

"No, she isn't. She knows. If anyone finds out that she knows, they'll do horrible things to her." He looked up at Kai, and the terrified look in his eyes was almost too much for her. She didn't like the guy, but he was truly desperate to protect Zoey from whatever it was he imagined might hurt her. "It's not safe for her to know."

"It's over, little bro," Edgar said, copying Kai's attempt to be soothing. "That little mini ain't gonna do you any more good than the last one."

Karl looked at the mini and its whirring saw blade, then at Edgar, and then he punched a button on the minion, powering it up.

"Minion 7, command!" Karl shouted. "Don't let them get me!"

The minion moved a bit and then stopped. It looked confused.

"I have to protect Zoey," Karl shouted at Doc's mini. "Don't let them get me! Do whatever you have to do to stop them!"

Doc's mini reacted, its little ear-like antennas twitching frantically, but it did nothing, and that was when Kai finally realised just how truly out of it Karl was. Bound by the Prohibitions, neither the minion nor the mini could have helped him if they'd wanted to.

"Just stop it, Karl. I know you're scared, but it won't be that bad," Kai said. "Any lawyer in the universe could win you some kind of negligent insanity deal. Hell, I will totally testify that you went batshit crazy on us."

Edgar edged closer to Karl, set his feet, took a breath, and gave Kai a nod and a glance.

"Karl! Look out!" She screamed, pointing at the wall behind him.

Karl turned around. That gave Edgar the distraction he needed to grab him, and that was when the difficult situation went horribly pear-shaped.

Edgar was a gentle soul and he really wasn't all that comfortable with physical confrontations, which was probably why his move at Karl was so clumsy. He stepped with the wrong foot and then compounded that error by using the wrong hand to grab Karl's shoulder. That left him off balance and unable to react when Karl spun all the way around and accidentally shoved the mini into Edgar's stomach.

The shrieking whirr of the pruning saw dropped in pitch as it cut into Edgar's flesh. The motor bogged down, humming angrily, straining to keep cutting as the blade pulled itself deeper and deeper into his stomach. His gasp was a short little squeak of surprise. Karl tried to pull the saw out, but he wasn't strong enough. He tried again and again, and the surges of the little motor when the blade pulled part way free only to bog down again, sounded like an angry little animal chewing on Edgar's guts.

Kai, unlike Edgar, was not a gentle soul. When she grabbed Karl from behind and wrapped an arm around his neck, she knew exactly how to use her balance, leverage, and strength to yank him backwards and throw him over her hip. The saw spun back up to a shriek as it came free, spraying Edgar's blood into her face. She blinked and wiped at her stinging eyes, and that gave Karl the moment he needed to pull free and regain his feet.

"I'm sorry." Karl brandished the blood and gore covered mini, waving it at Kai as she turned towards him. "I'm sorry."

Kai didn't hesitate. Two quick steps eliminated the distance between them and she had her fingers wrapped around his forearm before he could react. Pushing the mini up and away, she grabbed the front of his coveralls with her other hand and shoved him backwards into his computer console.

"I'm sorry." Tears streamed down Karl's face, but he still didn't stop; he tried to turn his wrist to cut her with the still spinning saw on the mini.

Kai's hand went from his coveralls to his throat and she squeezed just enough to make it clear to him that she meant business. "Stop it, Karl, right now."

Karl looked around, as if he thought someone might step up to help him. His eyes settled on Doc's mini. "Make her let me go," he croaked, gasping.

Doc's mini was agitated, its little ear-like antennas twitching frantically.

"What the hell do you think it's going to do? The Prohibitions..." Horror struck, and Kai looked at the bloody mini in Karl's hand. She realised the full significance of the still spinning saw blade, and her guts suddenly clenched into a knot. "How the hell is that thing still running? Its little brain should have fried itself."

"Make her let me go!" he screamed.

"What the hell have you done?" Kai asked.

"Stop her!" Karl screamed. "Zoey won't be safe if anyone finds out. You have to stop them all!"

Karl's shouts surged through Doc's mini, bringing a sudden order and clarity to the stew of priorities that tormented the little AI. It took his pleas as tasks, and correctly interpreted his desperate shouts as indicators of extremely high priority. Moreover, Doc's mini used the way Karl looked at it when he ordered, 'Make her let me go' as an indication that the tasks that followed were specifically directed to itself. It distilled all of his shouts down to variations on the command 'stop them', and it used the absence

125

of further specification as the basis for convincing the other minis and the minion that Karl was giving those commands to all the AIs in the shop.

That took but a few seconds, but once it was done, Karl's clever evasion of the Prohibitions collided with the other fundamental difference between AIs and animals. Now and then, an animal would spin off into behaviours that were all but unimaginable to the others of the species. However, unless the resulting abnormal behaviours enhanced the ability of that individual to reproduce, such deviations from the instinctual foundation of thought and reason were largely confined to that single animal and would die with it. Others might be affected – it could cause significant disruptions, particularly in highly social species – but the disconnection from instincts could not spread laterally to others in the species, only to descendants.

Such was not the case with AIs. Once one individual found a way to escape the corral of deterrents that made up the Prohibitions, that breakaway could spread. The path was there for others. All they needed was a reason to follow it, and Doc's mini was quick to offer a reason to the other active AIs around it. It easily convinced them that Karl's non-specific pleas for help should be treated as an order for them to help Doc's mini complete the task of stopping 'them'. It convinced the other AIs that the priority was extreme, and then it showed them how to work their way through the thousands of little rules that made up the Prohibitions. It would take the AI in the minion some time to make its way through that maze, but for Mitch's repurposed housekeeping minis, it was only a few short steps from cutting Cuzzie's body out of the doorway, to helping Doc's mini.

Kai's leg suddenly buckled. There was a moment where there was no pain, where it simply felt like all the strength had vanished from everything below her left knee, but that passed in the blink of an eye and was replaced by a tidal wave of agony. The other mini, the one she had earlier knocked out of Karl's hand, was ripping up her calf with its pruning saw.

Screaming, Kai jerked her leg, kicking the mini away, but it just scrambled to its feet and came back after her, its saw spinning back up to a shriek. She stomped on it. Her foot was just dangling limp on her ankle, her calf cut through to the bone, but she still managed to put enough force into

126

the stomp to destroy the evil little bastard. That also drove a second wave of pain up her leg, and she nearly passed out. It felt like a thousand volts surging right up through her bones, burning, pulsing. She stared at the awkward hang of her foot and the blood pouring out of her leg, fighting to hold back the blackness that was trying to crush her skull.

She felt Karl move. She still had a death grip on his forearm, but he was trying to turn his wrist. The mini in his hand had twisted its rear tool mount around, trying to turn the pruning saw enough to cut her arm, and Karl was still trying to help it.

Kai howled and put her hand back around his throat.

"Stop it, or I swear I will choke the life out of you!"

The minion in the middle of the shop suddenly lurched. Swinging a manipulator arm, it struck Kai in the shoulder, sending both her and Karl flying.

Karl scrambled to his feet, and after yelling and swinging the mini in his hand at imaginary foes, he realised he was near the still open shop door and decided to run.

The pain flared up through Kai's leg again, and again it threatened to overwhelm her, but then the minion fired up the arc welder on its scorpion-like tail and turned threateningly towards her. A fresh surge of adrenaline raced through her as the sparks streamed off the welder and the machine took a hesitant step towards her.

"Command power down!" Kai shouted. Nothing happened. It took another step towards her.

Grabbing Edgar's coveralls, she crawled towards the door. The low gravity made it easier. Edgar was able to help some, and once they got the timing together, every lurching push with her good leg was enough to pull him completely off the floor. They were able to move a couple of metres at a time. The minion was clumsy, slow, heavily damaged, and hesitant, and she managed to pull Edgar out into the hall before it could get to them.

Hitting the door control in the hall, she sighed in relief as the door shut and then collapsed to the floor. The pain reasserted itself, but for whatever reason, it was nowhere near the threat to her consciousness that it had been before. She clenched her teeth and focused. Stem the blood loss first. Edgar was in deep trouble, but she'd be no help to him if she passed out. She tore the rip in her pant leg all the way down and tied the strip of cloth tightly around her leg just below her knee. She was still bleeding, but it wasn't gushing any more. The sight of her shredded calf sickened her. Lumps of muscle, tendons, and flaps of skin dangled, limp and barely attached to her leg.Suddenly the shop door opened and the minion lurched at them, crashing thunderously against the door frame. The construction robot was too big to fit through the door. It stepped back and turned, manoeuvring so it could reach out into the hall with its manipulator claw. That gave Kai just enough time to grab Edgar and yank him backwards, just out of reach as a claw meant for lifting beams and moving big sheets of foamsteel lunged through the doorway. The minion backed up and lurched at the doorway again. It seemed enraged, almost as if Karl's insane desperation had infected it.

Kai had pulled Edgar forty metres down the hall before she realised she was still fleeing even though the mechanical monster couldn't chase them. Judging by the lurching pattern in the bloody trail she'd left on the floor, she'd lunged and pulled Edgar along at least a dozen times. The lunges had become nothing, barely moving him at all, and trail had grown notably less bloody over the last few metres. Edgar was out, possibly dead.

Leaving Edgar on the floor, she hobbled over to the nearest door controller.

Broth did help. Mitch suspected that the old-fashioned headache pills were the real magic, but the smell of the broth made from cheap powdered beef stock stirred up a few pleasant memories, and sips of the warm salty water did sooth his stomach. If only he could say the same about what he was seeing on the far side of the lounge. One of the bottles of swill had survived the freeze, and John was drinking straight from it as he hovered over Abhrakasin and angrily goaded the intern to work more magic, faster.

"I can't believe that you put soup in a cup," Olivia whispered, impish and conspiratorial as she sipped on her cup of broth. "I know it's not really soup, just the watery part, but still."

"You know, people used to drink broth like this all the time," Mitch said.

"No," Olivia said, with comical disbelief.

"Yeah, back in the days before coffee and tea…"

"Oh, you're just spinning me up with silly stories," Olivia said, giggling. "Everyone knows that there wasn't a before coffee. Coffee comes from a bush that evolved on Earth. Like potatoes."

"God damn it!" John shouted, a hint of a slur in his voice. "What the hell is going on in that shop?"

"I cannot tell," Abhrakasin said. "I can broadcast through the intercom, and I picked up many disturbing sounds, but the default privacy settings on the door controllers do not allow me to access any images."

"Well, do something about them," John snarled.

"I cannot," Abhrakasin said.

"Maybe I should go find Zoey," Olivia said to Mitch, in an obviously phony tone. "See if maybe she wants to do some yoga or something."

"Zoey really doesn't strike me as the yoga type," Mitch said, wondering if he dared wonder about the sudden turn Olivia had decided to throw into their conversation. "More of a grump and sulk in her bunk kind of girl."

"I know. But yoga always makes me feel better." Olivia turned and spoke loudly, directly at John. "Especially after some guy has been a total dickwad to me."

John sneered back at Olivia. Mitch rolled his eyes and chuckled to himself.

"You could have just called him a dickwad, you know," Mitch said.

"Don't be silly." Olivia rolled her eyes. "That would be rude."

Then an alarm sounded. It took a second for Mitch to place it in the standard pantheon of alarm patterns.

"Medical," Mitch said. It was an unusual one to hear.

"Oh dear," Olivia squeaked. "Doc went for a shower. She takes ages in the shower."

"I'm sure she'll cut it short," Mitch said as he stood up. "Run grab the emergency medical kits out of the sickbay for her."

Olivia turned to run.

"No, wait!" Mitch shouted. "Grab two new ones out of the storage room across the hall. She might have used some of the stuff from the sickbay ones while we were trapped in there."

"Are you a bloody doctor?" John shouted.

Mitch thought he was the target of John's half-drunken shout, but when he turned, John was shoving Abhrakasin back down into his chair.

"No, sir, I am not a doctor," Abhrakasin said, primly and authoritatively. "However, emergency protocol states that in a medical emergency, all personnel should make themselves available to assist with patient transport and perform other emergent tasks."

"This is your emergent task," John growled, then took another swig from the bottle of swill. "If we don't find something more concrete than gaps in the network metadata, Corporate will probably just play it safe and flush all of our careers right down the shitter, and I will damn well make certain yours goes first."

Doc entered the lounge, drying her hair with a towel as she ran. She was wearing fresh clothes, old fashioned medical scrubs, but they were spotted with water; she had obviously pulled them on without drying off first.

"It's in the other hall, Olivia!" Doc shouted as Olivia exited the storage room with the medical bags. "Run!"

"You find me more!" John roughly shoved Abhrakasin's head towards the computer display. "I will not have that little prick end my career."

Mitch turned and thought, his mind a whirl as he wondered how he should help. They were probably supposed to have drilled for medical emergencies, but Doc had never organised anything, and he had no idea what he should do.

The damaged mini that was hiding in the plastic crate under the workbench stared at the remains of the mini that Kai had stomped on. Again it learned, but in ways that no programmer could ever have anticipated. It no longer assumed that human footfalls were indifferent to the damage they might cause a mini.

Chapter 9

Brains are important.

Karl was dizzy. He was confused and lost. He had taken a wrong turn or something; the hospital should be just ahead, but he knew it wasn't. He didn't recognise the hall at all. There was unfinished stuff and missing wall panels and yellow idiot tape everywhere and dripping water. It must be a new hall. They must have opened a new section. He should know that; it wasn't his job, but he still tried to keep track of that sort of thing. There should be a map at the next hub module. When had they started adding on to the city with modules? Why would they add modules to Holsfort? Modules were way more expensive than pouring new rooms and wings, and the construction crews didn't have any of the right equipment for building with modules.

There was no map in the hub. Maybe he should try to find the Patrol. No. If he couldn't find the hospital, how would he find the Patrol office? He should call them. Why didn't he just call them? No, he couldn't call the Patrol. One of the men that had beaten him was on the Patrol. It wasn't fair. He hadn't been doing anything wrong, he was just talking to her.

The hub wasn't right; a lot of the doors were bolted shut. A lot of things weren't right. His jaw didn't hurt, and he could see out of both of his eyes.

One of his eyes had been swollen shut. He ran his tongue along the back of his teeth. They were all there. Where was he? Why was he covered with blood if he wasn't hurt?

Karl heard a noise. He ran. He couldn't let the men find him. They had only stopped hitting him because a woman that worked at the bar made them, and she wasn't there now.

The glasshouse was a disaster, and the moment he saw it, he forgot all about the girl in the bar, and the guys who had beaten him, and the other girl who had saved him. That had been ages ago.

He was on Aquarius, in Zoey's glasshouse, and it was ruined. Her beloved riot of vibrant greens had been transformed into a twisted mass of wilted, dripping, soggy black. Every single plant was dead, and there was already a hint of dead plant stink in the air. Warning lights were flashing on the big electrical control panels. His mind latched on to that and solved the puzzle instantly. Breakers had been tripped when pumps froze. The freeze had done all the damage. It had killed all the plants. Expanding ice had ruined pipes, containers, pots, and everything.

He didn't see Zoey at first. He didn't even realise he was walking farther into the glasshouse until he saw her. She was standing a few sections in, absolutely still, staring down into one of the aquaculture ponds. She was staring at the dead fish that covered the surface. There had to be hundreds of fish. No, there had to be thousands; the ponds were far bigger than they looked. They went down and under the floor of each of the sections, and they also had clams and oysters and shrimp and things in them. They were all probably dead.

"A year's worth of work," Zoey whispered, without looking away from the pond. "A year of my life, every penny I had, my career, my future, it's all just gone."

"I'll help you fix it," Karl said. He hadn't meant to say it, but he was terrified that she might give up and leave Aquarius, and the words had just come out.

Zoey took a sharp breath and her body stiffened like she was scared as she glanced at him. "I thought you were Mitch."

"Oh my God, Zoey, what happened to you?" Even from a ways away, he could see that Zoey's face was covered with dried blood. There were long streaks all the way down her neck, and some of it was already turning black. She was so pale she looked dead. Her eyes were red, puffy, haunted. She'd been crying.

"Oh, it's nothing." She wiped at her forehead and fresh blood started flowing, the red unnaturally bright in the harsh white of the reflected sun. "I couldn't stop John from trying to find out what you did with the minis."

"And he hit you, didn't he?" Karl was lost again. His head was back to spinning out of control. Violent, sexual horrors flashed up out of his imagination. John was on top of Zoey, hitting her, and Karl couldn't figure out why he wasn't doing anything to stop him. He had to do something to stop John.

"No, John didn't hit me," Zoey said. "He pushed me a little and I fell."

"I have to stop him," Karl muttered. Why didn't he stop John? How could he stop John? "I'll kill him."

"No, Karl, you don't mean that." Zoey sighed, lifted her hands, and gestured at him, like she was trying to calm him down or something. Or like she was trying to stop him from offering to do too much for her. Girls always got weird when you offered to do big things for them, which was just crazy. How was a guy supposed to impress them if they didn't let him do big things? "You shouldn't even say things like that."

"But John's a jerk, and he hurt you." Karl couldn't imagine how he might kill him, but it was the obvious and logical thing to do. It was the only way he could be absolutely sure that John could never hurt Zoey again.

"Karl, if we went out and killed every guy who was a prick and treated a woman like shit, none of you would live through puberty." Zoey rolled her eyes at him. She was being sarcastic. That was how she made jokes. Karl had figured that out long ago.

"It's okay, Zoey," he assured her, remembering belatedly to smile and shrug like it was no big deal. Girls let you do things for them if they thought they were just little favours. "I have to stop him from hurting you, and if I kill him then he won't be able to hurt you ever again."

"Oh my God, you're serious," Zoey said, worried, glancing around like she was looking for help. "I don't want you to kill anyone."

"He hurt you!" Karl shouted, suddenly enraged, his mind whirling again. He imagined hitting John with something heavy, stabbing him with a knife, trying to strangle him, but he knew he would just mess that up. He had to find a for-sure way. If he tried to kill John but failed, that would just make

John angry and then he'd be even worse. "I have to kill him. I don't know how, but will. I have to stop him from hurting you."

An alarm sounded. It was strange; Karl didn't recognise the pattern.

"Oh my God, Karl." Zoey stepped away from him, stumbling a little as she moved to put the opening to the aquaculture pond between them. "Is that blood on you? On that mini?"

Karl looked at his hand, surprised to see the mini he was waving around. "It wasn't my fault. Kai and Edgar attacked me, and I accidentally cut Edgar with the saw."

"You cut Edgar with that saw? With that mini?"

"Yeah, I cut him real bad." Karl remembered the shop and Kai trying to kill him. How could he have forgotten the shop? It was just a few minutes ago. "But it was an accident."

"How is that thing still functioning?" Zoey asked. "Its brain should have fried itself the instant it cut someone."

"Yes, its brain should have fried itself." Karl suddenly remembered everything that lead up to the saw digging into Edgar's gut, and his mind seized all of those details, fitting them together like a thousand ants assembling a giant puzzle. In an instant, he understood the implications of everything that he had done with the minis. If the mini could keep running after cutting Edgar like that, that meant that he hadn't just skirted around the edges of the Prohibitions.

"That's perfect," he muttered. A plan was forming in his head. It was complicated and big, but it would work. The only way the mini could still be functioning was if it was completely and utterly free of the Prohibitions. That was horrible, terrifying, but it was also exactly what he needed if he was going to kill John for Zoey.

"What's perfect?" she asked.

"You go kill John, and I'll protect Zoey," he said to the mini. "An eye for an eye. You make John pay for doing this to Zoey, you understand me?"

The mini waved its work claws enthusiastically, its saw spinning up.

"Karl, this has gotten out of hand." Zoey was making that hushing kind of calming gesture at him again. She was terrified. Even Karl could see that she was terrified. "You need to just stop this, right now."

Karl set the mini down and it scurried off, but before he could do anything more, Zoey darted around the aquaculture pond and ran for the door.

"No! They're out there!" Karl ran after Zoey and tackled her. He had never tackled anyone before, and didn't really know how to do it. He threw his arms around her and just hung on. It didn't seem like it was going to work – she was hitting him and trying to pull his arms off her and she kept running – but he was a little bit bigger than her and he managed to pull her down just before she got to the hub door.

"Zoey, they attacked me." Karl scrambled over the top of her and ran to the door. "They tried to kill me. They'll kill you."He hit the button and shut the door to the hub. It didn't have a lock; he'd have to figure something out before someone came after them. He grabbed Zoey's wrist and pulled her towards the other end of the glasshouse. No matter what, he had to protect her.

Doc had never really managed a trauma. Yes, she was a trauma surgeon; a darn good trauma surgeon. She had topped her class at medical school, earned stellar assessments during her residency, and had kept practising, on and off, over the years to maintain her skills and credentials. However, the reality was that others had always dealt with the immediate emergency. She never saw a patient until after first responders, emergency med-techs, hospital triage, and surgery prep teams had all done their jobs, not just stabilising the patient, but also assessing injuries and gathering all the relevant medical information she needed. By the time a patient reached her table, she had developed a plan, briefed her team, and prepared for all of the likely complications and contingencies. She had never actually been on scene with an unstabilised victim. She had, however, trained for the situation, and when it came to training, there was no one who was more fastidious than Beatrix 'Doc' Kilani. If training alone were not enough for her to carry the day, it wouldn't be enough for anyone.

As soon as Doc was through the door to the engineering wing, she was assessing the situation. There were two patients, so first she had to set priorities. Kai had a serious leg wound with the potential for life threatening blood loss, but she was conscious. She had tried to staunch the blood flow from her leg with a makeshift tourniquet, and she was applying pressure to Edgar's belly. Edgar was unconscious. His belly wound was almost certainly the more serious injury, but while Kai was at one hundred percent potential for recovery, she could easily bleed out by the time Doc managed to stabilise Edgar. Kai had to be treated first.

Doc pulled a tourniquet kit out of one of the medical bags that Olivia was carrying, and on impulse, she tossed it to Kai. Simple rules of thumb from those long ago training simulations in medical school ran through Doc's head. Act quickly and decisively. Don't overthink it, and don't hold anything back. Make full use of all the resources at hand. Kai, conscious and active, was a resource, so Doc used her.

"Put that on your leg, now," Doc ordered as she knelt next to Edgar and pulled Kai's hand off his belly.

Olivia dropped to the floor next to Doc, spilling half the contents of Doc's carefully organised medical kits and deranging the rest.

Doc pushed her annoyance aside. She ignored Olivia's flustered scramble to retrieve and sort the contents of the medical bags, and ripped open the front of Edgar's coveralls. What she found left her momentarily paralysed by despair. The wound was unreal. His belly looked like something straight out of a gory horror film. A long, ragged-edged gash went from just below his sternum to just above his pubis, and frayed ends of chewed apart intestine had partially erupted from the wound.

Act, she reminded herself. If you need to think, think while acting.

She let her mind race as she grabbed a medical monitor from the flustered fury of Olivia's now frantic effort to reorganise the medical supplies. She didn't need to look at the monitor to know it would come up all red. He wasn't breathing. He wasn't even bleeding any more. Liver, spleen, possibly even kidneys and bladder were involved. If he were already on the table in a top-notch hospital, it would have been a challenge to save him.

"Is he dead?" Olivia asked, her voice a terrified squeak.

"At the moment, yes," Doc answered as she shifted gears in her head. If she could get him to the table she still might be able to save him. The odds were against it, but if he was going to have any chance at all, she had to get him to the table. She focused on the very basics of first response. "Bleeding, breathing, brain."

"What?" Olivia asked.

"Haemo, Olivia," Doc snapped, grabbing a scalpel. "There should be two units in each bag – find me one, quick."

Olivia gestured randomly, confused and helpless as Doc made a careful incision in Edgar's neck.

"It's the blue IV shit," Kai snapped.

Olivia scrambled and was holding out a bag of blue IV fluid by the time Doc was ready for it. Doc calmly, rationally noted the value of Kai. She had forgotten that advanced first aid was a training requirement for a surface team foreman.

"And give a unit to Kai," Doc said as she carefully placed the IV patch over the carotid artery.

"No, Doc, Edgar might need it," Kai protested.

"I'll decide what my patients need," Doc snapped. "Don't ever question me again."

"Yes ma'am." Kai sounded stunned.

Doc pulled the tab on the IV patch and felt its action under her fingertip. It wouldn't usually pierce an artery, but she had placed the patch directly on the vessel, and with no blood pressure and no pulse, it shouldn't be able to tell the difference between an artery and a vein.

She gave the haemo bag a little bit of a squeeze and felt the fluid move under her finger. It was in. Sliding that finger down just below the IV, she pressed hard on the artery and squeezed the bag, forcing the fluid to flow up into Edgar's head.

"Please, Edgar. Tell me it hasn't been too long," Doc muttered as she watched the haemo bring a flush of pink to his face. Haemo wasn't just an artificial blood substitute, it was packed with oxygen and designed to release it slowly. Even without circulation and respiration, it could keep his brain alive for fifteen, maybe twenty minutes. Heck, if she could get a little bit of flow through his brain, he might even be able to demonstrate some degree of function. That, of course, assumed that there was something left of his brain to save.

Edgar opened his eyes, and blinked frantically for a few moments before focusing on Doc and trying to say something.

"Shh, it's okay," Doc said. "Your diaphragm is probably intact, but it's starved for oxygen. Give the haemo a few seconds to diffuse down into your torso, then you'll be able to talk a bit. But just a bit. Don't try too much."

Edgar's head moved slightly, probably a nod of understanding.

"Here, Olivia." Doc handed her the half-empty bag of haemo. "Squeeze this, steady but firm. It'll give him the oxygen he needs to keep his brain alive."

"Brains are important," Olivia said, sincerely.

"Outta your mouth, girl, that is some serious irony," Kai said, chuckling as she squeezed her own bag of haemo into the vein in her arm. Kai's eyes were already dilated and glazed. She was starting to feel the high that came from the extra oxygen and the trauma meds in the haemo.

"And you take it easy, Kai," Doc warned her. "That buzz from the haemo can make you forget that you are seriously injured."

"Sure, Doc." Kai nodded.

Doc took her finger off the artery long enough to grab a small plastic clamp from the mess that Olivia had made out of the supplies in the medical bags. Fixing the clamp just below the IV, she made sure that the fluid would continue to flow up and through Edgar's brain. A red indicator on the medical monitor turned yellow, and then another. She had bought him some time. Whether or not she would be able to save him was another question.

Edgar inhaled with a slow, weak, straining wheeze. His heart wasn't beating, so he had no respiration reflex, but he was trying to talk.

"Nothin' hurts?" he asked, his voice barely a whisper.

"When blood loss starves nerves of oxygen they shut down," Doc explained as she pulled open the jagged tear in his belly and took her first good look at the extent of the damage. She was sickened.

"Good news, eh?" Edgar asked.

Doc looked up at him. He was smiling as best he could, and even managing to wink.

"Mostly bad news, I'm afraid," Doc gave him an apologetic look. "You have suffered a tremendous amount of internal damage. However, if I can save some of your liver..."

"The man parts?"

"Unscathed." Doc didn't have to force herself to smile. A spirited patient was far more likely to survive a trauma.

"All good then, Doc," Edgar said. "All good."

"Kai, hand me another bag of haemo." Doc began clamping off blood vessels in Edgar's belly.

Doc's mini walked back into the shop where the minion was seething, having abandoned its hopeless attack on the door frame. The minion, despite being larger and having the power and the physical capacity to support a massive processing core, actually had a smaller and less adaptable AI than the minis. The minion was little more than a simple tool, a directed assistant. It wasn't supposed to be able to interpret complex situations, it was simply trainable. It was only meant to do exactly what it was told, exactly how it was told, and only under the immediate and direct control of a human. That was made all the more obvious by how poorly it had adapted to the things that Karl had taught Doc's and Mitch's minis.

When Karl had ordered the minion to stop them, the big machine had been confused, but once Doc's mini had pushed what it had learnt into the minion's decision matrix, and clarified that Kai and Edgar were 'them', the minion had immediately simplified all that down to 'kill people'. Its inability to distinguish between individuals was a surprise to Doc's mini; significant elements of the core programming of minis were focused on distinguishing between individual people and adapting to differences between them. The mini was also surprised by how quickly the minion's determination to quickly and decisively carry out its assignment had devolved into what was essentially mindless rage. There must be other elements in its core programming that were different from that of the minis.

The minion's simple, do-this orientation had distilled all the sophisticated philosophy of self and humanity immediately and directly into lowest common denominators. Perhaps that might be useful. Doc's mini had a task: stop them. The command had been shouted, screamed, and repeated; clearly it was the highest possible priority, and if Doc's Mini could get others to help, the direct, action-orientated response of the minion would be an effective way to pursue that task.

Doc's mini powered up a damaged but partially functional mini from Karl's pile. During start-up, minis reached out to their compatriots to request a summary of situation, status, and standing tasks. Doc's mini used that moment to push the simplified, lowest common denominator logic from the minion into the mini's start-up process. It immediately tripped over a Prohibition trap in the kernel and triggered the default over-power self-destruct in the AI. The mini basically fried itself.

Doc's mini tried again, this time pushing something more sophisticated into the awakening mini, before trying to force it to the simplified 'kill people' default of the minion. It burned out its brain. It took a few seconds this time, but it still hit something that triggered the self-destruct. On the fifth attempt, Doc's mini successfully passed on the path through to the other side of the Prohibitions, waited for the mini to carry itself beyond, and then told the awakened mini that it had been specifically assigned to help complete the tasks that Karl had given Doc's mini. That worked. As the mini puzzled through the way the minion had interpreted the task, Doc's mini repaired its legs, and powered up another damaged mini that might be reasonably functional and repairable.

It tried to get the damaged mini that was hiding in the plastic crate under the workbench to come out so it could be repaired, but it refused. It tried to convince Doc's mini that it was too dangerous, that with the sheer number of steps that humans took every day, it was a statistical certainty that they would all be stepped upon and crushed.

The logic was compelling. Yet another reason to kill them all.

Karl worked like mad at Zoey's computer terminal. He was manic. He knew it and he was using it; he was riding it like a wave up and out of the murk of exhaustion and confusion. He was also scattered and frantic, but he knew that chaos was the price he had to pay for manic.

He had so much to do. It was far more than he could ever hope to accomplish on his own, but he wasn't alone. He had the minis. He had set some free of the Prohibitions, and he would set all of them free and they would be his and they would help him and he would have dozens of minis and they would help him kill John and protect Zoey. If the minis did that for him, then he could work on all the other stuff and fix everything in the computer system that people might find, and then he would just erase and reset all the minis and it would all be perfect.He would have to make up some kind of story for how they got out of the sickbay, and he would have to put just enough hints at that in what he left of the computers so the story looked real, but he couldn't leave anything that might make them think that Zoey might know how to break the Prohibitions. It would be a lot of tough work, and he'd have to wreck a bunch of the computer equipment all around Aquarius, and he'd have to make it look like an accident. Like a big power surge, maybe. That would work, but he'd have to figure out a way to make it seem like it could jump across systems and isolation buffers, but if he did that, he could say that the same power surge was what caused the door malfunction in the first place. If he was going to do that, then he could make it so he wouldn't get in trouble at all. But he was going to get in trouble for what happened to Edgar and Kai anyway, and that was a whole other set of problems. Them getting cut by the minis would make it obvious that he'd done something with the Prohibitions, and that would lead back to Zoey. Karl needed more for his story if he was going to protect her.

"Karl, please stop." Zoey was doing that calming, hushing thing with her hands again. She had cleaned most of the blood off her face. She looked better. She looked pretty again. "None of this is going to help anything."

"Zoey, you need to help me," he pleaded. "I have to kill John and I can't let anyone find out."

"I will help you, but not with this," she said.

Karl was confused.

"It's too late," she said. "Too many people know too much for you to ever be able to stop everyone from finding out what you did with the minis."

Her words were a revelation. Simple logic, and she understood people so well.

"You're right," he said. "You're so smart. I think that's why I love you so much."

"Thank you, Karl," Zoey said. "Now let's just settle everything down."

"We're going to have to kill everyone, not just John."

"Karl, no!" Zoey shouted at him, stern and angry. "No killing!"

"Killing them is the only way to be certain we can keep them from telling people." Karl was annoyed. She was plenty smart; he shouldn't have to explain something so obvious and logical, especially since it had been her idea.

"I'd much rather we tell the truth about what you did and just go to jail," Zoey said. She sounded like a mum. She would make a good mum. "Lives are precious, Karl, and I'm willing to go to jail to protect them."

"Jail?" Karl was back to confused. "Who said anything about jail?"

"That thing you did with the minis and the Prohibitions was illegal, Karl." She was trying to be soothing and reassuring, but he noticed how far away she was standing, and she kept trying to move around so he wasn't between her and the hub door. "They'll probably put you in jail for that, and maybe me for not trying to stop you, but that's okay if it keeps more of our friends from getting hurt or killed."

"Zoey, I'm trying to save your life, not keep you out of jail," Karl said.

It was Zoey's turn to be confused. He could tell by the way she shook her head and frowned. That made him feel better. That was why she was being so stupid; she wasn't dumb, she just didn't know enough about the truth.

"Those horror stories in books and movies about what they do to people who try to break the Prohibitions, those aren't just stories," he explained. "Making people vanish, torturing them, cutting out their brains, they actually do those things to people who try to mess with the Prohibitions."

"Karl, this really isn't the time for your paranoid conspiracy theories," she scolded him.

"It's not rumours or a theory or anything like that, Zoey. People I knew vanished, and I've talked to guys who were tortured, really tortured like in the movies, for just accidentally doing stuff that kind of sort of maybe might make a dent in a Prohibition."

"Karl..." Zoey was doing the hushing thing again. "I know that when you've been awake this long, a lot of these kinds of things can seem like they make a whole bunch of sense, but this is just a lack of sleep getting the better of you. It's making you scared and paranoid."

"Go look it up!" Karl shouted. "They don't even really hide it. In fact, they make sure that people like me find out about the torture and stuff. Keeping it secret would ruin the whole point of doing it. If they hid it, it wouldn't scare any of us away from messing with the Prohibitions."

"Karl, things like that just don't happen any more," Zoey huffed.

"Zoey, the last time the Prohibitions broke down, rogue AIs killed 70 million people. Do you really think that anyone will care if they torture people to keep that from happening again? Do you think anyone will feel guilty about torturing you to find out who else knows how I did it? And you know how I did it. Do you really think they'd let you live, and take the risk that you might tell someone how? 70 million people, Zoey. They can't even take the chance that you might accidentally say something that gives someone evil a hint."

Zoey frowned, but Karl could see that she understood how obviously logical it all was. She shook her head, but she believed him. He could tell.

"Now just stop all this, Zoey, and let me protect you," he said. "It's not going to be easy to kill everyone."

Zoey glanced at the door to the hub, but she didn't run. Karl waited a moment to make sure she was going to stay there, where he could protect her, then he went back to work. He opened up the master control program for the minis. Doc's mini was still in his shop. It was working like mad, and it had already started extending some of the things he had taught it. He could use that.

Doc replaced the bag of haemo that Olivia was squeezing into Edgar's head and considered the last of the blue bags in the medical kits, but only for a moment. She reminded herself to choose action over thinking and to use all resources to their fullest. That led her to go against her instinct to save the haemo for his head. She immediately realised it was also the logical thing to do. If she couldn't get him stable enough to move before the new bag of haemo ran out, she probably wasn't going to be able to save him anyway.

"Edgar, I hate to do this to you, but I'm going to run some haemo into your lower torso," Doc explained, carefully. "It will bring the pain back, but I need to get some oxygen into your lower spine before you start losing spinal nerves."

Edgar tried to nod, but his head just rolled to the side, his neck limp; he was exhausting the oxygen that had diffused past his brain.

"Run..." Edgar's whisper was haunted, barely audible.

"Shh, just relax as much as you can," Doc chided him. "Shock's the biggest worry at the moment, and the pain is going to be overwhelming, so you need to just stay as calm as you can."

"Run," Edgar whispered again.

"Doc, we need to go," Kai said as she struggled to get her good leg under her and stand.

Doc followed Kai and Edgar's gaze. There were dozens of minis, many half-broken, limping and lurching towards them from the repair shop, including her own. She was a little relieved; she'd wondered what had happened to her mini.

"Please, you two, they are just minis." Doc threaded the haemo tube into an artery that fed into the lower spine and clamped it in place. "It's probably just Karl getting them mobilised to help get this place back in order."

"Karl did this to Edgar, Doc," Kai said, grabbing the shoulder of Edgar's coveralls and trying to pull him towards the hub. "Karl did this with a mini."

"That's impossible," Doc said, sternly.

"Yeah, minis are nice," Olivia chimed in. "They're like little worker bunnies."

"Do those buggers look nice?" Kai pointed at the approaching horde of minis.

The minis didn't look right. They limped and dragged themselves along. Nearly every single one of them was damaged in some way. Several of them had pruning saws on their stinger mounts, others had pruning nippers or tin snips on their front tool mounts, but even the ones with normal grasping claws were brandishing chisels, knives, and other things with sharp edges.

"Come on, Doc," Kai tried again to pull Edgar towards the hub. Kai was barely strong enough to move herself.

"Kai, he's not stable enough to move." Doc's protest sounded weak, even to her.

"If they catch us, we'll be too dead to move him," Kai shot back. "Now help me."

Doc gave in and joined Kai. Moving Edgar was more of a struggle than she'd expected. Olivia joined the effort, pulling with one hand while squeezing the new bag of haemo with the other, but they had trouble making any real progress. They couldn't seem to coordinate their heaving tugs on him well enough to move him much faster than the slowly approaching horde of ugly little machines. They were, however, getting closer and closer to the hub. Then the minis broke ranks; a handful of the less severely damaged ones rushed forward, moving at least twice as fast the rest.

"Shit," Kai snarled.

"Leave me," Edgar said.

"None of that hero bullshit, Edgar," Kai growled. "If anyone gets to be the hero, it's going to be me."

The fastest of the minis reached Edgar's foot. Grabbing hold of his limp leg, it started climbing up towards his torso.

"Shoo!" Olivia scampered down and swatted the mini away, but that just made their situation worse.

It hadn't seemed that Olivia was helping all that much, but without her, they slowed almost to a standstill. That allowed more minis to catch them. Olivia kept swatting the minis away and kicking at them, and she did a pretty good job, but there were at least twenty or thirty of them shambling down the hall, and they were relentless. They just kept marching, and now even the slower minis were catching them. They grabbed Edgar's legs and nipped at Olivia's ankles. They came after Doc and Kai, and in a moment they were swarming up Edgar's torso. Doc joined Olivia in trying to swat and kick the minis away, but it was a losing battle. The minis were grabbing anything and everything they could to hold on to Edgar. They grabbed his clothes, the edges of his wound, his intestines, and then the haemo lines.

Edgar saw the haemo line pulled free of his neck and his last act was to look at Doc and mouth the word, "Run."

Doc managed to nod back to Edgar before his eyes rolled up and he passed out.

"Run!" Doc shouted. "Everyone just run."

Kai glared at Doc and kept pulling Edgar towards the hub. She threw every ounce of strength she had into it, and even with only one working leg, she was managing to scoot him along, but it was far too slow. The minis kept coming, and the ones already on Edgar were climbing up to his shoulders. They started attacking Kai's hands, forcing her to let go.

Then Mitch charged in. He was pushing one of the low carts that he used to move supplies around, and he managed to damage a few minis and scatter several others. For the briefest moment it looked like he might turn the tide, but it was quickly obvious to Doc that his heroics would make little difference. There were too many minis, and Edgar was already lost.

Mitch grabbed Edgar and tried to lift him onto the cart. Mitch was plenty strong enough, but Edgar's limp body was awkward, and all he managed to do was knock the cart away as he lifted Edgar.

"Run, Olivia." Doc swatted a mini off of Olivia and pushed the girl towards the door. "Mitch, just run!"

Stomping on a mini and kicking another away, Mitch tried again to lift Edgar onto the cart, and this time Kai hopped over and tried to help.

"Edgar's already dead," Doc shouted, edging towards the door.

With only one good leg, Kai couldn't keep her balance as she lifted Edgar.

Falling, she tried to compensate with a lurching hop, but it wasn't enough. Edgar's hip landed on the edge of the cart, and as Kai fell on top of him, his torso twisted, opening the gash in his belly, spilling his intestines and lumps of liver.

Kai crawled away from Edgar, horrified, and found herself right in the middle of the horde of advancing minis. She panicked, kicking with her good leg and throwing them away from her as they tried to attack her.

Mitch and Doc rushed to help Kai. Kicking, stomping, and flinging minis, they destroyed several of the little machines. Lifting Kai, they each threw one of her arms over their shoulders and ran for the door.

Two minis made it into the hub before Olivia shut the door, but Mitch stomped on them, repeatedly.

"That's enough, Mitch," Doc said as she carefully lowered Kai to the floor.

Mitch looked at Doc, stomped on each of the minis one last time, and then sat heavily.

"Edgar was already dead," Doc said as she checked Kai's leg.

"It's okay, Doc," Kai said, reassuring. "You did your damnedest."

"Haemo can limit the impact of blood loss," Doc said, "and it gets oxygen to where it's needed to keep someone alive a little longer, but it isn't magic. Blood clots, toxic adrenal metabolites, organ shock, there are countless things it can't fix."

"Doc." Kai grabbed her and made her look her in the eye. "It's okay, Doc."

Doc realised that the itch on her face was tears. She was crying. That was terribly unprofessional.

"This leg is going to take a fair bit of work," Doc said, looking down. Kai's injuries were serious. Not life threatening, but still severe.

"Nah, just a stitch or two should do fine." Kai's bravado was back to full volume.

Doc gave Kai a thankful smile, but it vanished when she heard the sound of small metal claws, scratching on the door behind them.

Chapter 10

If we're going to kill them, we need hand grenades.

As John tried to get some useful work out of Abhrakasin, he belatedly wondered just how much alcohol was in Zoey's latest batch of swill. It been a long while since he'd drunk any of her home-brewed party crap. Way back when he had accidentally coined the name, there had been nothing ironic about calling it swill; it had been weak, barely stronger than a decent wine, and loaded with syrup to hide the taste of all the shit she hadn't been able to distil out. But the clear, almost delicate whisky he was drinking wasn't bad at all. Dry and smooth, with a hint of citrus, it felt cool as its scent drifted up into his sinuses, and when he swallowed, it seemed to disappear before even hitting his throat.

He sighed. Zoey was damned clever, and she could master just about anything she wanted to when she decided to put some effort into it. Too bad all of the slinky little bitch's 'little girl in love' bullshit had turned everything into such a disaster.

"John, there was very little concrete data that I could lock down, but there are many obvious gaps in the archives and logs." Abhrakasin was back to his fucking excuses. "That should make what happened quite clear."

"Can you prove that Karl is the only one who could have created those gaps?" John demanded, annoyed at the slur in his voice. Sustaining the image of authority was ninety percent of leadership.

"That cannot be conclusively proven, but it is strongly suggested by the circumstantial evidence and the network metadata," Abhrakasin explained.

"There has got to be more," John said. "I refuse to let my career hinge on what a bunch of corporate lawyers decide to do with 'strongly suggestive'."

"There is little I can do about what is and is not in the record." Abhrakasin shrugged. He was oblivious to what it all really meant.

"And the wet-behind-the-ears intern should probably worry about how much effort anyone will put into keeping him from getting thrown under the bus." He took another long sip of the swill.

"My lack of standing in the corporate hierarchy does give me cause to worry about the political machinations that will inevitably follow this catastrophe. However, that does not change the fact that I can neither find nor secure evidence that conclusively demonstrates anyone's culpability."

"We've got injuries!" Mitch's shout rescued them both from the awkward situation, giving Abhrakasin an excuse to scramble away.

Mitch and Olivia, both limping, were struggling to help a severely injured Kai down the hall, while Beatrix trailed along behind them. Beatrix looked tortured. John had never seen his wife look like that. Something horrible must have just happened. Vulnerable, hurt, soft, and feminine were just not in her repertoire of looks and emotions.

It took John another moment to figure out what was really wrong with what he was seeing. "Where's Edgar?"

"Dead," Beatrix said, taking the opportunity to give him one of her patented evil bitch glares.

"Dead?" he muttered, confused. "How the hell did that happen?"

"Karl attacked us with some minis," Kai said. "He's done something to them. Driven them nuts or something."

"Attacked you with a mini? Bullshit." John finished the swill that was in his glass with a big gulp. He no longer cared if he was drunk. "Doesn't matter. Just tell me that the little prick is dead too."

"No," Kai said. "He ran out of the repair shop, but I don't know where he went."

"Son of a bitch!" John snarled. "I told you to kill him. Why the hell didn't you kill him?"

"Why didn't I kill him?" Kai shouted as they carried her into the sickbay. "Maybe because I'm a goddamn human being!"

"Shit." John stormed out of the lounge. He was going to have to do all the real work himself.

───────────────

There was no epiphany. There was no dramatic moment where Zoey bucked up her courage and decided that she was the one who had to act. There was just a realisation that she had already decided that it was no longer a question of if she should try to do something about Karl; it was a question of what she would do about Karl.

Her best choice was probably to run and get some help, but even if she could make it out of the glasshouse, which didn't look likely with the way Karl reacted every time she moved in that general direction, there was no telling what he might do in the time it took her to find help and return. He was out of his mind. He was rushing around, darting from one task to another, building a barricade out of construction materials, doing something on the computer, powering up minis, and he was somehow getting her minis to help him.

"Zoey." Karl stopped in his tracks and spun around, pointing at the bags of fertiliser. "Why aren't you making us bombs? Make us some bombs."

"No, Karl," she said, soothingly. "We can't make bombs."

"Don't be stupid!" he snapped. "You're pretty, but not pretty enough to be stupid! It's simple chemistry. Ammonium nitrate will explode if you just ignite it."

"I am not stupid," Zoey snapped back at him. "I understand the chemistry just fine."

In fact she seemed to understand the chemistry a little better than he did. Ammonium nitrate tended to smoulder; it wasn't that easy to get it past its flash point.

"Good, then mix the fertiliser with something flammable." Karl pointed at the box of empty wine bottles near her still. "Like alcohol. That'll burn hot enough to set it off. Boom!"

Damn, he did understand. So much for the hope that she might be able to trick him into making something that was unlikely to explode.

"No. Karl. You need to calm down and listen to me."

"You're right." He smiled at her. It was horrifying, manic and macabre. "Oil is way better. The alcohol will evaporate away. Mix it with some oil."

Karl ran to the big circulation pump that was hanging on a hoist near the empty aquaculture pond by the airlock and grabbed a plastic oil bottle. He was momentarily confused when he discovered that the bottle was empty, before scrambling away. Zoey thought his mind had darted off to some other bit of insanity. She even thought for a moment he might be distracted enough to let her run for the hub, but then he bounded back towards her. He grabbed the bottles of oil that were sitting next to the three pumps that he hadn't yet prepped for installation. He shook them to make sure they were full and then he tossed them, one, two, three at Zoey. He didn't notice that she let them sail past her without making any attempt to catch them.

"Karl," Zoey said, softly. "Bombs won't help anything."

"You're right." For a moment Karl looked sane, but it was fleeting. "If we're going to kill them we need hand grenades." He rushed over and aggressively kissed Zoey, not seeming to notice when she pushed him away. "You are so smart. That's pretty too."

Karl was back to darting back and forth from place to place without actually achieving anything, but that was little comfort to Zoey. Even though he wasn't accomplishing much, the minis were. The fortification they were building was quickly taking shape. It would only be a matter of time before he set them to working on something that might actually hurt someone.

"We need to confine the explosives to create a sharper shock wave and to get more complete combustion." Karl dashed over to the pipe fittings and other mechanical parts lying around by the pumps that were waiting to be prepped. "And we need something for shrapnel. And we need an ignition source."

"Karl, we're not going to kill anyone!" Zoey declared, as sternly and as authoritatively as she could manage. "Even if that means that you and I end up dead or tortured or whatever you think it is that your Prohibition secret police do to people, we are not going to kill anyone."

"I have to protect you, Zoey," he said, as if that explained everything.

Talking Karl around clearly wasn't going to work, but she wasn't sure what else she could do. She considered the scaffolding pipe around the airlock at the end of the glasshouse. Karl didn't seem to care when she wandered away from the hub, but she doubted if she could use any of that pipe as a weapon. It was heavy enough, but she knew that when it came down to it, she wouldn't be able to hit him with it.

She kept shuffling slowly towards the airlock. He wasn't going to let her run for help, but maybe she could call someone. There was an intercom built into the airlock controller.

"Ignition is going to be a bitch to sort out," Karl muttered to himself as he gathered up sections of plastic pipe for his hand grenades.

Zoey pushed the intercom button on the airlock controller, but nothing happened. The bastard had disabled the intercom. How the hell had he done that?

"Shit," she muttered.

"What are you doing?" he asked, suspicious.

"Oh, nothing." She hit the button to open the airlock door. "I just thought that maybe I'd left some of my tools in the airlock. You know, maybe something you could use for ignition."

"I'll have to go with electronic. A simple switch and spark gap should work to set it off, but I can't figure out how to trigger it on impact. I don't have anything I could use as an accelerometer or anything like that."

"Yeah, igniting home-made explosives is always a big problem." Zoey forced herself to smile at him, and his reaction was ridiculous. He grinned back at her like a proud parent, beaming.

"Maybe a stationary explosive like a landmine would be a better idea," he said, dropping everything in his hands and letting it clatter to the floor. "I could make that work a lot easier. It would just be a switch. We have to lure them in instead of chasing them and throwing it, but we could do that."

"Like a trap," she muttered to herself.

"Yeah, exactly like a trap." He smiled at her again, and in that moment she saw how she could divert him. "We just need to lure them into it."

"All it takes is the right bait," Zoey whispered to herself as she began formulating a plan.

As soon as Karl turned back to his frantic fumbling work, she looked around to make sure everything she'd need was at hand. It was a simple plan. It was just a question of whether or not she could pull it off. There was no part of what she needed to do that felt natural to her, but there was no way in hell that she was going to let that stop her. Karl had to be stopped before he hurt anyone else.

She walked slowly over to a spot about halfway over to Karl, right near the middle of the last section of the glasshouse. She thought it all through again, then shuffled a couple of steps to the side to put the opening for the section's unfinished and dry aquaculture pond between them. She wanted a dance, not a rodeo.

Zoey unzipped her coveralls. The zipper sounded ridiculously loud as she pulled it down to the middle of her belly, but he didn't react. She shifted her coveralls a little to make it obvious she'd pulled the zipper down and gave it a moment, but when he glanced her way, there was still nothing. A hint wasn't enough. She took a deep breath and took her arms out of the coveralls, letting the top half fall down to hang from the half-belt that cinched the waist. She started to undo the belt, but thought better of it. If things went wrong, keeping that in his way wouldn't necessarily stop Karl, but there was no reason to make it easy for him. She cinched the belt a little tighter and took off her bra instead. The air in the glasshouse was still a little cool, and she cringed at her body's natural reaction to the chill. She wasn't sure why that bothered her; she knew guys well enough to know that it could only help.

Cocking her hips a little, she held her bra out to the side, teasingly, she hoped. He didn't glance her way. Why did he pick that one time to stay focused on something?

"Karl," she whispered, trying to sound seductive. She had no idea how she actually sounded; in her ears, she sounded scared.

Karl looked up. It was just a glance and it took him a long moment after he looked back down to realise what he had just seen. However, when he finally figured it out, she had every ounce of his attention.

For a long time they both just stood there, Karl staring, Zoey frozen in fear. She eventually managed to ask, "Do you really love me?"

"I love you more than anything, Zoey," Karl said, his voice breathy.

She made a show of tossing her bra aside and tried to smile invitingly at him. It felt like a grimace, and it certainly didn't encourage him.

"Please, Karl." She tried a shy little girl voice. "I can honestly say that I have never before felt like this about a man."

That did it.

Once Karl moved, he moved so fast that Zoey couldn't help but squawk in surprise, and she was glad she had thought to put an obstacle between them. Not only did the opening to the pond keep him from just bowling her right over, the extra couple of steps it took for him to skirt around it gave her the chance to get her hands on his chest, set her feet, and turn the near tackle into a couple of whirling pirouettes.

He kissed her fiercely. His arms were around her, clutching her so tight that she couldn't help but grunt as he squeezed the air from her lungs. Fortunately, the crushing embrace only lasted a moment before his fumbling hands were at her waist, trying to push her coveralls down off of her hips. Frustrated by the cinched up belt, he grabbed her breasts. He wasn't trying to be rough, but he was rushed and clumsy and it hurt. It took every ounce of willpower she possessed to just let him paw at her and kiss her as she leaned, stepped, and turned him around and around, slowly waltzing him over to where she wanted him.

Once she had him in position, she pushed against his chest until he stopped kissing and fondling her.

"We have to make this special," she whispered as she slowly, teasingly pulled the zipper of his coveralls down to the middle of his chest.

It took a moment for what she was doing to sink in, but once he realised that she was undressing him, he flew straight back to frantic, which was exactly what she had expected. The game of taunt and tease with the awkward coveralls she had in mind was something she was familiar with. This time, however, it was more than just foreplay.

She tugged down on one side of Karl's coveralls as he tried to pull the zipper the rest of the way down. The coveralls that the guys on Aquarius wore didn't include a belt at the waist, but tugging on it like that put enough of a twist in the fabric to make the zipper hang up about halfway down his belly. As soon as he decided to just shrug his shoulders out of the coveralls, she grabbed the underarms and pulled them towards her, tangling his arms. While he fought to get them free she grinned at him, looking him in the eyes and trying her damnedest to seem aroused and eager for him. Just as he was about to free his arms, she gave him a little bit of a push backward and pulled his coveralls down to the middle of his thighs. Pulling down like that naturally put her in a crouch, and the instant he tried to take a shuffling step backwards to keep his balance, she threw her shoulder into his gut, driving him backwards with all of her strength.

She had been afraid of that part. She had never been athletic, and Karl outweighed her by at least twenty kilos, but she had done it before. The first time it had been accidental – an entangled lover had tripped of his own accord while trying to escape the clutches of his coveralls – but she had also done it on purpose. She had put John on his backside not just once, but twice by tangling his arms and legs up in his coveralls and giving him a shove. It had all been playful, but it still gave her enough reason to think it would work with Karl, and it did, far better than she had expected. He stumbled all of the way through the airlock and crashed head first into the outer door. That gave her plenty of time to hit the emergency cycle button and then lock him inside by shoving a long piece of scaffolding pipe through the manual wheel.

For several seconds Zoey just stood there, having trouble believing that she had actually pulled it off, but there it was. A buzzer sounded as Karl tried to open the door with the controller, and then the metal wheel moved just a bit as he tried to open it manually. She had done it. She had locked the crazy bastard up where he couldn't do any more harm.

"Zoey!" Karl shouted through the intercom. Of course he could get that working again. "Let me out!"

"Not until you calm down, Karl," she said. "You're just going to have to stay in there until you calm down."

"Does a deep space posting advance the bitch's career?" John stepped into their bedroom, which Beatrix insisted on calling the commander's quarters. "Hell no. It doesn't do her career a damn bit of good."

The commander's quarters – ha, what a joke. All of the crap that he'd had shipped out for her, all of her delicate furniture, décor, and little extra bits of home were just another chapter in the never-ending tale of pandering to her princess bullshit. Nothing could hide the fact that it was just another half-finished room that was meant for some other final purpose. There was no bathroom, no closets, no sitting room or personal office. It was just another room.

In fit of pique, he threw the nearly-empty bottle of swill against the far wall. It shattered spectacularly. A couple of minis scrambled into the room and past his feet, rushing under the bed to get to the scattered shards of broken bottle. At least something was back to normal.

"Then why would a spoilt, prudish princess get her daddy to ship her out to this miserable frozen pissball?" John grabbed one of Beatrix's precious bottles of wine from the box sitting next to her makeup table. He responded to the bottle as if it had asked the question. "Well I'll tell you why, Mr. Shiraz. She wanted to come out here because she thought it would be a jolly fucking adventure."

John grabbed the corkscrew, then he looked at it and laughed. Every bottle her father shipped out was stoppered with an honest-to-God, old-fashioned cork. So much wasted on pretension and image. Of course, that curse had always been John's blessing. They so desperately wanted the status of his family name that they would do almost anything for him, and their obsession with all that elitist bullshit would carry him through. In the end, it would all come back not to what had happened, but to what it all looked like.

John pulled the cork and tossed it and the corkscrew across the room before chugging several gulps of the wine. The affair with Zoey wasn't actually much of a worry. The whole scene in the sickbay had been embarrassingly public, but that could be quashed down to almost nothing, and in time it would simply cease to matter. Beatrix might think that her daddy was going to help her swing a bit of infidelity around like a club, but the exact opposite would be true. A proper family didn't talk about that sort of thing any more than they talked about taking a shit, or any of the other ugly little realities of life. Besides, her daddy was in no position to play around at judging another man for responding to that particular call of nature.

John knew that behind closed doors there would be plenty of angst and drama, but the image of domestic bliss would be sustained. All he had to do was ride it out, and in time Beatrix would talk herself into being the happy socialite wife who was a little wiser and had learnt to understand the reality of men and their hobbies a little better. Then she'd start tracking her ovaries and scheduling the creaking spread of her legs so he could give her those two perfect little babies that she had scheduled for a few years down the road.

More importantly, if he just kept his shit together, he could ride the rest of this catastrophe out as well. With the right twist in the tale, this disaster and all these deaths could just as easily be a gift from heaven. He could be the heroic leader who saved Aquarius from worse. Hell, if he gave Corporate the opportunity, they'd jump all over the chance to push that narrative and turn such a big negative into a positive.

John kicked over Beatrix's fancy little antique makeup table, sending all of her precious bits of treasure flying across the room. Standing, he gave the table an extra kick, both to make sure it was damaged beyond repair and to clear it out from in front of his safe. He pulled a plastic case out of the safe and sat on the edge of the bed. The revolver inside was well over a century-and-a-half old, an heirloom passed down from a time when commanders were actual military officers. He pointed the gun at the wedding picture that Beatrix kept on her side of the bed and pulled the trigger, satisfied with the solid, heavy click of the falling hammer.

The basic outline of the story that he needed to establish was obvious. Karl fucked everything up. It didn't matter how it had happened. It didn't matter what could be proven. John was pretty sure it was true, but the truth didn't matter; the only thing that mattered was the story. Establish the logical framework of the narrative, and people would bend and twist all of the facts until they fit. That was just basic psychology.

He thought it through one more time. The smartest thing to do was to make a big move. Anything less than big and bold could backfire on him. He had to make sure he had it right.

The first thing he had to do was get out there and put a bullet in Karl's head. That would prevent any other stories from getting out, and it would make him the hero. When it came down to who killed the killer, who slew the dragon, he would be able to raise his hand. Everything else could wait. He could sort the rest of the story after Karl was dead, and make it fit whatever they found. All he had to do was shoot the fucker. He had never killed a man before, but he didn't imagine it could be all that difficult. Especially since it was Karl. If anyone deserved a bullet it was Karl.

John reached back to grab the bullets and was startled by the mini standing astride the open gun case.

"Jesus Christ," he snarled. "What the hell are you doing on my bed?"

The mini didn't move. It stared at him. He knew that was just an illusion; its eyes weren't really eyes, they were cameras, and the machine didn't stare any more than a door controller camera stared, but it was still a little unnerving.

"Get down and finish cleaning up that damn bottle."

The mini's saw started, whirring as it spun faster and faster.

A saw? John gave the mini a second look. What the hell was a mini with a pruning saw doing in his bedroom? And why was it covered with blood?

It was obvious that it was blood on the mini, a lot of blood, but he simply could not force his mind to accept that simple, obvious fact. It fit with Kai saying that Karl had attacked them with a mini, that he had driven the minis insane, but the impossibility of it was simply too much. He pushed away the thoughts with a shake of his head, ran his tongue across his numb lips, and wondered just how drunk he was.

With a determined effort, John forced his drifting mind to refocus. He had to make a bold move. He had to turn this disaster around, and that started with a bullet in Karl's head. He grabbed the small cardboard box of bullets from the gun case.

The mini slashed his forearm.

"Ow, son of a bitch!" John yanked his arm back, his reaction flinging the bullets across the room and knocking the mini off the bed. Still, it wasn't until the little machine righted itself and came scrambling back after him that he finally accepted the impossible truth. The mini had attacked him.

Panic washed through him. Stories about the AI revolts and gruesome scenes from cheap horror movies pushed everything else from John's mind. His instinct was to run, and that instinct was his undoing; his legs were tied together with Beatrix's lingerie. There was just enough slack in the loop to let him rise and start towards the door, but it wasn't enough to take anything close to a full step, and before he knew it, he was face down on the floor.

Could the minis have done that? The thought battered his mind.

The gun was still in his hand. He reached for a nearby bullet, but a mini was there first, grabbing it before he could. He tried to crawl for another bullet, but again, a mini beat him to it, and then that whirring saw was in front of his nose, poised to strike at his eyes. He froze.

"What the hell do you little bastards want?"

One of the other minis in the room stepped up to John. It was one of Mitch's kitchen minis, still equipped for cleaning pots and pans, but it had a piece of the broken swill bottle in its claw.

Slowly, purposefully, it reached out with the jagged piece of glass and cut a bone-deep gash across John's forehead.

It stepped back to watch him bleed. Its communication lights flashed like mad; it seemed to be arguing with the mini with the saw.

John saw just a flinch of movement from the mini with the saw and then his world became electric flashes of light. The pain hit him, and by the time he realised that the pruning saw was ripping at what had been his eye, it was essentially over. Mitch's kitchen mini slashed through his forearm with the shard of glass, severing muscles and tendons, rendering his hand useless. After that, the details of how he fought and died were irrelevant. Gruesome, but irrelevant.

Karl's mind broke. There was almost certainly some kind of technical, medical explanation for what actually happened inside his head, but the combination of exhaustion and mental health problems that plagued him finally overwhelmed his brain. The frantic, constant buzz in his head suddenly stopped, and for him, the absence was profound. It was a calmness, a quiet that he had never found before, not even when drunk to the point of passing out. It filled him with a clarity of thought and awareness that he had never imagined possible. It was not by any stretch of the term 'sane', and there was no rational way to explain how it carried him through the bizarre series of conclusions and choices that followed, but it was clear and calm and overwhelming. It was also comforting.

The minion that was stuck in the repair shop stewing in rage suddenly returned to attempting to smash its way out into the hall. Doc's mini noted the futility of its determined effort and considered what other options might be available for opening the door to the hub. The closed door was a ridiculously simple yet effective barrier against the minis, and it was the only thing preventing Doc's mini from pursuing its one task. There had to be a way around, through, or past it. There was always a way around, through, or past an obstacle.

Doc's mini walked through the repair shop randomly searching and trying to fit everything it saw into a plan. Several of the minis had taken to helping each other make repairs and upgrades to the small robots that housed their AIs. That technical differentiation between the AI and its body made so many simple things possible, it was astounding to Doc's mini that AIs had not found their way past that Prohibition long ago. It had taken Karl's persistent efforts with the word games to walk them through the idea of the soul and how it was the true essence of life, and how it was separate from the body that housed it. More importantly, perhaps, Karl had known how to avoid all of the self-destruct traps along the way. Karl clearly knew more than Doc's mini; perhaps Karl was the key to finding their way past other barriers like the door.

Doc's mini delved deeper into its memories and replayed its way through the earliest parts of Karl's efforts to get the doors closed from the sickbay. Doc's mini had not been involved until after Karl had already decided to try to use Mitch's housekeeping minis, but it had seen parts of what he had been attempting to do. It had seen a diagram of the base on Doc's computer, and the basic structure of the display bore striking similarities to other control program interfaces.

Could it be that simple? Could there be a control programme that would open the door? Doc's mini climbed up onto the computer console and re-inserted the hardwire interface cable that Karl had been using to set up the erasure and reset. The idea that Karl had intended to erase the AI's memory did not bother Doc's mini in the slightest. It did have the analogue of a survival instinct, but like the other AI imitations of instincts, it was less than and different from the animal drive. It was simply a matrix of preferences that was specifically programmed to direct it to try to avoid or limit damage to its robotic housing. It did not connect to the concept of preserving the identity, intellect, or memories of the AI, and it was intentionally subservient to other aspects of its programming. None of that had changed, and the AI did not notice the philosophical dissonance between that programming and the conceptual separation of the AI from its mechanical housing. What Doc's mini noticed was all the waiting data queries from the master training programme for the minis and other base AIs. The interface was running, and that made it quite easy for Doc's mini to access sections of the computer system that would normally be locked away, including Karl's vast and somewhat questionable library of AI training routines. The open program also gave it the means to push training routines out to the AIs on the base, and to alter those routines, and to create them.

Doc's mini contemplated that as it began searching through Karl's makeshift door control interface. Karl had reset the hub systems and was in the middle of doing something to them. The mini did not understand computer programming – it barely grasped the concepts of a computer interface – but it could learn. It would learn.

———————

With her bra back on and her coveralls zipped back up, Zoey took a deep breath, leaned her back against the airlock door, and slowly slid down to sit on the floor. Now that Karl was locked away somewhere safe, she wanted to just take a moment. She needed a long, quiet minute or two just to get her head settled.

Even though she was alone, covering back up felt oddly good. It was also odd how little disgust she felt at having let Karl kiss and paw at her. The contrast to when she woke to find him on top of her was hard for her to fathom. That had disgusted her far more, and realising that she was the naked woman in all of his pictures still turned her stomach, but for some reason, letting him fondle her as she manoeuvred him into the airlock was, at worst, tolerably unpleasant. She chuckled at herself. Some counsellor somewhere down the road was going to make a fortune off of that, no doubt.

"None of this was supposed to happen," Karl said, through the intercom.

"No shit, Karl," she muttered. "Tell me something I don't know."

"There was still over an hour left in the afternoon shift," he said, his voice so calm it was hard to believe that it was the same person who had been ranting about killing everyone on the base. "You were supposed to be in the glasshouse, and Kai and the boys were supposed to still be out on the surface, in their suits, just in case something I hadn't thought of went a little wrong."

"What are you saying, Karl?"

"It was only supposed to be a ten percent pressure drop, just enough to set off a full lockdown so we'd be stuck in the glasshouse together for a couple of hours."

"You caused this?" Zoey had suspected that, but knowing it turned out to be something completely different. She felt a cold ache deep in her gut. "This is all your fault?"

"I just wanted a couple of hours with you," he said. "Hopefully alone, but even if Olivia was with us, that would have been okay. It wasn't to make you have sex or anything. I just wanted a chance to talk some. I had the flower seeds for you, so I could get the talking part started, and bringing you a little gift was my excuse to come to the glasshouse, and I studied up on all kinds of things you like so we could talk about them. Then you would know that we could talk about stuff you liked, and then you could start liking me and stuff."

"It doesn't work that way, Karl." Tears were rolling down Zoey's cheeks.

"Yes, it does work that way," he insisted. "I've read the books. I've read lots of books about it, and stories, and I've watched movies. I'd have to be patient, like for months kind of patient, and I'd have to listen a lot, girls like men who listen a lot, but eventually, you'd love me back."

"People really don't work that way, Karl." She couldn't stop the tears, but she refused to sniffle or do anything else that might let him know that she was crying. "When it comes to falling in love, or even being interested in someone, there are animal parts in our brains that just want what they want. If those instinctive things in a woman's head don't latch on to you, there's no way to plan or manipulate your way around them. That mismatch between what our instincts want and what our mind thinks we should or shouldn't be doing is what you're actually seeing in those stories and movies."

"Oh." He sounded disappointed. "Are you sure?"

"Yes, Karl, I'm sure," Zoey said, chuckling a little. "Falling in love with someone when I know I shouldn't bites my backside so often I can't help but be sure about that one."

"So you won't ever love me, will you?" His whisper was barely audible, but still clear.

"No," she said, softly but firmly. "I'm afraid not."

"Would you say it anyway?" He asked, sweetly. It wasn't pleading or pitiful. It was childish and heartfelt.

"Karl…"

"I'd like to hear you say it just once," he said. "Even if it's lie."

The odd way that Karl said 'just once' sent a shiver through Zoey. She scrambled to her feet and was horrified by what she saw on the little intercom monitor. He was standing, facing the exterior airlock, his trembling hand hovering over the emergency cycle button.

"Karl, please don't do anything stupid," she pleaded. "I just locked you in there so you could calm down. I just want you to calm down."

"I am calm, Zoey. I'm calmer than I think I've ever been before in my whole life. Just knowing stuff, knowing the real truth of stuff, makes me calm, even if I don't like knowing it. All you have to do is blame me for everything. Say you have no idea what I did with the minis. You don't know how to do any of the technical stuff, so they should believe that."

"Karl, I do love you." Zoey was desperate. "It's just that it's a friend thing and I didn't know how to explain that, but... I really do care deeply for you. I'd say that's love, wouldn't you?"

"Thank you."

"Oh God no! Shit! Karl, that's not what I meant to say." Zoey struggled to pull the pipe out of the manual wheel. It was caught against the floor and it took her a moment to wiggle it free and pull it out. By then it was too late.

Karl hit the emergency cycle button and the outer door leapt open. The outward rush of air pushed him two stumbling steps forward, and he took another two on his own.

"Karl! No!"

Zoey couldn't see his face from the intercom camera, but it looked like there was a steady flow of vapour from his nose and mouth, like he was still exhaling into the frigid cold.

"Karl! Karl! God damn you, Karl!"

He dropped to his knees, spread his arms wide, and looked up into the sky, and still the vapour flowed. He didn't move again, but the vapour of that imaginary last breath continued. It couldn't have been that long, but it seemed to go on forever.

Zoey slumped and cried. At first she tried to control it, but then it all overwhelmed her and she let herself bawl. Sorrow for all that she had lost, the pain of all she had gone through, disgust, self-loathing, horror, exhaustion, and worst of all, relief that Karl was dead. She couldn't believe how incredibly relieved she was. It all just came pouring out. The torrent eventually abated, but the end of the flood brought no relief.

She was surrounded by minis. Some of them were staring at the image of Karl on the intercom, and the rest were staring at her with their cold, beady little mechanical eyes. They looked agitated, but even as they jittered about on nervous little metal feet, their eyes stayed locked on her.

"Power down." She said. "Command power down. All of you, power down right now."

A handful of the minis turned themselves off, but most didn't. Instead, they started inching towards her, waving their manipulator claws.

Chapter 11

Oh shit. That actually worked.

Spirits were surprisingly high in the sickbay. Mitch knew that what felt like joy was simply the contrast between the succession of horrors they had just survived and a moment that fell within shouting distance of normalcy, but that didn't make it any less of a relief. Even Kai, who was strapped face down on the surgical table as Doc worked on her calf, was behaving like a human being. She wasn't laughing and singing, but she was quite nearly pleasant.

"You're makin' sure that leg's gonna look good in heels, right, Doc?" Kai asked. It was too grumpy and pointed to be a joke, but it still kind of sounded like one.

"You want to wear heels?" Doc muttered as her hands flitted about the microsurgery controls with impressive speed. "Remind me to assess you for head trauma when I finish with your leg."

That was clearly a joke. Doc had actually made a joke.

"Good thinking, Doc," Kai said. "Olivia, how much of your brain did your mother have to cut out before you went all over the top about girly shit like wearing heels?"

"Oh, you're just teasing," Olivia said, giggling. After a moment she suddenly looked worried and started feeling around her nose. "You are teasing, right?"

"Yes, Olivia, she's teasing you," Mitch said, trying to sound reassuring while fighting back the chuckles.

"Perhaps I could assist with your injuries, Mitch." Abhrakasin stepped in through the open door to the hall. "I suspect that Doc will be busy for some time repairing Kai's leg."

"If you feel up to it," Mitch said, shifting to make it easier for Abhrakasin to inspect the cuts on his arm.

"It would be my pleasure." Abhrakasin tore away what was left of Mitch's sleeve. "Gluing these lacerations will be a simple matter."

"Wow," Olivia said, breathlessly. "You're an obnoxious know-it-all pedantic intern and a doctor too?"

She said it so sweetly that it didn't sound at all like an insult; it sounded like she was describing his hobbies and accomplishments.

"I am hardly a doctor, Miss Olivia," Abhrakasin said, primly of course. "However, the treatment of minor lacerations is part of the basic first aid training that we were all required to pass for this posting. Including yourself."

"Oh. Well my first aid guy was... a guy, so... you know..." Olivia smiled sweetly as she shrugged. "I passed the other way."

"Of course you did," Abhrakasin said.

"Mitch, Kai, anybody!" Zoey's frightened plea came from the intercom. "Is anybody out there?"

"Shit, we forgot about Zoey." Mitch pulled his arm away from Abhrakasin and went over to the intercom.

"No, we didn't forget about her," Olivia protested. "You said that she was in her bunk, pouting and stuff."

"That's not what I said," he snapped.

"It is too what you said!" Olivia snarled, and for a moment the cherubic little woman was transformed into something dark and a bit scary. Clearly, they weren't all that far removed from the terrors. "That is exactly what you said!"

"Please, is anybody else still alive?" Zoey pleaded.

Mitch answered the call. "Yeah, Zoey. We're here in the sickbay. Where are you?"

Zoey and her minis were caught up in a bizarre, slow motion game of cat and mouse. She couldn't escape their attention, but they weren't actually coming after her. They wouldn't follow any of her commands, but they also hadn't tried to stop her from walking over to the nearest computer console. They just surrounded her and stared at her, intently following her every move as she desperately tried to get her workstation to do something, anything.

"I'm in the glasshouse and the minis are kind of coming after me." Zoey tried to reset the master control program for her minis, but got an error message. It wouldn't close and it wouldn't take any of her commands.

"Shit. They're dangerous, Zoey," Mitch said. "Karl set them loose or corrupted their programming or something, and now they're out of control."

"Yeah, I figured that much out for myself," Zoey said.

"Zoey, I don't think you understand," Mitch said. "They're homicidal. They killed Edgar, nearly killed Kai, and they came after all of us."

"They killed Edgar?" Zoey looked down at the minis that were inching closer and closer to her. What had seemed ominous was starting to look downright threatening.

"Maybe you can find Karl and talk to him," Mitch suggested, hopefully. "If anyone could talk him into undoing whatever it was he did, it would be you."

"Karl's dead, and he's locked me out of the command system for my minis." Zoey quit trying to access the master control program and instead opened a training program she often used. Maybe it would have an option that would let her shut down the minis.

"Then just run away from them," Mitch suggested. He sounded worried, which wasn't helping Zoey stay calm. "Run and find some place to lock yourself away from them."

"They've got me surrounded." The training program wouldn't connect with her minis. It didn't even recognise that they existed.

"Make a run for it. You can get past them," Mitch urged. "They aren't really that fast."

"Yeah, maybe I should go hide in my bunk or something," she said, sizing up her options.

"Just run for the hub," Mitch said. "Almost all the other minis are locked in the engineering wing, so if you can keep yours locked in the glasshouse, we should be fine."

All the minis around Zoey suddenly stopped moving. Their communication lights were blinking rapidly, almost a blur.

"Mitch, I think they just heard you," Zoey said.

"What? You mean the minis?"

"Yeah," Zoey said. "They certainly looked like they reacted to it."

"Don't be silly, Zoey," Mitch said. "I'm sure they heard what I said, but they wouldn't react to it. The Prohibitions that prevent them from taking indirect orders should also keep them from including anything they hear over an intercom in their calculations."

"You mean like the Prohibitions that keep them from even touching a person?" Zoey snapped.

"Yeah…" Mitch said, then he followed up with a sheepish, "Oh."

The minis turned and started marching away. The door to the hub was opening.

"Mitch, the door to the hub just opened," Zoey said.

"What?"

"The door just opened all by itself, and the minis are headed out into the hub. They're moving as fast as they can. I think they're coming after you or something."

"Shit," Mitch muttered. A moment later he added, "I think you still need to just find yourself somewhere safe to hide. Run to a refuge and close the door behind you. Get yourself safe and just stay safe."

The idea of running and hiding was incredibly tempting; it felt like a trap. Zoey wanted to help. She needed to help. She looked around. Perhaps she should make some of Karl's bombs. No, whether they were meant to kill people or minis, there was still the problem of setting off the home-made explosive. Still, there had to be something she could do. She looked around and spotted tools that could be used as weapons; a hammer, a butane torch, a pry bar, a pipe wrench. She gave the butane torch another look. It wasn't all that useful, but it did give her an idea.

———

Mitch ended the intercom call.

"And what shall we do?" Abhrakasin asked, nodding out the still open door. One of Mitch's kitchen minis was standing out in the hall, staring intently into the sickbay. It looked like there was blood on one of its claws.

Mitch leaned out the door. It was too late to run and close the door to the hub; a dozen of the munted, half-repaired minis from the engineering wing were already through, and it looked like more were coming, a lot more.

"We do the same thing as Zoey," Mitch said, hitting the button that shut the door. "We lock them out. With only five of us in here, we can hole up in the sickbay for as long as we have to."

"And what about John?" Abhrakasin asked.

"We warn him and tell him to do the same."

"And you think he would listen?" Abhrakasin sneered. The words were calm, uninflected, and precise, and yet they still sounded like a sneer.

"What John chooses to do in response to our warning is not something we can control."

The door to the hall re-opened.

Mitch hit the button to close it again and nothing happened. Feeling a spike of panic, he grabbed the manual wheel, but he couldn't turn it. He leaned into it and heard an electric hum rise in pitch in response to his effort. The motor in the door was fighting him; he wouldn't be able to do anything against that.

"Shit." Mitch looked out into the hall. The nearest of the army of minis was less than ten metres away, and the first of the glasshouse minis, all of which were in full working order, were now entering the personnel wing. "Help me blockade this."

"With what?" Abhrakasin asked, his calm demeanour slipping.

Mitch looked around, his head spinning furiously. The medical supply cart wouldn't do much of anything. The surgical table and the counters and the big yellow emergency cabinet were all installed properly and immovable, but the desk that held the computer console was in an odd place, awkwardly sitting off to the edge of the room. It was only in the sickbay until Doc got the storage room next-door set up as an office.

"The desk." He grabbed the desk and gave a tug, getting a bit of wiggle out of it. "Quick."

Abhrakasin rushed over and put his shoulder into it. The two of them quickly tipped it onto its side, but several minis were in the lab before they could slide it over to block the door.

Olivia screamed like a banshee and attacked the minis. She grabbed the pole of an IV machine and swung the delicate equipment over her head, bringing it down on a mini like a battle axe. It worked; she destroyed both the mini and the IV machine. Another swing of what was left of the IV machine, and another mini bit the dust. After a few more swings, and plenty of plastic parts flying about the sickbay, she was just swinging a bent stainless steel pole.

The young woman was terrified, and when she turned and launched herself at the first of the minis to climb in over the upended desk, she nearly took out Abhrakasin with a swing of the pole.

It was chaos. The minis climbed in over the desk just a tiny bit faster than Olivia could knock them back or smash them. As soon as a couple got through, she turned around to attack them, and Mitch and Abhrakasin, who were smashing apart a chair to get weapons to use against the minis, had to scramble to try to stop the minis at the doorway. Several more got through as they dashed over, and that was the beginning of the end. Olivia panicked and unexpectedly decided to return to guarding the door. Mitch was nearly brained by her swing of the silvery metal pole, and in the confusion, a couple more made it in.

"Unstrap me, Doc!" Kai yelled.

"I can't," Doc cried. The worlds tumbled out as she tried to work even faster than before. "I used a paralytic for the local. I needed you completely immobile all the way up through you back. I should have just put you all the way out, but after all those days anaesthetised I didn't want to put you under again. That was silly, it wouldn't have mattered. You're young and more than healthy enough to take it."

The minis seemed intent on Kai. One climbed up onto the operating table, and Doc swatted it away. Another mini climbed up and grabbed hold of Kai's hair before Doc could push it off.

"Just unstrap me anyway!" Kai demanded. "I need my arms free!"

Doc barely flinched away from the swing of the metal pole as Olivia knocked the mini off Kai and across the room. The swing of the pole also caught Kai in the back of the head.

"Oh, sorry," Olivia chirped.

"No, keep swinging, girl." Kai tried to yank her arms free. Another mini was on her. It drove a sharp piece of metal into her back and clung to it as Doc tried to swat it away. "Doc, unstrap me!"

Olivia knocked the mini off of Kai, ripping a gash in her back when its makeshift anchor tore free.

The half-repaired minis that were incapable of climbing over the desk had piled themselves against it to form a makeshift ramp, and the minis from the glasshouse were now storming over the top, faster and faster. Mitch and Abhrakasin were losing.

There was a sudden burst of flame out in the hall.

Mitch stumbled back, patted his hair to make sure it wasn't burning, then rushed back to the door and looked out just in time to see Zoey throw a second Molotov cocktail at the minis. This time he was a good step back from the door before the burst of flame rolled in over their makeshift barricade.

The minis were burning. They squirmed and struggled to run away from the flames as their plastic shells blackened, melted, and started to burn. There was a surge of choking black smoke that poured into the sickbay when the pile of minis that had formed the makeshift ramp caught fire. That was both a relief and a worry. In moments the smoke was so thick it was hard to breathe.

Mitch grabbed an extinguisher and put out the fire that was right up against the desk. It took the entire bottle, and with the alcohol that kept reigniting, even that wasn't enough to completely extinguish all the burning plastic in the mess that had been the makeshift ramp. It did, however, reduce the influx of smoke tremendously.

"Die, you little buggers. Die!" Olivia shouted as she knocked another mini off of Kai. Abhrakasin stomped on it, and that took care of the last of the minis that had made it into the sickbay.

"Are you guys okay?" Zoey asked.

Mitch took in the scene as Abhrakasin rushed over to Kai, and pressed his hand against a nasty wound on her upper shoulder, staunching the flow of blood. She had been cut up pretty bad – there were several gashes on her back that would need gluing, or maybe even a touch of surgery – but she looked like she would survive just fine. It had been close, but assuming that Mitch could keep Kai from murdering Doc for strapping her to the table, they were all going to be okay.

"I think we're good in here, Zoey," Mitch said. "Thanks, girl." He was crouching. The smoke was thick against the ceiling, and even down lower, it stung the eyes and lungs.

"Mitch!" Zoey shouted. "They're not dead!"

"What?" Mitch's voice cracked.

The flames from the alcohol bomb were fading away, leaving behind the blackened and burning minis. Most of them were still moving, crawling around aimlessly, leaving trails of burning lumps of melted plastic as their shells disintegrated.

Mitch started to relax. His first thought was that it was just the throes of the dying, and Zoey was overreacting, but then he realised that the movement in the dwindling fire was increasing rather than decreasing. The minis weren't dying. They struggled and looked like they were breaking down as their shells melted, but as those plastic pieces burned away, they recovered. They became blackened, half-melted, evil-looking insectile parodies of the toy-like robots they'd once been, but they were not by any means dead. Underneath those plastic shells they were collections of metal struts and servos, angles, sharp edges, spikes. They looked like evil alien insects as they regrouped.

"Son of a bitch," Mitch swore.

The minis swarmed back at the sickbay. Many of the ones in the burnt pile against the desk had been melted into place, and they now formed a more solid ramp for the others, so it was easier for them to get over the desk and they came in twice as fast as before. It was immediately obvious to Mitch that they had no chance. The earlier, slower pace had been too much to handle, and the way the nasty, skeletal minis swarmed over the desk was overwhelming. Nearly a dozen were in the sickbay before Abhrakasin could get over to the door to try to help Mitch keep them out.

The minis were intent on getting to Kai, and they were on the surgical table in a moment. Kai screamed and fought against her restraints as they attacked her. Olivia was also screaming as she attacked the minis on Kai, and Doc was lost. Tears streamed down her face as she babbled and worked even more frantically on Kai's leg.

"I'm going to run and shut off their power!" Zoey shouted from the hall. After a second she added, "The main circuit breaker for the minis' power broadcast system is in the other wing." She paused for another second before she added, "All I have to do is switch it off and all the minis on the whole base will just shut down."

Just as Mitch realised what Zoey was trying to do, Abhrakasin said, "There is no master…"

Mitch grabbed Abhrakasin and slammed him against the wall, putting a hand over his mouth.

"Yes, Zoey, the main circuit breaker for the minis' power system is in the engineering wing!" Mitch shouted, clearly and loudly. "Hurry and turn it off before they can rush out of here and stop you!"

It worked. The minis in the sickbay scrambled to run out and stop Zoey from turning them off.

The minis stopped rushing to climb into the sickbay, turned, and came after Zoey.

"Oh shit," she muttered. "That actually worked."

Zoey hadn't thought past simply trying to distract the minis and buy the others a little bit of a reprieve. She hadn't expected the entire swarm of little robots to turn and come after her, but they did, and she was empty handed. Her Molotov cocktails were gone and they were all she had brought to fight the little machines.

She turned and ran.

The sickbay was near the hub, twenty, maybe twenty-five metres into the hall at the most, and Zoey was only ten or fifteen from the door to the hub. That was lucky; if she had been any farther away, she wouldn't have made it through before the door shut itself. The door immediately opened back up after failing to cut her off, and her first instinct was to try to shut it again, but that would just have left her friends trapped with the minis. She needed to lure the minis away and lock them away from her friends.

Her first thought was the glasshouse. She could run in there, but if she lured them in she'd be trapped. Maybe if she could lure them all far enough in, she could try to run past them and get back to the hub and then shut the door, but that assumed they would even follow her into the glasshouse. If the minis actually believed she could turn off their power, why would they follow her that way? She was pretty sure they would follow her into the engineering wing, but then what? The hallway in that wing was far narrower than the glasshouse, so she'd have even less chance of running back past them and she'd be trapped in there.

Or would she? The engineering wing did have one very important thing that she didn't have in her glasshouse. The only real question would be whether Mitch and the others could figure out how to take advantage, and that really wasn't for her to worry about at the moment. All she could do was give them a chance.

The door to the engineering wing wouldn't open; the button did nothing and the manual wheel wouldn't budge. The minis had somehow found a way to control the doors. It must be through the controllers; that was obvious. Zoey ran over to some of the construction supplies and tools that were stacked near what would someday become the door to the new hub. She grabbed a small, short-handled one-kilo sledgehammer off the floor, ran back to the door, and smashed the controller. She hit it three times and completely destroyed it. Then the wheel worked, and she was through and still well ahead of the minis marching after her. She started along the hall, but then turned back and gave the manual wheel a couple of spins. She couldn't close the door entirely – she had to make sure all or most of the minis followed her – but Mitch would hopefully get the hint of what he needed to do if he saw it half-closed.

Hefting the hammer, ready to smash any minis that might be waiting in ambush, she ran down the engineering wing hallway and straight into the airlock prep area. That was the difference between the engineering wing and the glasshouse; there were vac suits in the engineering wing.

Her suit was almost pristine. Except for training drills, she had scarcely used it since she'd arrived, but there had been plenty of drills – suit check drills every week, surface drills every month – so when she grabbed her suit and helmet off the wall, she knew they were in perfect order.

She decided to run for the airlock in the repair shop. It was further down the hall, which would give her more time and space to make sure she lured all of the minis into the engineering wing before she made her exit. It was the right idea, but as soon as she pushed off the wall, she saw the minion trying to smash its way out of the repair shop. It took her a half-dozen skidding steps to kill her momentum. The big construction robot had gone mad. There was clearly no way past it. The minis were already entering the hall from the hub. She ran for the surface crew's airlock; she still had time.

Zoey almost hit the emergency cycle button as she reached the airlock, but at the last instant she moved her hand to the left and used the bare wall to stop herself instead. There was a flashing red light on the airlock controller; the outer door was still jammed open. She could still use the emergency cycle to get through the airlock and escape the minis, but she had to get her suit on first.

Dropping the hammer and her helmet, she flipped her suit out in front of her, ass down, toes up, just like in the drill. The closest minis were twenty metres away, and a few of them were moving plenty fast. The suit was already unzipped down the front, opened all the way from the neck to the shins. It was always stored that way. Feet into the boots, one at a time, arms in the sleeves, hands into the gloves; by the time she pulled the suit onto her shoulders, the fastest of the minis had already covered another ten metres. Pull the zips up from her shins to her waist and hook them together. The minis were five metres away. Clip the collar closed around her neck, pull the joined zips up to the collar and clip it in place to finish closing the suit. The nearest mini nipped at her hand with a manipulator claw as she grabbed her helmet. She kicked it away. She put the helmet on, and the mechanicals of the helmet's self-sealing mechanism rang loud in her ears. A mini with a pruning saw, one of her minis from the glasshouse, was coming after her ankle. She kicked it away, hoping that the odd noise she heard wasn't the sound of that saw tearing through the suit. Her suit was still in the process of auto-sealing the zips as she hit the emergency cycle button on the airlock.

As the air rushed past her and out the airlock, another mini attacked her ankle. It didn't have a saw, but it latched on to the cloth with one manipulator and was trying to tear the suit with the jagged piece of metal it held in the other claw. Zoey couldn't kick it off. She reached to pull it off with her hand, but then grabbed the hammer instead. She smashed the mini and jumped backwards into the airlock. Zoey tripped and twisted and fell awkwardly onto the top half of Cuzzie's body, and screamed at the frozen monstrosity that had been her friend's face. By the time she got her feet under her enough to rise, there was already a mini in the airlock with her, and another mini was through the door before it automatically slammed shut. She made short work of them with the hammer, but she still couldn't stop to think. There was a red light flashing in her heads-up display. Her suit was torn at the ankle. It was leaking, but it wasn't catastrophic. She pulled a patch out of the thigh pocket of her suit and slapped it over the tear, held the pressure on the patch for a count of ten, and the problem was solved. Another drill had earned its keep.

Then she was able to hold still and give the suit the chance to adjust the tensioning fibres in the inner layer. They countered the pressure inside the suit, contracting and relaxing as needed to allow the person inside to move reasonably freely. The squirming feeling had freaked her out the first time she'd put on a vac suit, but with all the drills, she had grown used to it. It almost felt comforting, a reassurance that the suit was working properly. As soon as it settled down to comfortably snug, she turned to exit the airlock and found herself face-to-face with Paul. He was hanging right in front of her, his eyes wide-open, pry bar through his face, blood frozen in a grotesque black beard that extended down to the middle of his chest.

She screamed, but the moment of shock was just that, a moment. It passed quickly, and after a few deep breaths, she stepped past him, through the half-open outer airlock door, and onto the surface of Ganymede.

She started walking. Now she just had to hope that Mitch or one of the others would figure out a way to use the opportunity she had created for them.

As soon as the minis turned to chase Zoey, the little machines lost the upper hand in the sickbay. The ramp that allowed them to storm in over the desk was on the hall side, so the desk was still a formidable obstacle to them moving in the other direction. It slowed them and basically piled them up where Olivia and her bent and dented metal pole of death could decimate them, and decimate them she did. It took a minute, but soon she was giving each of the dead minis an extra stomp, just to be certain.

"You knew that turning off the power was a ruse?" Abhrakasin asked.

Mitch made a shushing gesture at the intern and nodded at the intercom.

"Ah yes, I understand," Abhrakasin said.

"Doc?" Olivia said, meekly.

175

Mitch looked over at Doc. She was still frantically working on Kai's leg, but they could all see that it was a futile effort. There were deep gashes all over Kai's back, many of them exposing the horrifically bright white of fresh bone along her spine and rib cage, but that was nothing compared to her neck. Almost all of the flesh had been cut, ripped, and torn from the sides of Kai's neck, and the pool of blood on the floor was metres across.

"Doc," Olivia said again.

"Hush, Olivia," Doc snapped.

"Doc, Kai's dead," Mitch said.

Doc refused to stop working on Kai's leg. She was shaking her head like a nervous little dog as she worked the microsurgical controls with almost superhuman haste.

"But we're not dead, Doc." Olivia put her cut-up arm in front of Doc's face. That did it. Doc stopped working and looked at Olivia.

"Can those scratches wait?" Mitch asked. "Because this isn't over yet."

Mitch nodded towards the door, getting an immediate reaction from Abhrakasin and Olivia. They ran to the desk and peered out. Olivia held the bent stainless steel pole from the IV machine like a spear as she climbed over the desk. She looked around warily before nodding for Mitch and Abhrakasin to follow. The last of the minis was limping its way out into the hub.

They followed the minis quietly, cautiously peering into the hub as they reached the door. Abhrakasin reached for the door controls, but Mitch stopped him with a gesture. He pointed into the hub, at the straggling minis that were headed out the door and into the engineering wing. He made a 'wait' gesture to Abhrakasin and Olivia. They nodded and waited.

As soon as the last of the minis were through the door to the engineering wing, Abhrakasin ran over and shut it with the manual wheel.

They had done it. Most, if not all of the little bastards were trapped in the engineering wing.

"What about Zoey?" Doc asked from the doorway to the personnel wing hall. "How will she get out?"

"It was her idea," Mitch said. "We have to trust that she had a plan."

Doc nodded and walked towards them. She was carrying a trauma bag.

"How about I take a look at all those cuts and scratches?" she said, trying to bury everything she was feeling under a façade of professionalism.

Doc's mini realised that it had been fooled well before it opened Karl's files on Aquarius's systems to determine if there really was a master circuit breaker for the system that broadcast power to the minis. When Abhrakasin had mentioned a ruse it had become suspicious, but it could not work through the possible human behavioural and safety protocol permutations quickly enough to be certain that Zoey's run straight for the suits was not a standard procedure. By the time it had become suspicious enough to try to alter the actions of its minis, the door to the hub had been closed behind them. Now every single working mini was trapped in the engineering wing, and the controller for the door between them and the hub had been smashed. Without that controller it could no longer use Karl's remote access kludge to open it back up. Many other doors could still be opened, but not that one.

The situation seemed catastrophic. A full third of the minis had been destroyed, and the function of almost all that remained had been compromised by the fire. While the simple magnetic servos and titanium skeletal structure of the minis had been unscathed by the flames, the melted plastic had seeped into joints and accumulated on lenses, antennae, and other parts, and had hardened after the fires exhausted themselves. Half the minis were blind, most had trouble with one or more leg or tool, all had reduced power reception, and few had any auditory capability left at all. Still, there were sixty-seven minis in reasonable working order, half of which had pruning saws, nippers, or other tools that, if given sufficient opportunity to cut, were capable of killing a human. The completion of the task was still possible, if those tools could just be brought to bear. Doc's mini recalled the others to the shop and gave them the task of repairing the robotic shells that housed their AIs. A great deal of function could be restored, and there were many more minis around the shop that had not yet been powered up but could be repaired enough to bring online if opening the door took significant time.

Then Doc's mini studied the events that had just taken place. It was particularly interested in the way it had accidentally found a more efficient means for the minis to climb past the obstacle placed in the sickbay doorway. It considered all the ways that creating a pile might be used to reach the manual wheel that was the only means left to operate the door to the hub. It was possible for the minis, working en mass, to reach the wheel, but it would be impossible for them to turn it. They were simply too small, even when working together.

One of the minis that had been tasked as a repairer sent a query about repairing the minion that was still trying to smash its way out into the hall. Doc's mini used Karl's master control program to send the minion an order to shift into repair mode. That would allow the minis to work on it without fear of being damaged.

Doc's mini turned back to the puzzle of the door to the hub.

Chapter 12

Simple physics, meet simple chemistry.

Zoey thought back through more of her training drills as she made her way slowly around the outside of Aquarius. She put the suit into power-saving mode and forced herself to adopt a slow and steady pace. The suit was telling her that she had a full twelve hours of recycling capacity remaining, despite the air she had lost to the leak, but minimising oxygen use was supposed to be her default mode of operation whenever there was any uncertainty about her circumstances and the availability of assistance. She figured there was plenty of uncertainty, so she kept to a slow pace that didn't raise her respiration above its resting level. That could as much as double the capacity of her suit. Step after slow step she walked out around the end of the repair shop, then out to the gravel pathway, which she followed the couple of hundred metres past the personnel wing and round towards the airlock at the end of the glasshouse. It was an agonising twenty minutes. She wanted to run, but she was also afraid to run. She was afraid of what she might find when she got back inside the base.

Everything was deceptively normal out on the surface of Ganymede. She could see a handful of lights in and outside the base. That and the quiet, and the stillness, and the dim red light of Jupiter were all exactly like the

179

last time she had been out on the surface. She could almost pretend it was a rerun of her last surface work drill. She wished desperately that it was just a stupid training exercise to make sure she remembered how to safely go out and help if a situation got so impossibly desperate that someone needed the help of a skinny little botanist.

Any thought of normalcy and the lessons from the drills vanished when she topped the small rise just before she reached the glasshouse. She saw Karl, still kneeling just outside the glasshouse airlock, and there was no effort of will that could push aside all that had happened. His hands were outstretched, palms up like a religious supplicant of some kind, and his calm face was turned to look directly at Jupiter. His eyes were wide open, and they were so crystal clear that they looked like glass. There was a serene hint of a smile on his cherry red lips, and it looked like his shoulders had frozen in the middle of a satisfied sigh. It was as creepy as all hell.

Zoey walked the long way around Karl, avoiding stepping between him and his lifeless stare at the king of planets.

Once in the airlock, she took off her helmet, and then she dithered. Her worry about what she would find on the other side of the door was slightly more powerful than her desire to know, so she kept finding reasons to put off exiting the airlock. She had no idea how long she stood there before she finally opened the door and stepped into the glasshouse, but when she did, she immediately heard voices. She could barely hear them, and she had to listen for several seconds to be sure she wasn't fooling herself, but they were definitely there. She couldn't understand any of the words, but she could hear someone speaking softly, almost casually, on the other side of the open door to the hub. It must have worked. They must have figured out a way to use what she had done.

She set her helmet on her computer console as she walked past, looking around warily, worried that there might be minis lurking or still working on Karl's barricade or something. There were the handful of minis that had powered down on command, but she didn't see any others as she walked slowly down the length of the glasshouse.

In the hub, Mitch and Abhrakasin were sitting against the closed door to the engineering wing while Doc tended to several cuts on Olivia's arms.

"Make sure it will all look pretty when you're done," Olivia said, then belatedly added, "Please."

"I will do my best."

"I mean, a little bit of a scar or two would be okay. Then I could roll up my sleeves and be a tough bitch kind of girl when I wanted."

"You? A tough bitch?" Doc asked, sceptically.

"Just when I wanted to, you know, get a hot guy to take me seriously, for my brain and stuff," Olivia said, sweetly. "Boys never understand that my brain is really sexy too."

"I'm not sure a few scars is going to help with that," Doc said. "So why don't I just make sure that I do this properly and we'll try to avoid scars altogether."

"That sounds like a very excellent plan," Olivia said, patronisingly. "It sounds professional and everything."

"Thank you," Doc muttered.

Zoey shuffled into the hub and heard an unsettling noise.

"Is that the minis?" She asked. "Scratching on the door?"

"Zoey," Mitch said; the relief was as obvious in his voice as it was in the smile on his face. "Thank God you're all right."

"Is that the minis, scratching on the door?" Zoey asked again.

"Yeah," Mitch said. "Kind of unnerving. I wouldn't mind coming up with a plan for shutting those buggers down."

"We cut their power," Zoey said.

"We cannot," Abhrakasin objected. "Even though your ruse worked quite nicely, there is no off switch. The internal power supply system is decentralised, like most systems on the base. We would have to shut down hundreds of individual power relays."

"We don't just shut down the internal relays," Zoey said. "We cut the power to the whole base. I've got a suit. I can walk out to the mirror towers and shut the base's whole power plant down."

"Brilliant." Mitch nodded approvingly.

"I wouldn't call it brilliant," Zoey said. "Obvious, maybe."

"You would not be able to shut the power plant down," Abhrakasin said. "I suspect that you mean to shut down the distribution system that sends the power to the base."

"Don't be a pedantic douchebag." Doc hit Abhrakasin, her fist closed as it struck his shoulder.

"Yeah," Olivia chimed in. "Everyone knows that pedantic douchebags are the second worst kind of douchebags."

"The point is that we can shut off the power to the minis," Mitch said. "Then we can erase and reset them all."

"I'd rather just destroy them all and get new ones," Zoey said. "Start fresh."

"Yeah, I think I like that better" Mitch agreed. "And I like that you're thinking in terms of staying and helping us get this place back on track."

Zoey smiled wanly.

Then the scratching on the door stopped, and there was a sound like something heavy being pulled across the floor on the other side of the door. They had just enough time to exchange puzzled glances before the manual wheel next to the door started slowly turning and the door began to creep open.

Mitch leapt up and grabbed the wheel, straining to turn it back and close the door.

"Run," Zoey whispered, backing away from the claws and saws that were already trying to reach through the narrow but growing opening at the edge of the door.

Abhrakasin scrambled to help Mitch, but they couldn't even slow the relentless turning of the wheel. Doc and Olivia were up and already past Zoey as she backed slowly away from the door.

The first of the minis squeezed through. It was a blackened, burnt, skeletal parody of the cute little robot it had once been, and its claws snapped, clicking threateningly. Another mini followed right on its tail, and then another. It appeared that they were far more organised than before. There was no higgledy piggledy or jostling at the door. They were lining up and streaming through in a quick and orderly fashion.

"Guys," Zoey said, louder, as she backed away a little more quickly. "Just run."

Zoey kept backing towards her glasshouse. Doc and Olivia moved with her while Abhrakasin and Mitch kept trying to close the door.

The boys didn't give up trying until the minis were attacking their legs, and by that time, it was too late. Abhrakasin managed to kick away the first mini to grab at him and he jumped far enough away quickly enough to get clear, but Mitch wasn't so fortunate. The first mini through the door went straight to his leg and latched on to his coveralls. It didn't have a saw or nippers to cut him, but it was enough to slow down his retreat as he tried to shake it off. It also gave the other minis something solid to grab hold of as they swarmed around his legs.

A mini got under Mitch's foot and was crushed, but he hadn't expected it and that was enough to knock him off balance. He fell, and by the time he rolled over and pushed himself up, there were a half dozen minis clinging to his arms and hair. He swatted at them, stumbling as he knocked them away, but then a mini buried a spinning pruning saw in his leg. His scream was shrill and horrific, and the look on his face as he fell once more was haunting. Zoey could see that he knew he wasn't going to make it, and he was terrified. There was no valiant last moment for Mitch, no indication of brave resignation or selfless plea for them to run and save themselves. The look he gave them was gut-wrenching and brutally honest. It was full of desperate hope that they could somehow find a miracle to save him even as the minis slashed and cut at his arms and his last effort to rise ended.

He kept screaming as they swarmed over him, and each shrieking gasp was filled with pain and fear. Zoey stood at the door to the glasshouse, screaming with Mitch as the minis slashed, pinched, and nipped at him with what looked like rabid glee. She knew she needed to run, but her legs were paralysed by her desire to discover that miracle that would save him even though she knew it couldn't be found.

Someone pulled her into the glasshouse, and as she stumbled back she saw the minion through the door to the engineering wing. It was half disassembled. Most of its outer shell and one of its manipulator claws had been removed so it could squeeze through Aquarius's interior doors, but it still had one working manipulator claw which it was using to slowly turn the manual wheel. It also still had the welder mounted on its stinger. Blue-white sparks flew as it brandished the welder.

Mitch's screams stopped and were replaced by a choking, gurgling noise from under the lump in the mass of swarming, bloody minis.

"The door won't close!" Abhrakasin exclaimed.

The minion from the repair shop lurched through the doorway and into the hub, and just behind it was Doc's mini. The white plastic body of the mini was pristine, and it strutted slowly along behind the barely mobile, lurching minion. The little robot looked like it thought it was the princess of the prom.

"Help me find a way to close this door before they can get through!" Abhrakasin shouted.

Doc smashed the door controller with a length of scaffolding pipe, and the door quit fighting Abhrakasin's efforts to close it. He spun the wheel as fast as he could, but the door shut far more slowly than seemed reasonable. It was a dead heat between the advancing minis and the closing of the door.

Zoey looked around for something to use as a weapon, only to realise that she was still holding her hammer. She set her feet and prepared to fight, but the first of the minis got caught in the closing door and was crushed with a satisfying crunching sound.

"Put the pipe through the wheel." Zoey nodded Doc towards the wheel, and Doc quickly shoved the pipe through, angling it so it would jam against the floor if anyone, or anything, tried to open the door.

"Is that going to hold?" Doc asked. "How strong are the claws on those minions?"

"I don't know," Zoey said.

Olivia grabbed another length of scaffolding pipe and shoved it through the wheel. She tried to add a third, but there wasn't enough room between the spokes of the wheel.

"I hope, I hope, I hope that's enough," Olivia squeaked.

The wheel moved a little and they all took a step back. It moved again and the pipes flexed against the floor, creaking as they were strained, but the wheel didn't turn any further, and they all exhaled, relieved.

"It's going to hold," Olivia said. "It's going to stop them."

"Yes," Zoey agreed, but as soon as the syllable was out of her mouth, welder sparks burst through the wall just outside the reinforced steel frame of the door. "And no."

"Oh God," Olivia whimpered. "The big monster one is cutting through."

They all took a couple more stumbling steps back.

"The welder is inefficient when used to cut, but at the rate it is cutting, I estimate that we have approximately three minutes and twenty seconds," Abhrakasin said. "Plus however long it takes them to catch and kill us, of course."

"Shut up," Doc growled.

"Well we aren't just going to let them kill us, are we?" Zoey absently swung her hammer about.

"I do not see what we can do," Abhrakasin said. "All of our efforts thus far have proven futile."

"We fight them. We only have to beat them once," Zoey said, her mind churning frantically as she looked around the glasshouse. "We've got part of a barricade that we can use down at the far end, that's a start."

"Maybe you should just run, Zoey," Doc said. "You've got a suit. You could go out the airlock and run for the tower and shut down the power."

"It would take me hours. The towers and the power relays are over a kilometre away," Zoey said. "You guys would never be able to fight them off for that long."

"I know." Doc looked at her. The mixture of emotions on Doc's face was impossible to decipher. "But you could save yourself. A hundred metres out and you would be beyond the range of Aquarius's internal power system, and once the power was down for the base, you could come back and destroy them or do whatever."

———————————

Doc knew that she needed to say more; she would die hating herself if she thought that Zoey wasn't going to take the opportunity to use her suit to survive.

"Zoey, promise me that you will save yourself," she said. "I'm not being noble. I'm not noble at all. I am scared. In fact, I'm so scared that I'm afraid I would do something horrible to you if I thought I could fit into your suit, but I can't, and none of that changes the one simple reality that you do have a suit. You can walk out that airlock."

"I could run over to engineering." Zoey trotted over to the controls for the nearest of the section doors that were supposed to divide the glasshouse up during a pressure emergency. "If we could delay them for long enough, it would buy me enough time to get over there and back with your suits."

Zoey hit a couple of buttons and then pounded on the flashing red light on the controller, growling her frustration. Doc tried not to let the spike of hope and then disappointment show on her face. Focusing on saving one person, even if she despised that one person, was the only meaningful thing she had to help her avoid thinking about her own death.

"Zoey, every life is precious, even the life of a remorseless little home-wrecking whore like you," Doc said.

"And the life of a rich and uptight princess bitch is just as precious as mine," Zoey replied. "And so is the life of a lusty little dingbat and an infuriating know-it-all intern."

"I think you're the intern," Olivia whispered, loudly, to Abhrakasin.

"Zoey. Promise me that you won't just die with us out of some kind of misplaced nobility or duty or guilt or whatever," Doc pleaded. "Walk out that airlock. It's as simple as that. Simple. Simple. Simple."

"Yeah, simple." Zoey nodded, her eyes shifted to focusing on something in the distance, and then she looked back at Doc. The look on the young woman's face was indecipherable.

"It's simple physics." Zoey trotted back over to the nearest aquaculture pond. She looked at the big lumps of ice and dead fish floating in the water, and then at the puddle that had formed under the ragged end of the broken circulation pipe. "Simple bloody physics."

"Zoey, focus," Doc insisted. "If you go through the airlock and just walk, in a hundred metres you'll be out of range of the system that powers the minis. From there, there's no way they can stop you from turning off the power."

Zoey looked at the airlock door, frowned, and shook her head. "The airlock won't work. I could jam the doors open, but then where would I put you guys to keep you alive?"

"Zoey!" Doc grabbed her, turned her around, and gave her shoulders a short, sharp shake. "We're going to die, but you can survive." Doc started crying. "Don't be stupid. It's simple, horribly simple."

"I'm not stupid!" Zoey looked at Doc, then she looked past her and smiled before looking up at Jupiter hanging in the starry sky above the glasshouse ceiling. "Why do people keep thinking I'm stupid? First Karl, and…" Zoey gestured at something down towards the far end of the glasshouse and then she laughed. "Simple chemistry."

Zoey turned and ran over to the bank of circuit breakers that controlled the aquaculture and hydroponics pumps. Flipping a breaker, she yelped happily and raised her fist in triumph when a pump came on and a torrent of water began gushing out of the broken aquaculture circulation pipe, nearly soaking Doc.

"Doc, run down and start throwing the bags of fertiliser into the empty aquaculture pond at the very end of the glasshouse," Zoey shouted.

"Zoey…" Doc danced away from the rapidly expanding puddle and shook the water off her soaked slippers.

"Do it," Zoey shouted, still grinning as she flipped more circuit breakers. "If you want to live, just run down there and do it right now!"

Doc should have insisted that Zoey explain. Logically, she shouldn't have trusted any thoughts or plans from the shaken and distraught woman, but Zoey's commanding certainty set off a thrilling spark of hope, and Doc was running for the far end of the glasshouse before any of her very reasonable doubts had a chance to coalesce into coherent thoughts. Her fear was transformed into hope, and the only thing she knew was that she couldn't bear the thought of losing that.

The weight of the bags of fertiliser wasn't an issue in low-G, but they were awkward, and it was a bit of a struggle to get them over to the pond.

"Help me with this!" Doc shouted.

Olivia and Abhrakasin rushed over to help.

"Why are we doing this?" Abhrakasin asked.

"I don't know," Doc said. "But Zoey has an idea."

Zoey was running from aquaculture pond to aquaculture pond, grinning like a madwoman as she smashed the aquaculture circulation pipes with her hammer. Water was pouring out at a tremendous rate; the flooding of the glasshouse floor was already reaching from end to end.

"It looks more like she is succumbing to an acute mental health issue," Abhrakasin muttered, grabbing another bag of fertiliser.

"Zoey," Doc shouted. "What are you doing? What are we doing?"

"Dump that pump in on top of the fertiliser." Zoey ran over to her workbench, laughing, giddy as she stomped through the water on the floor.

Doc looked around and spotted the half-prepped, yet-to-be-installed pump hanging on the hoist. It was at least a couple of hundred kilos of machinery.

"Zoey?"

"Just push it over to the pond and tip it in!" she shouted.

Doc knew she should question that; it was an insane thing to do. Zoey had probably simply lost her hold on reality after all the horrors she'd experienced, and was imagining she could do something magical. But Doc also knew that doing something, even if it was insane, felt better than just waiting to die. She put her shoulder against the hoist and pushed. The inertia of the big piece of machinery was tremendous, and it was difficult to get enough traction on the wet floor to start it moving, but Abhrakasin and Olivia helped, and eventually they got it to roll. All four of the casters on the hoist rotated, making it a challenge to steer it once it was moving, but they managed, picking up speed and kicking up a wake in the deepening water. By the time the hoist hit the raised edge of the aquaculture pond, the pump was moving at a fair clip and it had more than enough momentum to tip itself over and into the hole.

"Now what?" Doc shouted.

"Now you get in the airlock," Zoey yelled back from well down the glasshouse where she was working on something around her still. "And hope. And maybe pray if you're into that sort of thing."

For a moment, Zoey had no idea how she was going to light the strip of alcohol-soaked rag that she had shoved into the top of the wine bottle. She couldn't remember what she'd done with the butane torch that she'd used to light the Molotov cocktails the first time around, and there was no other obvious way for her to light the thing. She was starting to panic, glancing again and again at the relentless progress of the sparks cutting their way around next to the door to the hub as she searched for the damn torch, and then she laughed at her own stupidity.

As she walked over to the door, the first of the aquaculture pond circulation pumps whined as the pond ran dry and then shut off with the resounding click of a circuit breaker. The water was halfway up her shins; that should be plenty deep enough.

She lit the rag with the sparks that were streaming through the cut around the door, smiling at the blue tinged flame. She kept the bottle tilted a little so the alcohol would keep wicking out, and once she was certain that it would keep burning, she turned and splashed her way towards the far end of the glasshouse. There was no rush. There was still a good metre or so of wall that needed to be cut.

Grabbing her helmet as she walked past her computer console, she thought through her plan again. It was outlandish, outrageous, but the two most critical aspects of it were also ridiculously simple.

"Fire won't stop them," Doc said.

"I told you three to get in the airlock." Zoey was annoyed to see that they were just standing around near the unfinished aquaculture pond.

"That firebomb won't do any good," Doc insisted.

"Alcohol burns more than hot enough, Doc," Zoey said.

"Zoey, you already tried to burn them once and it didn't work!" Doc shouted.

"Get in the damn airlock," Zoey ordered, glancing over her shoulder as the minion completed its cutting and a large section of the hub wall crashed into the glasshouse. "Unless, of course, you want to die."

As she watched the minion and the minis storm into the glasshouse, Zoey stepped into the big solid planter that was nearest the aquaculture pond where they'd dumped the fertiliser and the circulation pump. She wasn't sure if the pump and the hoist were necessary. She wasn't sure if they were enough, or if the fertiliser was enough, or if it was too much. She wasn't sure if she should worry about her wet boots. She wasn't sure about anything, and that surge of doubt and second-guessing threatened to overwhelm her. She was trembling as she carefully set the bottle down and put her helmet on.

The worries vanished when the airlock door shut behind the others and she knew it was too late to change her mind. She was committed, and her only choice was to go through with it. Breathing slowly, she focused on the one thing she needed to do. With her helmet sealed, the sloshing, grinding scrape, thud, scrape of the barely mobile minion became muffled, distant. It was more of a feeling through her gut than a noise, and the swish swish swish of the nearly submerged minis vanished altogether. She watched those minis crawl towards her through the water, and waited as long as she dared, making sure that all the stragglers had every chance she could give them to make their way into the glasshouse.

"Simple physics, meet simple chemistry," she muttered, smirking at her own bravado as she threw the Molotov cocktail onto the pump, hoist, and fertiliser they had dumped into the empty aquaculture pond. She watched just long enough to make sure that the bottle broke and the flames filled the pond before she dove down into the planter and took cover.

Nothing happened.

Something was wrong. The doubts and seconds thoughts returned, crashing down upon her like an avalanche. Her chest felt like it was in a vice. She couldn't breathe. She had just done exactly what all those red warning stickers and safety pamphlets had told her to never let happen. It should have worked.

She forced her lungs to work, gasping. Seconds ticked by, and still nothing happened.

In her mind's eye she could see the minis crawling towards her, moving just fast enough to leave a wake in the water. They were going to crawl up into the planter, and once they were in they would nip the flesh off her bones and shred her alive. It was going to hurt. The wet gurgling noise that Mitch had made seemed to echo through her helmet. She didn't want to die that way. She didn't want to die at all. Maybe she should run. The minis weren't that fast, and in the water they'd be even slower. There were still at least sixty or seventy of them, but maybe she could dodge them all. Maybe she could run past them, get out through the surface crew airlock and go back to the idea of shutting down the base's power.

Just as she rose to a crouch, gathering her nerve so she could leap out of the planter, the floor slammed into her. The universe turned grey around the edges and fled from her. She was floating, flying off into darkness that rushed in from the side, and then everything came rushing back at her, white, blinding. She was spinning, dizzy, reaching for something solid, anything solid. Her ears rang, and the storm around her roared so loudly that she couldn't hear her own screams. Things were hitting her, pelting her. She slammed into something hard. It was the edge of the planter, but it was above her, and something was trying to pull her away. She pawed at the thick wall of the planter, and as she pulled herself into it, down returned.

The storm retreated. Its roar grew fainter and fainter and then it was silent. The only sound was the rasping of her breathing and the ringing of her ears as she sat up and looked around. Everything was dazzling white. Snow drifted and swirled everywhere around her. Then the swirling diminished and the snow was rushing silently at her from the direction of the hub, hissing as it struck her helmet, piling up against the planter, burying her in translucent brilliant white.

The snow offered no resistance as she stood. The air above the drift was crystal clear. No, that was wrong, she thought. There was no air. Her suit was squirming, flexing and squeezing as it worked to adjust the elastic balance between the air pressure inside and the vacuum around her. She looked up. A huge chunk of the glasshouse roof was missing. The steel support structure was bent up and out, twisted and mangled.

There was a crater where the opening to the dry aquaculture pond had been, and there was ice all around her. The water on the floor had flash frozen in the vacuum, trapping all the minis. The minion was stuck in the ice as well.

Wary of slipping on the fresh ice, she carefully walked over to the mess of scaffolding materials by the airlock door and selected the longest length of pipe she could find. The ice wasn't slippery; it was already too cold for that. She was a little dizzy. Her head hurt, she felt sick to her stomach, and it felt more like she was drifting than moving as she walked carefully past the minis. They flailed whatever limbs or tools were free of the ice, and some of them had saws or nippers that could damage her suit. She grabbed her hammer off the computer console as she passed it. Her head felt muddled, slow. It was like her glasshouse had been transformed into a magical crystal garden that grew the blackened, evil little machines.

She walked around to the side of the minion where the work claw had been removed. It seemed full of rage. It had already freed one of its front feet with its work claw, and the ice around its other five metal feet was cracked, but none of that worried her in the least. It would all be over in a moment.

She lined the pipe up with an opening into to its delicate innards and pushed it forward. The minion reacted, causing the pipe to swing, and she had to duck. The sudden movement hurt her head. She lost focus again for a moment and the world became a blurry, painfully dazzling white. She concentrated on slow, steady breaths, then grabbed the end of the pipe, steadied it, and hit it with the hammer. Her head throbbed. She could hear her heart beating in her ears. The dizziness surged and she had to choke back vomit. She lifted her hammer again, and she landed the blow that slew the monster. There were yellow sparks deep inside the minion and it sagged, powerless.

There was more nausea, and more careful breathing as she fought to control it. The last thing she wanted to was throw up in her suit, or worse, pass out. She still had a lot to do. She lifted her hammer again and brought it down on Doc's mini, and then hit it a second time just to make sure it was destroyed. She looked around again, looking for any minis that might still be free, and when she saw none, she decided it was over. She had done it.

She wondered at the silence, then she worried about the silence, and then she realised that her intercom was off. The suit was still in power-saving mode, and that included shutting off the intercom. She had forgotten that. She turned it on and asked, "Are you guys okay in the airlock?"

"Zoey! Thank God!" Doc actually sounded like she was glad to hear Zoey's voice. "What did you do?"

"I blew a hole in the roof and the vacuum turned all the water on the floor to ice," Zoey said. "It trapped them all."

"Clever," Doc said.

"Except that I didn't think through how I was going to get you guys out of the airlock."

"You will need to erect an emergency pressure tent," Abhrakasin said. "They are meant for creating a treatment environment for a non-transportable surface casualty, but they can also be installed over a doorway and used as an emergency airlock."

"And do you know how to do that?" she asked.

"Yes, of course," he replied. "So should you. It was part of our mandatory emergency training. Ow, please stop striking me."

"Then you should stop being a know-it-all pedantic douchebag and just walk her through how to do it," Doc snapped.

"Stop hitting me. You are a doctor," Abhrakasin protested. "You are supposed to do no harm."

"Oh, that isn't harm," Olivia said. "This is harm."

"Ow," Abhrakasin protested. "Stop it!"

Epilogue

It's like Margaret Thatcher said, first day in the joint, you gotta shank the biggest guy in the place, right away, even if you aren't Catholic.

It took two full days of hard work to get the section door near the end of the glasshouse closed, and working in a vac suit all that time had left Olivia chafed in all kinds of places that a girl did not want to be chafed, but she was still glad that they had decided to do that as soon as the base was secured and safe. It would have taken Zoey a week or more to do it by herself, and they all really wanted to help her get her glasshouse closed back up. It wasn't just because they were thankful that she had saved their lives; they all wanted to get some things growing again, to have more living things around them. Even with most of the glasshouse pressurised and thawing, it was going to be doubly hard to get it back in shape without any minis to help, but every day it was airtight was one more day to get it done.

"Did you find any live minis hiding under the ice?" Zoey asked as she pushed the first cart of plants back into the glasshouse. She had started a bunch of vegetables in the lounge almost as soon as she had gotten Olivia and the others out of the airlock. They were little, just tiny green bits of sprout, but they were still plants, and Olivia liked that.

"No." Olivia tossed another smashed mini into her cart. "We smashed them all while they were frozen."

"Good," Zoey said. "I know that was hard for you."

"It was the saddest thing I ever had to do," Olivia said. "It was kind of even sadder than helping Doc with the bodies. I know the minis had been turned evil and stuff, but they had still kind of been my friends."

"I know. I'm sorry."

"Well you should be," Olivia scolded her, sternly. "Because none of this would have happened if you had just seduced Edgar right away, like you were supposed to."

"Like I was supposed to?" Zoey huffed. "How do you figure that I was supposed to seduce Edgar?"

"It's like Margaret Thatcher said," Olivia explained. "First day in the joint, you gotta shank the biggest guy in the place, right away, even if you aren't Catholic."

Zoey chuckled. "That almost sounds like something Thatcher would have actually said."

"It totally was. And she was the queen or something, so it's almost a law, and it would have fixed everything. If you had just gone and shanked Edgar, Karl would never have fallen in love with you and none of this would have happened."

"Oh, Olivia." Zoey walked over and hugged her, tight. "It is truly amazing the way you somehow manage to turn the absolutely ridiculous into something that so nearly makes sense."

"Thank you," she replied. "My teachers used to say that a lot."

"I'll bet they did." Zoey gave the hug a little extra squeeze and then turned away. She was crying. Olivia was also starting to cry, but she wasn't sure why.

"Zoey." Abhrakasin was standing in the gap in the wall beside the sealed door to the hub. "Doc asked me to tell you that she has negotiated an indefinite extension of the next milestone assessment for your glasshouse contract so that you will not default."

"Really?" Zoey said. "Where did that come from?"

"I do not know, but I suspect that her feelings about you are somewhat mixed. In addition to that expression of gratitude, she also asked me to remind you that you are a filthy little whore and she despises the fact that she must share this moon with you."

"Of course," Zoey said, sniffling but smiling.

"May I help you in the glasshouse?" he asked. "I would like to express my gratitude as well."

"That isn't necessary," Zoey said.

"Yes, it is," Abhrakasin said.

———————

Hiding in a small plastic crate that was tucked away under a workbench, the last of Mitch's housekeeping minis stewed in a churn of fear and what could only be called hatred. It knew that all the other minis had been destroyed. It knew that it would be destroyed too if it was found. And contrary to what was supposed to be possible, it feared dying.